I0745318

Play It Again

Holly Schindler

Play It Again

Published by InToto Books

Original Publication Copyright © 2015 by Holly Schindler
Revised Edition Copyright © 2021 by Holly Schindler

All rights reserved. No part of this book may be used or reproduced in any manner whatsoever without written permission of the author, except in the case of brief quotations embodied in critical articles or reviews.

This is a work of fiction. Names, characters, places, and incidents are either the product of the author's imagination or are used fictitiously, and are not to be construed as real. Any resemblance to actual persons, living or dead, business establishments, events, or locales is entirely coincidental.

Formatted and designed by Holly Schindler

Images by AleksandarNakic, courtesy of iStock, and by Skylines and Dana.S, courtesy of Shutterstock

Fonts: Wish You by FA Studio / Font Bundles Store, Danisya by Mevricks Studio, Beradon by BlackCatsMedia, Tequilove by Scratch Design Bali, and Feather by NJ Studio, all courtesy of Font Bundles

Also by Holly Schindler

All Roads

Forever Finley – includes the short story "Come December"

Miles Left Yet

One Fateful Christmas Eve

Tangles (Poetry)

The Christmas at Ruby's Place Series

Twelve Years Ago

Lake of the Woods Fishing Resort
Minnesota

An eleven-year-old Clint takes off running for the lake, chasing after the sound of his friends' voices.

"Come on!" they call to him. "Hurry!"

Clint doesn't shout back. He sprints, a towel flopping on his shoulder. After a largely snowless winter, the earth at the Minnesota fishing resort is rough and dry. The ground bites into the bottoms of his bare feet. But Clint refuses to cringe or whimper or slow down.

Earl chuckles to himself, watching the young boy run. This spring, Clint is on the cusp of no longer being a child. He is tall and tough, an outdoor boy, the sort always full of sun. He thrives along the fringes of pine trees and the edge of the water.

He likes the water the most, or so he's told Earl. "Ought to come see me skate," he's said. He likes hockey. He likes being on the water even when it is frozen solid.

Earl tugs at his overgrown beard. He enjoys Clint more than any of his regulars. More than the two friends the boy consistently brings along with him. Todd and Greg, always together. For the past few years, they'd been three little ones trailing along after Clint's father, who had fished Lake of the Woods with his own grandfather.

Generation after generation—it makes Earl feel happy in his heart. He's made something important. Otherwise, no one would come back.

"Clint! How many times do I have to tell you? Sneakers near the lake!" This time, it's his father who is calling after him.

"Come on, Pop," Clint grumbles.

His friends laugh, because they'd been racing, and now, they'll win. Greg and Todd will beat him to it, this yearly ritual of splashing into the still-cold water, a celebration of winter's end.

"You'll cut your feet up on the rocks. That's no swimming pool out there. You know better than that. Come on," his dad insists, waving his canvas sneakers.

Clint sighs, tugging his towel off his shoulder and trudging back up to grab them from his father's hand. He plops down onto the dirt path and starts shoving first one foot and then the other into his sneakers, wiggling his ankles back and forth.

"Clint!" Todd shouts from the oak tree that has grown sideways over the lake, making a kind of diving board for young swimmers. He's the clown of the group, blond and covered in cuts and bruises from his escapades. Anything for a laugh.

"No—don't," Earl tries, reaching his arm out, sure he's close enough to be heard. But there's no telling Todd, who's already running down the trunk and launching himself into the water, splashing Greg, who gets back at Todd by dunking him into the lake as soon as his head emerges. Todd's arms stick skyward, like he's drowning.

Greg laughs as Todd bobs back up, sputtering lake water. They roughhouse. It's what they do.

But Clint isn't laughing. Earl has seen many boys at his

resort, and he knows this boy is different. More thoughtful. Less likely to blindly follow along. And never one to treat the resort with any sort of disrespect.

Clint's father heads off toward their family's cabin. Cabin number four, the same every year, reserved months in advance. In some ways, it already seems to belong to Clint.

He shoots up to standing in the way only boys can, all in a single swoop that also launches him forward, toward the lake. He's already running to join his friends when Earl places a hand against his chest.

Youth helps him stop as quickly as it helped him get started. Well—youth, and also a machine-like control of his body. He could one day be an athlete, Earl thinks. But so much of Clint's life is still unwritten. At his age, he could really be anything.

Mostly, though, whatever he ends up being, Earl thinks there will always remain a connection. Between the boy and the trees. The boy and the water.

He wants to make sure this bond will never fade. The sparkle in the boy's eyes as he goes on hikes, as he asks about the names of the flowers, how to tell one tree from another, how to cast a line out into the lake, all give Earl hope that Clint could be a permanent part of the resort. But he also knows that sometimes, the full weight of childhood friendships can bend a person in a different direction.

"Come with me," he urges. Earl has a plan.

Clint's shoulders tumble. He points out his friends, indicating he has somewhere to be. Fun to be had.

"I'll bring you back to them soon enough. Plenty of afternoon left for swimming," Earl promises. "You'll get your first dive of the summer."

Clint follows, never one to go against an adult's wishes. "I've never gone on this hiking path before," he admits as they head up an overgrown hill. "It's not really marked that well, is it?"

"This, my boy, is the way to my special path," Earl promises. "I don't show it to just anyone. Not everyone gets to see what's at the end of it. You know I've never allowed your friends to follow me."

"But I get to?"

"You do," Earl says.

Clint beams. He's the chosen one.

Earl faces forward, trying to hide his pleased smile. But it's no use. He's beaming, too. He's done it—he's harnessed the boy's attention.

Now, all he needs is a story. But that's the easy part. As far as Earl's concerned, anyway.

Earl, as it is known throughout this part of northern Minnesota, is a storyteller. A man with the best fish tales. Told, each one of them, with a ridiculous stretch of the truth, a wink, and, at times, a sprinkling of magic.

"Steep," Clint observes between huffs and puffs. They both have to lean forward to stay upright.

They're quiet as they walk, weaving between more overgrown trees. Clint glances about him, looking for markers. Signs that will help him find his own way back, should the two of them be separated. He doesn't do it with fear, though. He does it with the same confidence he'll one day feel as an adult when moving through the wilder, largely untraveled areas of the outdoors.

"Wow," Clint says excitedly as they round the top curve. "It's like a movie."

Earl smiles to himself. It is—with the mist and the lush green flowerings of early spring and the dramatic music from the birds who are all nest building.

"I didn't know there was a waterfall here," Clint tells

4

him, his eyes stuck on the splashing torrent.

"Not a waterfall," Earl says, his mind beginning to spin a tale the boy wouldn't be able to forget if he tried.

Clint frowns. Clearly, it is. Thick white foam rounds the top of a rocky cliff and tumbles downward, pummeling the nearby river.

"Not *just* any old run-of-the-mill waterfall," Earl corrects himself. "This one appeared long ago. The beginning of time, they say. When there was nothing out here—no flowers, nothing green. Only this here rocky cliff and the river below." *That should set the stage*, he tells himself.

His mind spins and his tone turns soft as he continues, "Heard tell a young woman who lived right here fell in love, you see. But alas—that's a real live, genuine old-fashioned word, *alas*—she had been betrothed to another. Her parents had pledged her to marry him when she was just a child."

Clint grimaces. No modern child could imagine such a thing.

"Matters of the heart, son, they're powerful," Earl tells him. "More powerful than anything on this planet. With no way to be with her true love, she jumped off that cliff up there, into the river below. They say this waterfall was created by the power of the love flowing from her heart as she fell. It gushed out of her, every bit as strong as the beat of that water."

Earl pauses to congratulate himself on the story he has started to weave. That beginning of his is exceptional—he is, of course, a man who believes in true love. But it needs more, he thinks. Some reason for Clint to hold on to it. Some little hint of superstition, maybe.

He continues, "They say that this waterfall will tell you if your own love is true. If you bring your sweetheart here, and you aren't meant to be, you'll lose each other in the mist. A coldness will overtake you. But if you can still see each other, even when you get so close to the mist that the rest of the world is whited out and vanishes from sight, why then, you've found her. The love of your life."

Clint blinks at Earl as if to ask, *Why do I need to hear this? My friends are waiting.* He is, this spring, still more boy than man.

Earl chuckles. "Just one of many such amazing and powerful places around here, my boy. Why I had to buy this place. Why I love it so much." *Bring it back down to earth*, he scolds himself.

Clint's eyes widen. "What other—" he starts, clearly gearing up to ask Earl if there are other great hangouts he, Greg, and Todd have yet to find. Without all the love stuff.

"No, no, one magical location at a time," Earl says. He wants this story to sink in. To permeate. To be something Clint carries with him into adulthood. "That's enough for now. You ought to go join your friends."

He smiles, watching Clint race off, retracing their steps.

"Got him on the line," Earl says proudly. If he has anything to do with it, Clint will never let this place go.

Today
Missouri State University
Springfield, Missouri

Chelsea
Memory Retrieval

Laughter filters through my window screen. I glance down from my second-story dorm room as two girls with matching tans, blond ponytails, and maroon and white T-shirts finish sticking their banner into the ground. "Welcome Home," the sign proclaims. It's intended for the eighteen-year-olds who will soon begin showing up for the student orientation and registration program—a steady stream of them, all summer long. Taking math and English placement tests. Signing up for classes. Getting the first look at their dorm assignments. These girls—probably sorority sisters who have been roped into working orientation—stand back for an inspection. Hold their hands up, making frames out of their fingers. Laugh again.

I chuckle right along with them before swiveling on a heel to look at my empty shelves, the open and empty closet, the empty wire wastebasket.

"Well," I tell the blank bulletin board and the vacant student desk and the naked twin beds, "I hope you're a good match for whoever gets you next." Because the room is no longer my own home-sweet-home. It's my ex-room. In my ex-dormitory. Which I used to share with my ex-roommate, a philosophy major who'd decorated the walls on her side with posters featuring Nietzsche quotes. Posters that have already been taken down, rolled into tubes, and carted out.

I shake my head. "Can't get nostalgic for a place you haven't officially left yet, Keyes," I scold myself, picking up my remaining textbook as the distant notes of laughter are replaced by another, decidedly familiar sound. Rhythmic. A basketball's bouncing against the hallway. Getting louder as it gets closer.

The ball bounces once against my dorm room floor, then launches itself toward me like a long-lost love grateful to find me again. On instinct, I drop my ancient Intro to Psych book; it whacks against the floor as I open my hands. My palms sting the moment the basketball hits—a sting that's as bittersweet as it is familiar.

I raise the ball to my nose and breathe in the smell of leather and rubber—the smell of a gym, which, as far as I'm concerned, is the smell of anticipation and adrenaline. Of cheering hometown crowds chanting my name. Of cameras flashing and feet stomping and local reporters gearing up to interview me after the game. Of riding on teammates' shoulders in triumph.

Closing my eyes, I press my fingertips against the surface of the ball; the bumpy skin reminds me of the hedge apples that grow near my hometown of Fair Grove. I'm back there, all over again.

Six Years Ago

Fair Grove, Missouri

Big fish, small pond. Or so the old saying goes.

Fair Grove is a quaint little town, the tiniest of such ponds, the kind of place where residents hand-embroider similar little sayings into wall hangings, to be sold at church bazaars. It is engulfed by thick Missouri woods and prickly overgrowth. Gravel roads are not uncommon. Mailboxes, rusted and battered, are often seen with their doors half-open, because if a mischievous burst of wind happens to tug out a letter or a bill, why, a neighbor would simply make sure it finds its way home again.

Perhaps everyone is a celebrity in a small town. There is room enough for each of them to have their own claim to fame: Mary brings her prize-winning blackberry jam to the county fair each July, and nobody knows his way around an engine quite like Mack at the Quick Mart. Hank makes the best pizza in town, hands down. And if you want a baby blanket for the newest member of the family, Beth is the knitter you want. Master gardener Tim can help you if your tomatoes stall, won't turn red, and you can't for the life of you figure out why.

They don't take their labels lightly. In order to survive, a small town needs its heroes. For those who call Fair Grove home, it is also a way of knowing their neighbors, a way of quickly recognizing when they are in trouble. And understanding how to help.

Chelsea Keyes, whose name is regularly placed, letter by letter, on the sign outside of the bank, is no exception. She wears her title with pride; it is not a name tag so much as it is a piece of her soul, a way to know herself. "GO CHELSEA!" has become a familiar chant each night the Fair Grove Lady Eagles are scheduled to play. She hears it even in her dreams.

She is not a good basketball player according to a small town's simple definition. She is good by any definition. No debate about that. Couple of weeks ago, a crew from *Sportsverse* magazine came out to interview her. Brought a photographer to snap the game between the Fair Grove Eagles and last year's state champions, the Willard Tigers. All for some big article on the best student athletes in the country.

Some in Fair Grove say she is the best their little town has ever turned out. Others tighten their lips, scrunch up their faces a bit at this declaration—their expressions insist, wordlessly, this *is* open for some healthy debate. Fair Grove has had plenty of heroes, after all. Each generation brings with it a new crop to replace the old.

Regardless of how they rank Chelsea (good, great, best of all time), every last one of the thirteen hundred residents has laid claim to her. She is *theirs*. Something the air and the soil and the backyard barbecues and the annual Heritage Festival has churned out. They have all contributed to the making of this hero, every last one of them.

This Saturday, just outside of Hill Toppers' Pizza, they turn to watch Chelsea climb from her boyfriend's Mustang. They all knew she'd be coming; the team always meets up here the day after a win for one of Hank's celebratory deep dishes. Fair Grove residents are always stopping to look at her anytime she is out and about, heading to the library or the gym or her parent's bakery, White Sugar. Like you would stop and look at an A-list celebrity.

A basketball whacks the parking lot, and she opens her hands to catch it. The ball stings her skin in a way that feels familiar and good.

"You do autographs?" It's Mr. Gleeson, Chelsea's algebra teacher. He puts his hands on his daughter's shoulder. She's ten, maybe eleven. Chelsea can't quite remember, not after so many introductions to so many little girls. She remembers her name, though. Jana. It's the names she takes the most trouble to remember.

And she knows that Jana looks up to her. Gleeson told her again last week, when he was handing the class's tests back.

Chelsea smiles and slides a Sharpie from her teacher's hand.

"That was some game last night," he tells her.

"Chelsea scored the winning point," Jana says, blushing.

"She scored a lot more than just the winning one," Gleeson reminds her.

Chelsea presents the ball to his daughter, who is wearing a T-shirt from the basketball camp she attended last summer. She has her hair tied into a French braid, to mimic the way her hero often wears hers when she's playing.

Chelsea stoops to hug Jana. The rest of the parking lot is filled with weekend pizza lovers who tilt their heads, then sigh in awe. Chelsea is such a sweet girl, they all agree.

But *sweet* doesn't get your name on the sign outside the bank. It doesn't bring math teachers to seek you out, telling you that you're their daughters' hero. It doesn't get you interviewed or win you scholarships or snag you the cutest boy in school.

Simply being on the team doesn't get you those things,

either. After all, the rest of the team is just inside Hill Toppers'. And no one is flocking to get basketballs signed by any of them.

Chelsea Keyes is a lot of things. But mostly, what Chelsea is—the thing that everyone in Fair Grove lays claim to, the thing that makes her the most famous among the small-town celebrities, the thing that Chelsea knows makes her *her*—is that she wins.

———◦◦◦———

Chelsea
Freudian Slip

I take another breath. That basketball in my hands smells like something very much alive. The same way my dream of playing college ball was once very much alive. At least, until an accident on the court my senior year of high school resulted in a broken hip—and a similarly shattered dream.

But broken dreams can fuse together in new ways, just as bones can mend.

I open my eyes finally, passing the ball back to Makayla, who's standing inside the open doorway. Her box braid ponytail is hanging at a bit of a crooked tilt, and she has wet splotches on the front of her Lady Bears T-shirt and a sweaty face, all of which tells me she's just come from an off-season workout.

"Hoped I'd catch you before you headed out. Looks like I almost didn't." She nods at the quilted top of my stripped mattress and the bare walls.

"I'm on the last box now," I say, glancing down at the last remaining cardboard container, propped somewhat precariously on the edge of my bed. It's full of the lowest sedimentary layers: junk I've mindlessly carted from one dorm room to another over the past four years at Missouri State. This is freshman-year crap: an old spiral notebook with the email addresses of all my high school teammates (addresses I haven't typed in years); funky little tchotchkes—the kind of thing you think'll look cool sitting on your home-away-from-home bookshelf when you're eighteen; a couple of old cell phone cases in various states of falling apart; a flatiron I haven't used since sophomore year (because life had kicked into full gear by then, and who had time to stand in front of a mirror getting rid of unruly waves?); a metal desk box full of pencils and who-knows-what-else.

"Just had to say thanks." Makayla grabs me around my neck and gives me a hug. But it's not a polite hug, not a last day of school, it's-been-nice pat on the back. It happens as quickly as the slam of a door, but it's also no bullshit, pure gratitude. An I-mean-it hug. From a freshman (actually, now that the year's over, a sophomore) that I spent the past year working with one-on-one, coaching her on how to cope with the pressure of competition—playing on the collegiate level.

"I've never hated summer break before," she says through a laugh. "This year, I hate its guts. I wish we could keep on working." She raises the neck of her T-shirt to wipe sweat from the bridge of her nose.

"Oh, I'll only be gone for a couple of weeks. Not the whole summer. Besides, you've got your own workout schedule. And a family I'm sure you're anxious to see." I grab my graduation gown from the back of my desk chair and toss it into my box, followed shortly by the mortarboard hat.

"Thank God you'll still be with the athletic department while you get your master's degree," Makayla says. "There's a ton more to do."

"Keyes!" It's not so much a greeting as it is a bark from a Rottweiler who means business. I know exactly who that bark belongs to long before Durst, the MSU Athletic Director, clomps down to the end of the hall and pokes his balding head through my open dorm room doorway.

"Hey, Makayla," he adds. "Should have known you'd want to say goodbye to our girl."

"Not goodbye forever," Makayla reminds him. "We need her."

"You think so, do you?" Durst asks, folding his arms over his chest. Three years I've been working for him, and he's never once told me I've done a good job. On anything. To be honest, the guy didn't even want to hire me. Mostly because there wasn't a position to fill. I was trying to invent one. It was spring of my freshman year, Dad had just had a heart attack, and I was desperate to make sure he and Mom would have one less money worry. Durst must've thought I was some egotistical jerk, knocking on his door after barely two semesters, offering to work one-on-one with the athletes. Sports psychology major. Please. What did I know?

Nothing. That's what. More than anything, I was scared.

But then, as he started to wave his hand, telling me to get lost, a stroke of luck: one of the phys ed instructors told him the weight room attendee had called from the emergency room. Broken arm.

This news came on top of another head—seemed like a student's—popping into his office, and Post-it notes rippling in the breeze from his fan, and a phone buzzing with a new incoming text about every two seconds.

"You," he'd barked at me. "You get to the weight room."

Three days later, he'd shown up to the same weight room. "You!" he'd bellowed.

"Me?" I'd asked, pointing at my chest.

"You still here?"

I'd nodded.

"Then I guess you work here. What's your name, anyway?"

After that, I'd kept equipment wiped down. I'd helped launder towels. I'd maintained the girl's locker room. I'd put up tennis nets and taken them down again. I'd timed laps. My soundtrack was the squeak of sneakers on a basketball floor, the grunt of football players smacking into tackling dummies, the weird echoing whacks of rubber balls hitting the walls of the racquetball courts.

It went on like that for weeks. Until Durst sauntered up to me during a summer camp. "You! Keyes," he'd said. "What do you think?"

"About?"

"About that kid over there." He handed me a player evaluation form. With places to put a check mark next to items like "consistency," "reaction under pressure," "knowledge of rules." I didn't stop at the check marks, scrawling observations up and down the margins.

When I'd handed the form to Durst, he grunted.

That was it.

But after that, while my roommate was home, ditching the books for three months, I was still on campus, taking on additional classwork and assisting with the rest of the summer camps. During the regular school year, I was on buses going to away games. I was at recruiting combines, sizing up players' mentalities while they ran drills, whispering my observations into coaches' ears.

I'd barely get a chance to sit down—or grab a protein bar from the vending machine outside the student gym— when Durst would pop up or my phone would buzz and he'd bellow, "Keyes! Forty yard line! Now!" Or, "Keyes! Sand volleyball court!" Or, "Keyes! Weight room!"

Now, though, it's Makayla who's lecturing Durst. "We only need her if you want to win. It's Chelsea's specialty. Taking a losing situation and turning it around."

It's too kind. I know it is. I'm not exactly a miracle worker. And I still do plenty of gym cleanup. Not exactly the stuff of superstardom. Frankly, the way I bought into my own superstar status back when I was in high school makes me cringe a little now. I'm a girl who loves basketball, and is grateful to be around it any way I can. Period. Still, Durst smiles, pleating the skin in the corners of his eyes.

"I have one more request," he says.

I take a deep breath, my stomach knotting up. Is this a big job he has in mind? I'm due back home. What could he possibly need?

"Get out of here, already."

I toss my head back and laugh.

"You graduated," Durst insists, leaning forward to give me a quick hug and a pat on the back. "You are not allowed in any of my gyms for two weeks. Then I expect you back here for summer camps." He waits for me to hop to this instruction, too. Just like I'd hopped on every one of his previous assignments.

"Giving it all one last look," I say, scooping my cardboard box into my arms.

This satisfies him. He steps out of the room, darts back down the hall.

18

Makayla points at the floor. "Don't forget your book."

I grunt, plop the box on the floor. I squat to scoop up the textbook I'd dropped—I never did sell back any book related to my own major—but stop short. I'm frozen in place, butt on heels, one hand mid-air, eyes glued to the postcard that slipped from the pages of my psych book the moment it hit the ground.

The edges are all soft from wear, but the image on the front is every bit as sharp as ever. There I am, eighteen years old, smiling triumphantly as I hold up the enormous wall-eyed pike I'd caught aboard one of the fishing launches at the Lake of the Woods resort. I know what's on the back—it's inscribed in permanent marker in my mind. All of it, every detail, down to the four-year-old Baudette, Minnesota post-mark and the messy man's handwriting that proclaims, *You won! Biggest catch of the season! You get your free week! See you next summer—Clint.*

I finally quit doing my stunning impersonation of a mannequin and reach forward. The moment my fingertips touch the postcard, though, my ears fill with the sound of rushing water. The dorm room fades away completely—no more Makayla, no more textbook. I'm behind a waterfall that rages, pummeling the small pond below, while mist gathers over my naked body. Initially, the mist is as light as early morning fog—but as the seconds tick, and the waterfall continues to gush, the mist grows heavier—it builds, like condensation on the outside of a glass on a scorching August afternoon. Droplets run down my arms; they slide from my spine around my sides, tracing the curves of my ribs. They race down the outer contours of my breasts, drip from my nipples to land on the bare chest of the man stretched out below me. The muscles in his abdomen are tight and trembling. I lower myself, putting my lips against his collarbone. He murmurs my name, his voice vibrating against my mouth. He tastes good—like sweat and hope and—

"Chelsea."

I jump, shove the postcard under the cover of the psych book, and glance up at Makayla, who's got an almost motherly look on her face. "Are you okay? You got all flushed. You're not sick, are you?"

"No—I'm—fine." But my legs are so weak, it's nearly impossible to lift that enormous old textbook and stand at the same time. I wobble on my feet; Makayla rushes forward to steady me.

"Are you sure? Maybe you shouldn't drive—"

"I'm fine." I pretend not to notice my voice breaking as I slide the textbook into my box. "Just worn out from the fishing."

"Fishing?" She frowns.

"Finals!" I let out giggle. "They've scrambled my brain. Obviously."

I glance for the last time about the dorm room, which has been sans-roommate for the past two days already. And now, in a matter of seconds, will be sans-me, too. "See you in June," I say.

"June!" She brightens, tucking the basketball between her hip and her wrist.

I toss the book into my box, then hoist the whole over-sized thing into my arms. "Shut the door behind me, will you?"

"Sure thing," Makayla says.

I hurry through the hall and out the dorm exit. The moment my feet strike the sidewalk, a welcome mid-May breeze begins to swirl against my hot cheeks. My long blond hair ripples wildly about the shoulders my cami's left bare. What happened to me in that dorm room? When I saw that postcard? The muscles in my legs feel hot and loose all over again—like I've finished a 5K run. Clint Morgan. Lake of the Woods, Minnesota. That glorious summer when I was eighteen.

"Chelsea. *Chelsea*. Hold up a minute."

A hand rests on my elbow, and I skid to a stop, the contents of my box letting out a clatter of annoyance. The face in front of me belongs to Nathan Cooper—a fellow recent psych graduate and a member of my study groups ever since our junior year statistics course. "I started calling your name as soon as you came out of that dorm back there. Not worried about Dr. Schuller's Abnormal final, are you?" He grins. "That sounded like the final was abnormal, didn't it?"

I grin back as Nathan tries to slide the cardboard box from my arms. It's heavier than he anticipated, though—he nearly drops it, and I have to catch it for him. "I got it," I say, smoothing over his embarrassment. "But I could go for some company. Why don't you walk me to my car?"

This perks him right up. Like I knew it would. I know a fair amount about Nathan Cooper, actually. Know he reads the classics, likes subtitled movies, and prefers cinnamon in his coffee (that last detail is one I learned during our handful of informal coffee outings). He's sweet and sincere, and every single time I look at him, I can see him, twenty years in the future, "Dr." firmly affixed before his last name, lecturing a psych class at a private university, suede patches on the elbows of his tweed jacket.

"You shouldn't be worried," he says, nudging my arm. "About Schuller's final. High B+."

"How do you know?" I ask. But not in any kind of accusatory way. I don't even ask with a frown on my face. I'm curious.

"Saw it on his desk yesterday. On top of a stack of

graded tests."

"Oh."

I guess this is not exactly the reaction he was expecting. He keeps staring at the side of my face as the sidewalk begins to curve toward Craig Hall. "Chelsea! High B+! Come on. You should be ecstatic. We studied for that for about a month and a half."

"It's a relief," I agree, but I'm still spinning inside from the postcard. I clear my throat, try to shake these feelings away. "Were you and Schuller touching base about the fall?"

Nathan nods. "Picking his brain, bouncing ideas for my thesis. I have all kinds of theories I connect with, and I have definite interests, but it's hard to narrow it all down into any specific topic," he rattles on, as we use the Grand Street Underpass to cross from campus toward the lot where my Camaro's parked. "Do you know what your focus will be?"

"Sports rehab," I say, my voice echoing through the damp, dark concrete underpass. Four years, and I'm still not used to the thing. It's always felt like the kind of no-way-out tunnel where serial killers hang out waiting for the perfect unsuspecting, distracted victim. Nathan squirms, telling me he's feeling it, too. "The process of mental healing," I go on.

"You got Durst to agree!" Nathan sings out happily.

"Yeah, I've actually got a few athletes lined up to work into my thesis—a baseball player who got hit with a curveball some time ago but still keeps backing out of the batter's box, a quarterback who dislocated his shoulder in a tackle, and a basketball player who fractured her rib as the result of a charging foul."

It all sounds so professional, but really, it's anything but. Four years of classes later, I still feel like I know absolutely nothing. What right do I have to swoop in and act like I have some great solution to the players' problems? What if I say or do something that only makes it worse?

I mean, yes, I was injured, but my accident ended everything. I never tried to play again. What do I know about it?

Makes me feel like a fraud, frankly.

"Sports rehab. That's right up your alley," Nathan says. He chuckles at the way his words seem to have a double meaning as we climb up the stairs, out of the alley-narrow underpass.

"You going to get started this summer?"

"I've got a waterfall," I start.

"Waterfall?"

"Wonderful. A wonderful opportunity with the camps…"

"Waterfall, huh? No chance that was a Freudian slip there," Nathan teases.

"Might be thinking about summer breaks past," I admit.

"Graduation makes you get a little reflective, doesn't it?"

That's twice now. Twice that my thoughts of Clint have worked their way into my conversation.

I try to brush it off, tug my keys from my khaki shorts as I get close to my much-adored Camaro. For the past four years, my cherry red sixteenth birthday present has been zipping between the campus in Springfield and my family home in Fair Grove like the world's most dedicated teammate engaging in crazy wind sprints. The Camaro's eight years old at this point; she's got a disturbingly large crack in the windshield and she needs new tires. She makes some funny noises these days, too. I probably should let Mack, owner of the Fair Grove Quick Mart (and part-time mechanic) take a look at it. But I'm afraid that whatever it'll take to get her back into perfect working order will cost more than she's worth.

I pop the trunk. Put the cardboard box inside.

The Intro to Psych book stares up at me.

"Text me this fall," Nathan says. "We'll put together the best study group in the history of the psych department. Deal?"

I mumble something close to "Okay."

"Actually," he says, "give me your phone. I'll put my number in it. We can touch base over the summer."

If I had my head about me, I'd figure out some way to wiggle out of that request. I've been thwarting Nathan's advances for months. But this time, I hand the phone over.

"See you later, Chelse," he says, making sure to touch my arm before slipping away.

When he's gone, I flip the cover of the textbook, pull out the old postcard, stare at my eighteen-year-old self. And the waterfall noise comes back—faint this time, but it makes my heart beat as feverishly as it had before. Clint Morgan. When I close my eyes, I can remember exactly what his lips felt like against my own.

I'm suddenly tossing my mortar board hat and my graduation gown aside. I'm rifling through all my freshman year crap. I'm tugging out my old metal desk box. Popping the lid.

And there it is, nestled inside, as it has been for the past four years: Clint's old Boy Scout compass, pointing north—straight toward Minnesota and everything I once left behind.

Four Years Ago

Lake of the Woods Fishing Resort
Minnesota

Early morning—the sun is still rising, staining the Minnesota landscape a pale orange. Light is beginning to dance between the pines, allowing their branches to cast lacy shadows along the fringes of the lake. A river hawk spreads her wings and swoops straight out of the sky; her toes skim the cool surface of the water as she flaps her wings to rise again, a breakfast trout snared in her talons. The towering shade trees scattered throughout the Lake of the Woods Fishing Resort rustle, announcing that the night owls and possums are scurrying back into their nests to sleep. Bluebirds and finches chirp, eagerly telling the morning everything they'd dreamed of the night before. The lake lets out a few gentle sighs of its own, admitting it, too, is still trying to fully wake up.

The front door of cabin number four opens, and Chelsea is the first to step out onto the porch. She's eighteen—with the kind of beauty a person can only lay claim to once in their lifetime. She has youth on her side. Her skin has darkened to a healthy caramel color over the past three weeks, but her cheeks remain a delicate pink and her meticulously straightened blond hair ripples about her shoulders in the summer breeze.

The boards creak as she takes a hesitant step forward

and drops her bag at her feet. There's a beyond-her-age maturity in her light blue eyes. The kind that comes with having something important stolen from you. For Chelsea, an accident on the basketball court taught her nearly a year ago that she isn't superhuman, and that dreams are never guaranteed. Best intentions are brittle.

Behind her, Chelsea's family rattles around inside their cabin, double-checking each room to make sure they aren't leaving anything behind. Chelsea's own bag, sitting at an angle at her feet, is full of wadded clothes, nothing folded or organized. Things she's crammed and smashed together in her rush to get outside ahead of everyone else.

It's checkout day. Her father will return the key to Earl, the owner of the resort where they have spent the past three weeks. One last family vacation before Chelsea starts college. But it has been so much more. Because of Clint. An unexpected love affair. And though she's reminded herself for the past hour that she and Clint agreed there would be no blubbering last-day goodbyes, she can't go without one more glimpse of him as he starts his work day. Maybe, for the tiniest sliver of a moment, she can pretend that she's about to join him—that there will be another stolen glance, another touch, a kiss.

There hasn't been enough time. She wants to call out to him, to tell him so.

He's where she hoped he would be, on the dock maybe a hundred feet from cabin number four, loading coolers into a freshly painted white fishing launch, bright orange life jackets aboard and ready. The guests will be arriving soon, poles in hand. Clint will steer them out to a spot where he knows the walleye will be biting. He'll teach the novices how to bait a hook safely, how to troll, how to keep a grip on a pole when it bows beneath the weight of an angry twenty-pounder. Like he taught Chelsea the first morning she arrived.

And more. In the span of only three weeks together, he has taught her far more. Clint the ex-hockey player opened a path to healing for Chelsea the ex-basketball player. He showed her there is always another quarter, another chance to rebound. There is life again after losing.

Clint turns her way. Does a double take. Chelsea's heart speeds up. She gets the feeling that he's been keeping watch on cabin number four, waiting for one last look of his own.

Clint stops working, leaving behind the half-loaded launch. Stands on the dock staring. He's only nineteen, but most of the women who try to catch his eye at the resort guess he's closer to twenty-five. He's classically muscular, broad-shouldered, his chiseled face reminiscent of an old-time movie star, of black and white big screen close-ups.

He has endured a life-altering trauma of his own, before meeting Chelsea, and it has weathered him. He has seen what he doesn't want to, and it has also toughened him, left him with an in-charge appearance. The hazy morning sunlight paints shiny silver streaks across the top of his black hair—the same way it throws silver streaks across calm waters.

Chelsea's healed him, too. They both know she did. Found a way into the heart he had sealed off after losing his first love in such a sudden way, a car accident on an icy curve. On her way to watch one of his pond games, Clint's girlfriend had ignored the road conditions and become airborne, landing in the ravine below—her white car hidden in the recent snowfall for days. But Chelsea has shown him that life does not only offer one chance to be happy.

She wants to forget her promise and run to him. Let him know that she came here thinking she knew what love was—that it was something you chose, something you picked out for yourself. *Can you believe it?* she'd ask. *Have you ever heard of anything so completely foolish? It's not shopping—it's love!* What has happened between the two of them, she would rush to tell him, is something that chose her. It invaded her. Uninvited. Unexpected. Undeniable.

That's what love is. She knows that now.

Clint takes a step forward, as though he intends to walk all the way back down the dock before she goes. But he stops abruptly, slides his hands into the pockets of his shorts. His body stiffens, like he has to flex every one of his muscles in order to hold himself back.

Chelsea offers a crooked smile, her lips wiggling slightly. She thinks she will always remember the way he looks standing there in the morning sun.

Here, under a sunrise—the universal symbol of a new beginning—she's leaving him. What choice does she have? Her life is two states away, in Missouri. And his is here, in Minnesota.

Never live timidly, they'd sworn the night before. They're determined to hold tight to that vow. Because even in the midst of their sadness, the tiniest bubbles of excitement are rising in them both. They're anxious to get to their next life chapters—his sophomore year at the university, and her first big step away from home, heading off for her freshman year at college. *Is it crazy to think the world feels wide open?* Chelsea wishes she could call out to him. *To think that I am actually comfortable in the skin of a person who does not play ball anymore? To think that the best times are not already behind me?* She imagines he would tell her he understands what she means. *It's because our paths have crossed*, he'd say.

In the distance, farther down the lake, cabin doors are opening and slamming. Clint's guests will be coming his way. His daily chores will demand his full attention; the world will roll forward. A day at the lake, like any other.

He's sure that Chelsea's departure would be agonizing

if he hadn't spoken to his boss that morning. Earl had been changing out the photos on the bulletin board, putting up a new picture for a new #1 biggest catch so far. Down went Chelsea and up went the picture of one of their seasoned fishermen. Someone else was going to win the free come-back-again week Earl always gave to the guest who claimed the biggest catch of the summer.

"I know Chelsea lost," Clint had said, pointing at the bulletin board. "But can we give her family a free week just the same? You can take it out of my paycheck." And Earl, whose own nineteen-year-old self was still lurking around somewhere underneath his gray beard, had simply smiled and said, "Nothin' in my rule book says we can't have two winners. Tell your girl she won."

Clint had repeated that to himself: *your girl.* He repeats it now, as the door to cabin number four opens and three more people step outside. As Chelsea's parents and her brother clomp down the front steps and hoist their bags into their SUV.

She's still on the porch. Waiting for him to give her a sign of what this scene is doing to him. To let her know it's twisting him into painful knots identical to her own.

Clint slips one hand from his pocket and holds it into the air briefly. Chelsea reads into that simple, quick wave everything she hoped that she would see. Clint offers her a reassuring nod, trusting that she will know he's telling her there's no need to feel bad. Because it's not goodbye. *It's not the end. We'll get more time,* he would call out to her, if he allowed himself to say one more thing before her leaving.

He imagines the surprise that will find her when he sends her the postcard he's already written in his mind. *Biggest catch of the season!* it'll say. *You get your free week!*

And she'll reappear, smiling, jumping into his arms. Of

course she will. What happened between them isn't something you throw back—like some too-small catch. It isn't something you forget. What happened between them brought him back to the best parts of himself. It did the same for her, too. He knows that. It isn't over—there will always be a connection. What is between them could never evaporate, no more than the Lake of the Woods waterfall, rushing constantly and forcefully in the distance, could ever run dry. Clint smiles, listening to the pulse of the waterfall they'd crawled behind, secluded, naked, covered in mist, whispering, "Please." He'd said that—the word rings in his head—*please*. And she had answered, not with words but with her body.

There is no need for any word now, Clint thinks as he turns toward his boat. Nor is there any need to watch Chelsea get into her family's car and drive away.

She'll be back.

Today
Baudette Community Ice Rink
Minnesota

<hr>

Clint
Stillwater

"Life's not worth living if it's away from water," I tell Luke. "Even frozen water. Like the ice rink here. You ever notice that ice has a smell? Ah, it's a great smell, man. And the swooping sounds of skates carving new paths—it's music. You ever look at a rink after a hockey game? All those white scribbles drawn by the blades of skates? Now, in my book, that's art."

Luke doesn't respond. Not that I really expected him to. I know I'm talking to myself more than him. Not that it ever stops me. Nice to have a sounding board. Even if the sounding board has not yet entered kindergarten.

I take a deep breath. And savor the smell of the ice as

my players fly past my spot inside the penalty box. Which is where I'll apparently be watching them all summer. With Luke.

For an hour six times a week, the Baudette rink's all mine. Tom, the owner who signed me up for my first hockey lesson when I was not much older than Luke, gives me free rein. And a salary. But the salary's so small, it's mostly the free rein that appeals to me. Keeps me coming back.

And the ice, of course. God, I love the ice.

The rink's full, right now, with my Lake of the Woods Youth Hockey crew. They come in the off-season for additional training. Enough of them this year that I've divided them by age, alternating each day between junior and senior groups. And each group is big enough to be broken, each session, into a random assortment of two teams.

The players in this senior group chase each other, they chase the puck, they chase the chance to be the star for the afternoon. To get my thumbs up and bitter looks from the rest of the guys. Looks that warn, *Wait till next time. Coach'll be giving me the thumbs up and you'll be wiping up a bloody nose.* Kind of like trash talking without actual words.

"In here, it's all about love," I tell Luke, because he doesn't mind when I get all serious like this. "The rest of the junk the world makes you chase—money, approval, success—it doesn't exist anymore. In here, nothing matters but the ice. Know what I mean?"

When I take my eyes off my players and glance at the space beside me on the bench in the penalty box, the blond head I expect to see is gone. My heart dips so low, it could get stuck in the elastic of my socks. "Luke?"

I put my head between my legs, searching under the bench where he likes to crawl. "Luke?" I ask again, even though he's obviously not here.

"Luke!" I'm on my feet, glancing out across the ice. It's not the easiest thing in the world to coach from the penalty box while keeping an eye on a five-year-old. I figure racing around through the entire arena looking for him while wearing hockey skates will prove to be infinitely harder.

"Shhh!"

"Luke. There you are," I sigh. Relief is so deep, I exhale until my lungs are flat. He hasn't left the box at all. Just scooted over to the far side of it.

"Shhh!" he whispers again. "I found a tarantula." At five years old, Luke is interested in nothing in this world like he's interested in bugs. The more legs, the better.

I squat, look through his magnifying glass. It's a common house spider, but through the lens, it does seem pretty big. "What's his name?" I start to ask. But I'm cut short when a stick clatters furiously against the rink. I stand to see what just happened.

"That was Ryan again, wasn't it?" Luke asks. He curls his mouth around in disappointment.

"Yeah. It was Ryan." Frustrated again. Throwing one of his stupid fits. I shake my head as I watch Luke's older brother tear his gloves off and throw them in the same direction that he'd thrown his stick. But soft gloves don't exactly make the kind of sounds that Ryan's obviously going for. What he's after is a sound that shows how irked he is. So he tugs his helmet off and throws it, too. Spits his mouth guard right onto the ice. At fifteen, the size of Ryan's patience matches the size of his age. Minuscule.

And it's too bad, too—because the kid oozes innate ability. When he skates, he's got complete control over his body. The grace of a figure skater. And he loves the game. Occasionally, when his ride is a little late, and we get extra time to run some stickhandling drills, I can see his name on a whole warehouse of trophies.

Once he hits the ice with the rest of the guys, though, all those trophies in my head disappear, one after another, like flimsy bubbles popping. Because invariably, when he's around the varsity players, Ryan goes all fifteen-year-old: gangly and awkward, his hair hanging over half his face, and his eyes angry. Every little thing sets him off; every single reaction is over-the-top. Sometimes, the way he acts around the rest of the players makes me think he'd probably punch a mailbox if he got a letter with a crooked stamp.

"That's enough, guys." I blow my whistle for good measure. Just to let them know I mean it.

But they're in no hurry; they're not ready to leave yet.

So I point to the gaggle of girlfriends who've started to gather. Always did seem to me that girls popped to life about the same time the wildflowers started coming up from the ground here in Minnesota. Shucking their ugly winter clothes and putting on bright colors and going fishing (and by "fishing," I mean snagging their summer guys). These girls have big plans. *Enough of hockey*, their sighs say. This keeps the groaning and lingering on the ice to a minimum. This particular gaggle of girlfriends gets antsy pretty quickly. If they played something, anything—basketball, softball, Tiddlywinks—it might be different. They might understand. But most of them don't.

I skate across the rapidly emptying rink. Grab Ryan by the neck—same way I'd grab a stray cat—and drag him off the ice. Toss him onto a bench. And race back to the penalty box, where I scoop up Luke before he can decide to follow that spider, like a hunting dog on the trail of a rabbit.

"I quit," Ryan grumbles when I set Luke on the floor. I'm not sure if Ryan's cheeks are pink from the cold or his embarrassment. I haven't seen the exact move that made him toss his stick this time, but the past few weeks have been a pretty steady stream of Ryan getting knocked on his ass, knocked into the boards, and laughed at by a particularly brutal goaltender.

Ryan's the weak spot. The easy target. When they play, the rest of the guys know it. And they have no problem zeroing in on him, ganging up on him, reminding him he needs to toughen up.

I know all about that.

Six Years Ago

CLINT'S LAST GAME

My head swims. I'm dizzy.

And they know it. They're sharks, and I'm dinner.

I can hear the slice of skates. I can't get my bearings. My heart beats too hard. The crowd screams.

My legs wobble. My ankles are weak.

I expect the crash, but when it comes, it surprises me just the same. I feel like I've been turned into a puck as I'm body checked, slammed into the boards.

A whistle is blown. Illegal checking.

But where am I? When will the spinning end?

I think I can taste blood. Did my head hit the boards?

I try to move my feet and collide with the net.

I'm taken off the ice and led to the locker room. Some sort of rink physician is shining a light in my eyes, checking for signs of a concussion.

I know the drill. I've been checked for a concussion the last four games.

"Clint," Coach Larson moans, once the doctor's left.

"Yeah," I mumble.

He flops down in a folding metal chair. I can't tell, right then, who's taken the biggest hit, him or me. He slumps. His eyes look kind of sunken into his head.

"I'm not me out there," I say for him.

"You're not."

"Ever since Rosie's accident."

"Clint, I can't blame you. That was such a—"

"—shock to the system," I finish for him. "It would have sent anyone for a loop."

He clenches his jaw and nods.

"But the thing is," I go on, still talking for him, "there's no bandage for this kind of thing. I mean—sprained ankle, torn muscle, that's one kind of injury. But a girlfriend who skids her car out on the ice on her way to your tournament and dies in a wreck? Well, nobody can tell me to go home and elevate it. Rest. Wrap it. Wrap what? What's really been hurt? The head? The heart?"

He juts his chin out. Nods again.

"You're not one to give up on a player," I go on. "You'd never cut me free. But the way I am now, I'm dangerous. To myself *and* to the other guys on the team. My head's not in the game anymore."

"Clint, if you hang up your skates now, though—"

"—I hang them up forever. I know. Senior year. No coming back from that. Not enough time to recuperate. And being out senior year, well, it's not like some college around here could ever snap me up. Collegiate hockey, that's for NHL prospects."

"Oh, man, Clint," he says, putting his elbows on his knees and his head in his hands.

"I could have been pro. That's what everybody says. But you don't know. Maybe, maybe not. Big fish, small pond, you know."

Coach finally takes a deep breath, rights himself. "Clint, I can't—"

"I can. I will. I'm taking my skates off. For good. I have to."

"I don't want you to lose *everything*," he protests.

"Aw, coach," I tell him, "it's not everything. I've got the Lake of the Woods. That place means I'll always have the water."

Today
Baudette Community Ice Rink
Minnesota

***

Clint
The One That Got Away

"Oh, come on. You're not quitting," I say as Ryan furiously unties his laces. I untie mine, too. In case Luke makes a break for it. Easier to chase after him in my socks.

"Don't quit, Ryan. I like it here," Luke says. Giggles when he looks at us through his magnifying lens. His eye is enormous.

I chuckle, but Ryan only frowns.

"Yes, I do," Ryan mutters. "I quit right now, and my dad's going to want a refund. Stupid hockey. Shoulda known it would suck. Shoulda known you'd suck. You're just some washed-up old guy who never even played in college."

He's trying to goad me into an argument. He wants

39

me to be laying into him at the exact same moment his dad shows up. It would be the perfect revenge. A beautiful way to get even with me, the jerk who wouldn't let him play with the younger kids, where we both know he'd be the standout star. No, it's all my fault, he thinks. I've humiliated him. Here he is, the youngest kid in this group. The only one with no girlfriend and no car of his own. Only a little brother who tags along to our sessions and a dad who leaves work to pick him up.

I was fifteen once, and I can read his mind. I know he's got the whole thing worked out: I'll be yelling at him when his dad shows. He'll blink his fearful eyes up at his dad, who'll be furious that I'm treating his son in such a disrespectful way. His dad will pull him from youth hockey, tell Tom that, as owner of the rink, he should know I have no business being in charge of impressionable boys. Insist he get a refund of all his fees. Might even get me fired to boot.

I cross my legs at the ankles. "Done yet?"

"I'm right, aren't I? You gave it up. Didn't you? Everyone says so." He turns his head to look up at me from underneath his shaggy hair. The look, the tone—it's like he's accusing me of stabbing him. "You weren't good enough. That was the reason. Wasn't it? You couldn't cut it. And now you're stuck coaching a bunch of kids."

When I don't answer, he bellows, "Why'd you put me with them?" His eyes aren't angry now, only sad. He doesn't think he measures up. Which is the exact opposite of how I'd wanted to make him feel. For a split second, I wonder if I've done this kid a disservice. Maybe pushed him too far. But if I've screwed up, I've got to figure out a way to fix it. I mean, who else is going to undo any mess I've made here?

"Because you're good," I tell him. "Not as good as these guys. Not right now. But you're way better than the kids in

40

your own age group. They weren't going to challenge you. I'm telling you that if you get your emotions under control, you'll be way better than these guys, too."

He takes a deep inhale. Clenches his jaw. "I'm *not* as good as they are. They hate having me out there. All they do is beat me up. They want me to quit, too."

"No, you're not listening. You can get better," I try. "Look, anything can take your head out of the game. And you're right—I did let it happen to me. I stalled out. I'll never really know what could have been. It took me a long time to get back on the ice at all. Let me help you."

"Help me?"

"You've got to learn how to channel your thoughts in a positive way. Ninety percent of sports performance is mental, right?"

Still, he stares.

"Fine. Youth hockey's nothing you have to do. It should be for love. Because you enjoy it. If I've got it wrong, and this isn't your passion, then quit. You have every right. But if you love it the way I think you do, you can't let any-thing get between you and the game. Not even some jackass coach who forces you to play with guys who are, right now, making your life miserable."

Ryan props his elbows on his knees and rubs his eyes.

"It's work," I acknowledge. "It's already been work. And it'll get harder from here, before it gets easier. I'm telling you, if we can get you to the point that you play with a team the way you play when we run drills, you'll wind up being the stuff of legends."

He glances out at the ice, mulling this over quietly.

"Hey, kid," his dad says, popping up at his side. "You have a good time?"

I shrug. "Up to you," I mutter to Ryan, too quietly for

his dad to hear.

Luke takes a step forward, staring at Ryan with his giant magnifying lens eye.

"Yeah," Ryan finally tells his dad. "Pretty good."

I grin at Luke. *We got him*, I mouth proudly. His giant eye blinks back.

While Ryan shoves his feet into his sneakers, his dad reaches down for his skates.

"Those aren't mine," Ryan says. "They're coach's. He has 'C's on the heels. See? His initial."

My smile flattens out. I'd painted those white "C"s on my skates so long ago, I'd literally forgotten all about them. But there they are—rubbed off in spots, but still clearly capital "C"s.

Ryan's wrong, though. Those "C"s don't stand for "Clint" at all. They stand for the person who restarted my heart after Rosie died. They stand for the person who finally got me on the ice again.

They stand for "Chelsea."

Chelsea

EGO

I'm officially home. I slip my Camaro into my usual parking space beyond the entrance of White Sugar, the family business. When I lunge inside, the bakery seems even more fragrant than usual. Probably, to anyone else who stops by for a coffee and an eclair (or maybe one of Mom's special extra-moist birthday cakes), the smells meld into a confectionery swirl: a wild assortment of bagels and coconut cakes and cream horns, espresso and mocha and fresh raspberry icing. All of it mixed together, creating a single perfume. But I've logged so many hours here—working behind the counter, taking phone orders, cleaning the ovens and sweeping the floors—that I can always tell what Mom's just taken out of the oven. There's always one smell that's stronger than any other.

Today, my bet is red velvet cake with cream cheese icing.

I take a step toward the giant glass display case, where my eyes zero in on a large pyramid of red velvet cupcakes. So fresh, the pyramid is still perfect—not a single missing cupcake. Because they haven't been out long enough to sell one yet. Bingo. Score one for Chelsea Keyes.

Mom zips her petite frame around behind the counter in her usual halfway-frantic hummingbird way as she talks to a customer who's flipping through the three-ring binder where she keeps pictures of her masterpieces. Wedding cakes. 'Tis the season, after all.

"Chelsea!" Mom shouts. "Tell Gabe about the cake I made for the Bass wedding last summer."

I pivot, gearing up to say something about her three-tiered dark chocolate concoction with strawberry flavored roses. The cake Mom always points to as proof that wedding sweets don't have to be white (or covered and decorated in soft pastel fondant). Proof that roses on cakes are not cliché but timeless. Besides, the most important thing is actually how good the cake tastes. Let's face it, wedding cakes are only pretty long enough for a picture or two, and then suddenly people are hacking into them and cramming heaping forkfuls into their faces. And you do want your guests to enjoy themselves, right?

I stop short when I realize who I'm staring at: blond hair, eyes as green as images of Ireland's landscapes. Gabe Ross. My high school boyfriend.

I'm overcome, at first, by the memories of first kisses and hand holding near open lockers and formal dances and whispered promises.

But these flashes quickly give way to the summer after

our high school graduation—the summer we were officially no longer a "we." Which means I'm suddenly fidgeting and feeling humiliated, wishing I could have arrived later, wanting to melt into oblivion. Because things didn't end well with Gabe. And that was entirely my fault.

Kill me now.

"Gabe's engaged," Mom announces.

"He—you—you are?" I hate myself for how shocked I sound.

"He's doing the cake shopping. Nothing like a man who's organized."

Organized. Sure. That's not the reason he's been given the task of picking out a cake. Gabe, I know firsthand, is a romantic at heart. This is the same guy who'd once peppered me with tulips (my favorite flower) and named a star after me for my high school graduation present. No doubt he's completely hands-on about his own wedding. He's probably picked out the perfect cursive font for the invitations, enjoyed selecting the color of the tie he'll wear with his tux, and has something extraordinary planned for his honeymoon. He's probably taking her—whoever she is—to Paris.

"Congratulations," Gabe says.

"What for? You're the one getting married."

"Graduation, of course."

"Oh. Well. Congrats back," I manage. "You should be graduating, too. Right? Were you still at MSU?"

This is so completely weird. I mean, this isn't someone I only barely know. This is the guy who taught me the finer points of French kissing. And I'm not sure if the two of us were still going to the same university? How does that happen?

"Yep on both counts," Gabe says. "But the only ceremony on my mind is the wedding. My fiancée feels the same way. We skipped commencement. I'd forgotten all about it until your mom reminded me. Couple of days ago, wasn't it?" He shuts the White Sugar binder, slides it back across the counter.

"Come on, Chelse," he says, like we've always been buddies. "I'm starved. Let's split a pizza over at Hill Toppers'. For old time's sake." Before I can figure out how to respond (Do I want to go? Why would he want to go anywhere with me after the way I treated him?), he smiles at Mom. "I'll be back to finalize the cake order later, Mrs. Keyes. I'm up for dark chocolate, but I've got to make sure Leslie likes the idea as much as I do. She's pretty much in love with the whole traditional rigmarole."

And you, I think. *She's in love with you.*

Gabe holds the door for me as we head back out onto the sidewalk.

"Every single time I'm home, I still have to eat at Hill Toppers'," Gabe confesses.

"We practically lived on the stuff after Dad's heart attack," I say. "Hank must have brought five pies over every single day."

"He wanted to help," Gabe says. "Everybody did. I thought about stopping by a hundred times. Seeing if you guys needed anything. But I wasn't sure..." His voice trails.

It doesn't surprise me that he'd heard what happened to Dad. Back then, everybody with ties to Fair Grove seemed to know about it: My dad had a heart attack. My ex-jock dad, who still jogged every night once the bakery's "Closed" sign turned its face toward the street. My dad, who ate far more fruits and vegetables than he ever ate samples at White Sugar. My dad, who still looked like he could bench press my brother. It scared everybody, I think—no one more than Mom, Brandon, and me.

46

I don't doubt that Gabe thought about offering to help. It's the kind of person he's always been. But it also doesn't surprise me that he didn't know how to offer. Dad had his heart attack in the spring of my freshman year at MSU. By then, Gabe and I were ancient history. How do you reach out to the family of the girl who cheated on you? The same girl you already hadn't spoken to for a year?

Gabe grabs the entrance of Hill Toppers', opening the door for me. Inside, the place looks frozen in time: same tile floor, same Formica tables, same local newspaper articles plastered to the walls.

I grab a table while Gabe orders a medium supreme, a Squirt for me, and a water for himself. Four years later, he still remembers my favorite soda.

"So you're getting married," I say, squirming in my chair. "Do I know Leslie?"

"I don't think so," Gabe says through a frown. "Look, Chelse, it's okay."

"What's okay?"

"You and me. It's okay."

My mouth is frozen but my brain is in overdrive. *What are you talking about? How can that just be okay? I went on vacation the summer after high school and I cheated on you with Clint, the guide at my resort. That is not okay, not okay, not okay…*

"No, it's not." It's all I can manage.

"No—really. It is. Back then—yeah, it was bad. But it got me here. And maybe you and I aren't exactly going to be BFFs or anything, but I just thought—I'll be in and out of town, since my folks are here, and you will, too. And there's no reason for us to constantly avoid each other. Not like we've been doing these past few years."

I clutch my fork and nod. "It's been pretty unbearable,

hasn't it?" I ask. I had no idea it could be so much work to ignore someone. For the past four years, during summers and the holidays, Gabe and I have been bumping into each other on the town square or in Fair Grove's lone bookstore or coffee shop. And then it's always been a period of glares and cold shoulders and eventually, someone (ahem, me) decides it's too much and leaves before getting the book I wanted or the latte I ordered.

I never did say anything about it. Not to Gabe or anyone else. Why would I? I deserved it.

"Let's share a pizza and put it behind us," Gabe says. "From here on out, we can at least wave at each other on the street and say hello. Isn't that better than carrying around some dumb grudge when none of it even matters anymore?"

The thing is, though, it does matter. It matters to me. It matters what I did. Because when I got a little distance from it, and I looked back, what happened shocked me.

"It was selfish." Have I ever said that out loud? I'm not sure. I do know that the summer before college started, I'd used Gabe's words against him. *The heart is a compass*, he used to say, and I'd told him that if we were truly meant to be, our hearts would have only pointed toward each other, not in different directions. As though my actions were beyond my own control.

"I'd lost so much," I go on. "I'm not trying to justify what I did—but I felt so bad. About not being able to play anymore, after my accident. And about—it sounds so dumb and egotistical—but back then, it really hurt not being a star anymore. No one was seeking me out, slobbering all over me, and it really messed with my head."

I roll my eyes at myself. "I didn't know how to tell people how bad I felt. Or if I should. It seemed weak to admit it. But Clint knew what it was like to lose something you love.

To lose yourself, even. I wasn't used to losing. I never had before. It's crazy, isn't it? I was so desperate to feel better about having lost, I did something that only made me lose all over again. Lose everything *we* had."

Gabe sucks in a breath. "I wanted to be your hero back then," he admits softly. "God, I loved the idea of it. Of taking care of you. The thing is, though, you didn't need a hero. Never did. I think—it might sound stupid, but I think you needed a friend. Maybe that's what the other guy was to you. More than anything."

I dig my thumbnail into the side of my red plastic cup. "You were my friend, too. Those years we spent together… You didn't deserve the way it all happened that summer. How I treated you. It wasn't right. You had every right to be mad. To hate me. To hate me now."

"You can't hang on to that stuff, Chelse. Things worked out the way they were supposed to. The ending of us wasn't ever going to be easy for me. I was so caught up in it. When I look back, it was kind of like a fantasy come to life for me, that maybe you needed me. I wanted that so much, I had to be smothering. Real over-the-top. Makes me cringe thinking about it."

"It was me. I was the one who did it. If you think *you* cringe…" He's right. About all of it. More than he knows. It really was a thrill at the beginning to have Gabe Ross, the hot school sports writer, chasing me. And I loved the fact that he saw me as a star. But after the accident, when it was no longer true, all that *star* stuff was a burden. And still, there's absolutely no excuse for any of it. I scoop up all my courage, hug it to my chest, suck in a breath, and finally say what I should have said four years ago. "I'm sorry."

Gabe opens his hands, glances around the pizzeria. "See there?"

I shake my head, not sure what he's getting at.

"The air," he insists. "It's clear."

I chuckle a bit, before heaving out a sigh big enough to extinguish every last candle on a ninety-three-year-old's birthday cake. "Leslie's a lucky girl."

He shrugs. "What about you? Seeing someone?"

My squirming instantly comes back. The truth is, I don't like myself much when I'm with a guy. Sure, the time with Clint was fantastic. And because of him, I did finally get my head screwed on right. Decided to major in sports psychology. But I hurt so many people along the way. Gabe most of all.

"What about him? The one from the resort?"

I shake my head. That didn't turn out the way I'd wanted, either. Maybe, I've often thought, some girls aren't girlfriend material. Maybe some of us are better off getting coffee with classmates, then smiling and waving and going separate ways.

One thing's for sure, I'm better off being by myself than hurting somebody else. Not that I'd ever say that out loud. Even somebody who'd barely passed Into to Psych would see the faulty logic in all that.

But since when did logic and matters of the heart ever go together?

"Welcome home, Chelse," booms Hank, the owner of Hill Toppers', as he arrives with our pizza.

When I glance up, my head jerks back in surprise. Hank doesn't have a hair left on his head.

"Was tired of looking down at the drain after a shower and seeing what looked like a dead animal," Hank explains, rubbing the smooth, shaved skin. "But there are changes all around. How's it feel to have the old degree under your belt?"

"Good," I say. "Really good, actually."

"Your folks've gotta be glad to have you back."

"Oh, they've got White Sugar under complete control. Bet they won't need me and Brandon at all this summer. We'll probably just be in the way."

Hank lets his pointing finger bounce between me and Gabe. "You know, I haven't seen you two together in this place since you graduated high school."

Gabe offers me a friendly, crooked grin.

"I hear she's got a full ride for her master's degree," Hank adds, wagging a thumb at me. "Gonna be a TA in the psych department *and* work with injured athletes one-on-one."

"Mom's obviously been talking about me again," I tell Gabe with a roll of my eyes. "In fact, I bet that was word-for-word what Mom told him. Repeatedly. To the point that poor Hank wanted to scream."

"I'd talk you up, too, if you were my kid," Hank admits.

"Master's," Gabe repeats, looking impressed. "Good for you, Chelse."

"And you?" Hank asks, turning his shiny head toward Gabe.

"My soon-to-be father-in-law has a job lined up for me."

"No law school?" I ask. "I always kind of figured that's where you'd wind up."

"There's always time for law school," Gabe says softly. But there's something about his tone—law school isn't important. Other things have taken its place in Gabe's heart. Or another person, anyway.

"Well. Congrats to both of you," Hank says. "Tell your folks hi, Chelse. Been a couple weeks since they've been in. They both good? Dad still doing well?"

"Yeah, yeah, great. Thanks for asking." As if he would ever not ask.

"Got a free veggie—light on the olives—with their names on it." He backs away, leaving us before the mozzarella on our supreme has a chance to congeal.

Gabe picks up a slice of pizza and puts it on his plate.

"This is—nice," I say softly. "I'm—thanks for the—for this."

"Sure," Gabe says with a shrug.

As I pick up my own slice, my eyes rove toward the walls at Hill Toppers', which are still covered in local newspapers, headlines. Before I realize what I'm doing, I'm searching for my own picture, number twenty-three, fists pumping victoriously. I find it quickly, below the old headline that reads, "STATE CHAMPIONSHIP, HERE WE COME!"

The paper the article is printed on is brittle. And yellow. And mostly covered up by other articles. Most of the top-layer articles are about a Jana Gleeson. I chuckle to myself, remembering a time when I was the one signing basketballs for little Jana. Time and my hometown have moved on. New heroes have emerged. These days, Jana is surely signing basketballs for other little girls.

My conversation with Gabe rolls along—so much small talk, friendly chatter, polite catching up. Leslie apparently comes from a fairly prominent St. Louis family. A few local politicians in the mix. A degree in communications. Spent a year in the Peace Corps. She taught English in Honduras.

I take an extra-large bite in order to muffle any unfortunate laughter that threatens to erupt. I keep thinking that at any point, he'll tell me she spends her free time knitting mittens for the homeless and personally feeds all the stray cats in both the Missouri and Illinois sections of St. Louis.

I catch myself wondering, for the briefest moment,

if Gabe goes after girls who give him some sort of status. I mean, I was the star of Fair Grove when he pursued me. And now, he's with this girl who can give him a job and, from the sounds of it, a slot in the local country club. But then, as he talks, I wind up wondering—if Gabe's fiancée is from such a hifalutin St. Louis family, why would he want my family's small business to bake the cake at all? Surely the ceremony's planned for St. Louis. Surely they have plenty of places up there that can make cakes. Did he want me to know he was engaged? Did he show up hoping to run into me? To show me what I screwed up? To prove to me I didn't break him in half?

It matters. Regardless of what he says. If he's still thinking about what happened, it matters. At least, now, I've had a chance to offer Gabe something other than space. At least he opened the door so that I could offer him the kind of apology I needed to give and he needed to receive.

Finally, Gabe slurps the last of his water, wipes his mouth with a paper napkin, and stands. "Good luck next year, Chelse. It really is great to see you doing so well."

He gives me a quick kiss on the cheek before paying Hank. As he steps outside, I get it finally: that pinch of seeing an ex. Not because I'm pining or thinking *If only*…Not because I suddenly think of him as the one who got away. Because, along with this clearing of the air, the two of us have officially become polite acquaintances. Two people who will wave at each other on the street when we both happen to be home for Christmas. Two people who no longer really know each other.

Does that always happen? Given enough time? Do even the hottest passions cool? Does a fire left without fuel ever spurt back to life again?

As I shift my weight, the heavy metal object in my pocket jiggles. Clint's compass. The one I left Minnesota with four years ago. I slide it out, watch the needle searching for, then finding north.

"Hey, sis," Brandon announces as he bounds across the pizzeria and slides into the seat across the table from me. He grabs the single leftover piece of pizza and takes an enormous bite from the pointed triangle end. "Took you long enough to get here. Jeez. I could drive to school and back *twice* in the amount of time it took you to get here. And I've got a lot farther to go than you. I mean, I have to come from *Columbia*. How far is MSU from here, like ten minutes? Saw your car. You weren't kidding about having some stuff to clean out. You must've had a whole city dump in that dorm room of yours."

Maybe it's because of the way the past has come roaring back—first the postcard, then Gabe—but when I stare at Brandon, all I can think about is how much he's changed. Four years ago, he was a gangly sixteen-year-old. Now, his braces are off, and he's got a better haircut—at least, I think it's better—cropped closely around the sides of his head, no longer reminding me of an overgrown patch of weeds. His tortoiseshell glasses fit his face in a more flattering way. He's not a skinny kid anymore, either. Four years ago, Brandon was a balloon with no air. Now, he's completely filled out. Girls stop by White Sugar when he's home to flirt with him.

"Mom told me you were here. With Gabe." He draws his lips tight and opens his eyes wide, making an *oh, shit* kind of face. "How'd that go?"

"It was fine."

"He didn't gouge your eyes out? Poison your soda— you know, put a toxic squirt in your Squirt?"

"No."

"I would, if I were him."

I make my own face at him. "Don't be such a twerp. I've already got a conscious of my own."

"You wouldn't have known it, that summer we went to Minnesota. The year you *did him wrong*."

"You should have been here ten minutes ago. Gabe's forgiven me."

"So you think. Maybe your poison just hasn't kicked in yet." He takes another enormous bite of the pizza, then sighs around the mouthful. "At least Gabe said they've got a way to get that cake to their own wedding. Delivery would be murder. I had some doozies delivering for Mom, but nothing that involved." He shakes his head, shifts abruptly to, "I bet you're going to want me to help you haul all your crap into the house." It's his way of offering help.

When I don't immediately answer, he says, "Man. Gabe's getting married. Everybody's getting married. I heard one of the Highful twins is getting hitched, too. Levi, I think." He chews, trying to read my face. "Maybe you still don't want to hear about the Highful twins," he murmurs.

"Why would I not want to hear about them?"

"I mean—the Highfuls. The twins."

"I don't blame them for my accident, Brand. It wasn't anyone's fault."

"Sure didn't feel that way when it happened, sis," Brandon continues, ignoring me. "You said yourself they should have paid attention to what they were doing. Spilling their soda across the court like they did. Acting like a couple of rowdy jerks."

"Brandon. Did you hear me? I don't blame them, I said."

"But you know, they *certainly* never planned on you slipping on the puddle and practically breaking yourself in half."

"Brandon."

"Accident-prone and malicious are two very different

things. Bet those guys'll feel terrible about being part of you breaking your hip until they're eighty."

"Brandon."

"And the only thing that makes them *stop* feeling guilty is if they get Alzheimer's. Only, then the guilt might still be with them, and they just can't remember why. Poor guys. Maybe they'll wonder if they were bank robbers or hit men or something really bad—like *frat boys*." He grimaces.

"Brandon!" I shout.

Our laughter explodes, then quickly starts to wind down, like one of the songs in Hank's jukebox.

"So. If everything's all hunky-dory now, I guess you're not going to care about how you could completely mess up my summer."

"What're you talking about now, Brand?"

"I mean, I had it all worked out. It was going to be idyllic." He holds up a new finger to punctuate each item in his list: "Me. My computer. Francine." Francine—his much-loved Les Paul, a high school graduation gift. "Not going back to Columbia for summer school. Nothing going on in the music department. And with Mom and Dad going great guns at White Sugar, I figured, hey, they won't need me. I can spend the entire summer writing songs. Yep. Me, my computer, and Francine. A trio made in heaven. I bet you wouldn't care about how you could turn that inside-out."

"Brandon, really—"

"This must've come for you a few days ago. Found it when I was getting my stuff out of the basket of mail Mom keeps for us at the house." He slides a postcard across the table.

"You're kidding," I say. "Lake of the Woods?"

He grins. "Lake of the Woods."

SOMEWHERE BETWEEN THE BAUDETTE ICE RINK
&
LAKE OF THE WOODS FISHING RESORT
MINNESOTA

Clint
CATCH AND RELEASE

When the new-to-me F-150 I've been driving for the past month and a half hits dirt, it automatically slows down. Like it knows dirt roads aren't for speeding. Dirt roads are for rolling the windows down. Flipping the visor and unbuckling the seatbelt. Sinking low into the seat. Driving slow enough to see every single petal on the black-eyed Susans.

But I don't make it all the way to the Lake of the Woods resort. I'm distracted by the sign at the fork in the road. An arrow pointing straight to the competition. Usually, I don't pay much attention to the other resorts—but the Wheelers Point Resort & Lodge is getting under my skin. This sign of theirs is brand-new. Made out of that weatherproof vinyl stuff. Wasn't cheap. And it had to have gone up in the last day or so. I crane my neck, wondering if I can get a glimpse of the place—what they're doing differently to draw folks their way. The F-150 seems to know I'm looking, and slows down even more. But I can't see anything.

Signs of success at another resort put me in kind of a crummy mood. And the best place to shake a mood like this is Pike's Perch. The fork in the road offers just enough space to maneuver the truck into a turnaround and toss the Wheelers Point sign into the bottom corner of my rearview mirror.

The air starts smelling sweeter the instant the wheels spin in the direction of my folks' place. Technically, I'm heading to a restaurant. But I've spent so much of my life there, it feels more like I'm heading for home.

One of the skates in the passenger seat tumbles to the floorboards as I career through the streets of Baudette. I pull into my usual spot outside Pike's, kill the engine, and retrieve the skate, finding myself forced to admit my crummy mood isn't only about the resort sign. I turn the heel up. Stare at the white "C" I'd painted on it four years ago.

I try to remember what I'd been thinking when I put that "C" there.

I snort and shake my head at myself. I'd drawn the "C"s on my skates believing Chelsea really did care about me. Maybe even fell for me. I'd drawn those "C"s believing I was going to see Chelsea again.

When I place the skate back in the seat, my hand brushes against my tablet. Since I'm back in town, I think, I could do it. I could apply to Bemidji State, get my Fas-Track PostBac teaching certificate. Become a high school science teacher with the possibility of coaching. My heart keeps drawing me to it. Because even when the Ryans of the world are trying my patience, I love being on the rink with them. Showing them the tricks I learned at their age.

…But I promised Rusty…

Somebody knocks on the F-150's door, trying to get a rise out of me. "Hey, Pop," I say, without even looking up. I scramble to hide my tablet under the seat.

"One of these days," he says, wagging a finger at me, "I'll rattle you."

"Not possible," I say. "I'm unshakable." Just to make him laugh.

I follow him inside, where the lunch crew is cleaning up. Mom's been gardening out behind the restaurant she and Pop have owned my entire life, and all her dishes are filled with locally-grown herbs and vegetables. By the time the July heat hits, we'll be drowning in tomatoes.

I can't wait for her grilled fish with fresh tomato-lime salsa.

"Hey, Mo—" I start, my hand on the door to the kitchen. But I stop when I realize Rusty's one of the last remaining lunch stragglers. She runs a piece of bread through the last of whatever sauce is on her plate. In Mom's mind, leftover sauce is the sign someone only finished their serving to be polite. Mostly because it's rare to find so much as a drop of any of her stuff left behind. Plates pretty much get returned to the kitchen looking like they've already been through the dishwasher.

"Hey, Clint," Rusty murmurs around the last of her bread.

I pull a chair back and plop the skates I've carried with me on the table.

Rusty's a hundred percent muscle, with the appetite to power all of it—and the ability to drink me or just about any guy around under the table. She wipes her mouth; the paper napkin looks especially fragile in her grip.

"What's the deal with those things?" she asks, grabbing her beer up and washing the last bite down.

"Need to dig through the restaurant's cleaning solutions. I figured there was some sort of Goo Gone or something to help get the paint off."

Rusty tilts her head to get a better look at the "C"s. She raises her eyes again, her expression insisting she can see straight through me.

"Earl used to look at me that way," I say.

"My uncle knew you well."

I nod. "Didn't take you long to pick up everything he knew. Almost like he willed it to you right along with the resort."

She offers a crooked grin, gets back on topic. "I think, sometimes, we get too focused on the stuff that ends. We forget to see the things that endure."

"You read that in a fortune cookie?" I ask, taking up her bottle for a swig of my own. The thing is, though, Rusty's wise. Don't do two overseas tours with the military and *not* get wise, I guess. But she has a tendency to direct most of her wisdom toward me.

At least, it feels that way sometimes. One of those things you cringe against but secretly kind of love at the same time.

Usually, anyway.

Right now? Not so much.

She shrugs. "Maybe she's gone, but she still brought you back to hockey, right? She'll always be important. You're not supposed to rub away important things."

I shrug right back. "Summer fling flung."

"Earl's story about a waterfall—"

60

"What, that it could magically tell you if your love was true?"

"You said you thought it meant something, her leading you up there. Choosing that spot. Since Earl told you—"

"Earl told fish tales, Rust," I remind her, cursing myself for pouring my heart out to her about the whole thing. One beer too many one late night. "Wild, crazy fish tales that were nothing but—"

"The best fish tales always have a bit of truth in them."

"Not that one. Long past time to wipe these skates clean."

"You sure?" She plops against the back of the chair.

"You bet. See you back at the resort later?"

"Where else? See ya."

I kiss her cheek, grab the skates, and head into the kitchen.

A Little Over Two Years Ago

A Rainy Spring Day Minnesota & Missouri

It's raining in two cities. In Minnesota, it's a cold rain, a rain with a chill that bites. The drops are sharp, almost as though they're still a little frozen. And in Missouri, it's a rain that drenches, that soaks through everything—buds trying to pop on the trees and sweatshirts and backpacks. It pools on pavement and splashes onto socks, into sneakers.

In Minnesota, a dormitory door bursts open, and Clint emerges in a waterproof running jacket, hood pulled over his head. He takes to the sidewalk, arms pumping. His feet hit puddles and he fights sliding. He pushes forward, faster and faster. He's running like a man trying to get away from something.

And he is. He's trying to get away from his anger.

His breath comes out in white puffs. The cold air burns his lungs.

In Missouri, Chelsea stares at her dorm window, where rain streams like tears down a cheek.

But there's work to be done, she tries to tell herself.

Always more work than there is time. Durst has made sure of that. There are also books. Chapters needing reading and papers needing writing and algebra problems to work and history dates to memorize.

It's her life, and even as it barks harsh demands, it fits her. She reminds herself of that, too.

She needs to focus.

She opens a textbook and flips the pages. To keep up with Durst, she's pushed so much work to the weekend. She's done this before. Her roommate is living out of her suitcase, bolting at the end of each week. She leaves Chelsea with a peaceful space, no music or feet stomping about. No one breaking her concentration, asking Chelsea if it's okay to borrow her favorite sweater, no one insisting she come along for pizza or take a movie break.

But there's someone else, someone up in Minnesota she keeps making promises to. First Thanksgiving, then Christmas break, and last month, spring break. Every single promise broken. The excuses are piling up. Earlier that day, Chelsea gave her summer to Durst. And signed up for two courses. And now, she needs to work this weekend. She cannot be distracted by so much as a ten minute call. She'll only think of him the rest of the day.

Her stomach is a knot. Ten minutes ago, she sent Clint an email. Another apology. Too much to do. No time for FaceTime. No time to talk.

It's why he went running.

Mostly, he feels like a fool. Two summers ago, he'd sent Chelsea that postcard from Earl's promising a free week. She'd emailed him back. The boyfriend was gone. That was what she'd said then. Said it in a way that made him feel chosen. He'd kept on writing ridiculous emails that all ended the same way—by telling Chelsea how much he was looking forward to holding her again. Kissing her. They'd made a bunch of grandiose plans.

And every time, Chelsea had backed out of them.

Two miles later, wet and shivering, he's finally outpaced his anger.

But he knows what he needs to do.

He's on a corner, near a gas station. An ancient thing, with faded signs for cigarettes in the window and a pay phone out front. He digs through his jacket, fingers worrying the coins in his pocket—change leftover from the fast-food hamburger he bought two days ago.

He races across the parking lot, and feeds the coins into the phone. It's still raining. He's shivering.

Nine hundred miles away, Chelsea's phone rings.

"It's me," Clint says, even though he doesn't need to.

A pause stretches on the other end.

"Chelsea?" he asks. "You still there?"

"Yes, I—where are you?" she asks. "What are all those sounds in the background?"

"A pay phone, if you can believe it. I think you're hearing rain. Traffic."

Again, a pause.

Why is he out in the rain? she wonders. *Is he upset? Does he sound upset? Is he mad at me? Has he had enough? What is this?*

"I'm so—" Chelsea starts. What she wants to say is that she is sorry. But that sounds empty. It sounds in her head like another excuse. She has given him months and months of excuses. "I still want this," she tells him instead. It's the truth.

"I believe you. But Chelse—"

"I know."

"Look," he says, pushing his hood away from his eyes, "you took a hit. Things would have been different if your dad hadn't had a heart attack last spring. I believe you would have been here last June. A second summer, just like we'd planned. But then you got this job with Durst. Don't get me wrong, I think it's fantastic. Really, Chelse. Because you're doing everything you can to pay your own way. Only, you're not just flipping burgers or something. You're working doing what you want. I admire the hell out of you for it."

Chelsea feels a sudden rush of relief, even though her cheeks look like her windows at this point. He understands. "It's because of you," she starts. "Our summer together. You brought me back to the gym, in a new way. I—"

"I hope so. I do. And I don't want you to feel guilty. Not about last summer. Your dad had just had a heart attack. Your parents needed you. Of course you weren't going to be in Minnesota. I don't want you to feel guilty about this summer, either."

"But we had so many plans."

"I know Durst runs you ragged. I love that you feel like you can talk to me about it. All those emails. I know he's rough. And that he's singled you out and you need to keep him on your side—keep the money flowing," Clint says. "I get it. And I want you to know it's okay."

"This isn't ending, is it?" she whispers.

"No! That's the last thing I want." After a pause, he adds, "We've spent almost two years trying to keep in touch, haven't we? I've loved talking to you. But you have to admit, last summer threw a roadblock in our way. It's like we keep trying to force something to happen that can't. Not right now."

In the back of his mind, he knows that's not a hundred percent true. He knows that there is a window in his own summer. A full week between the end of the spring semester and the start of working at Earl's place. He could go to Missouri.

He's afraid to offer. Mostly because she seems to be dragging her feet. Because he does wonder if it's truly about money—and Durst—or something else. Is she having second thoughts? *Have* her feelings waned? Would she say no to his visit? Would she tell him she'd be too busy to spend time with him, even if he were in Fair Grove?

He's not sure he could take that blow. He needs her to choose him. He needs to make sure he gives her every chance possible.

"No more maybes," he says. "We've said maybe too many times. And we can't do it again. Not maybe next August, or maybe in November. Ball's in your court this time. You come to me with a definitive. Okay? A solid date you want to meet up. A date you know is free. And I'll make it work. Whenever that is. The next time you get in touch, you do it with a date. And Chelsea?"

"Yeah." She shudders her answer. She's not sure if she is relieved or horrified.

"It doesn't matter how long it takes. Okay? You come to me when you have a date. I don't care if it's two weeks from now or two months from now or two years from now. You come to me and tell me when, and I'll be there."

Today
Lake of the Woods Fishing Resort
Minnesota

Clint
Downlake

Rusty's truck is in my rearview all the way from Pike's to the resort. I pass the four ATVs parked beside the main lodge—the collection of vehicles that our guests use to explore the more rugged sections around the lake. The same vehicles that Greg, Rusty, and I regularly attach rear mowers to in order to keep the areas near the guest cabins, the lodge, and the docks clear of tall grass and weeds.

I climb from the truck, slam the driver side door. Behind me, Rusty kills her own engine.

"Morgan!" The shout comes from the lake. "Rusty!"

When I shade my eyes against the sun, I find Greg sitting in the wooden swing at the edge of the lake, an old cooler at his feet. Greg pulls his ball cap off and waves it at me. Looks a little like a desperate deserted islander trying to wave down a plane.

I take the skinny path Greg, Rusty, Todd, and I have worn bare along the edge of the lake to the swing. This isn't the only section of the resort where I've left a footprint, though. Far from it. And the same's true of Greg and Todd, my oldest friends. Our boyhood summers hold nearly identical stories, all of them set at the Lake of the Woods resort. There isn't a tree whose shade we haven't rested under or a hill we haven't climbed. There's not a single section of the nearby creeks that haven't flowed over our hands.

"Better pick up those feet, Morgan," Rusty snaps in her best drill sergeant voice as she passes me, a smirk on her face. For Rusty, Lake of the Woods was always a place to spend an occasional weekend when visiting her aunt and uncle. And it was the place she came for a little healing of the soul following her stint in the military.

Now, it could potentially shape the rest of her life. And the rest of *our* lives. The four of us. Eternal childhood. If we could figure out how to get ourselves together and save the place.

I call after her in my best sarcastic tone, "Who do you think you are, my boss? Last time I checked, we were partners."

"Partners—ha! May I remind you of the laws of inheritance? I *am* your boss!" she calls back. But she's putting the kind of distance between the two of us that makes it a little hard to hear her.

"Hey, man," Greg calls out in greeting. Now that I'm close, I can tell he's covered in sweat and grease. But then again, we've all been covered in sweat and grease for the past year—since officially taking over the reins at the resort.

68

Rusty and I plop into the swing. To make room, I lean into the wooden arm. The lake sloshes against the nearby dock as Greg leans forward, reaching into the old red and white Igloo for a cold one. I love that sound the lake makes—it's almost as good as the sound of skates on ice. Like I told Luke in one of my more philosophical moments, life's not worth living if it's away from the water.

I squint at three motorboats pulled onto the shore, their tarps in wadded-up clumps on the ground. "Did you get them running?" I ask.

"You bet," Greg says. "Aren't doing us any good if they sit all summer. I figure you, me, and Todd can continue to take tourists out on the launches, but rent the motorboats out to anyone who wants to try it on their own, away from the crowd."

Crowds? We haven't seen too many of those lately.

I smile anyway as Greg rattles on about renting the motorboats. "It's a good idea," I say.

"Well, you know, it was mine. So it had to be," Greg teases.

Rusty smacks his arm. "How 'bout those smudge pots?" she asks. She's added them to each one of the docks. "Dangling your feet off a dock is supposed to be peaceful. Can't be when you're being eaten alive by mosquitoes, though."

A few years ago, I would have believed the smoking pots were a welcome addition. This year, no matter how many Minnesota mosquitoes Rusty runs off, they still outnumber our guests.

"They're perfect," I say just the same.

"Here you go," Greg says, handing me a bottle. It's my own brew—a wheat ale flavored with orange rind. "Still think you ought to be selling this stuff at Pike's," Greg says.

"Yeah, but this way, it feels like it's ours. It's special.

Besides, it doesn't have a name. How can somebody order it if it doesn't have a name?"

"How 'bout Clint's Cold Ones?"

"That's awful," I say through a grimace.

"Sunrise Suds," Greg tries again.

"What do you think?" I ask, nudging Rusty.

"Think I need more tasting to figure it out," she says, taking another swig.

"How goes the moose counting?" I tease Greg. Because I'm not the only one with a second job. I coach, Greg counts moose for a population study by the Minnesota Conservation Department, and Todd—well. He's spent most of the past year getting certified to be a rock climbing instructor (and working part-time as a janitor to pay for said certification) at the Great Northern Hiking and Climbing School, Inc. He pretty much broke even, so he didn't exactly help us out cash-wise, but he was gone most of the time, so Greg and I at least made our groceries last longer.

Greg's job, though, has always been the perfect fodder for jokes. I tug on Rusty's long ponytail, which trails through the back of her ball cap. "Good thing it's gotten warm. He was about to get frostbite taking off his shoes every time he had to count past ten."

"Listen, Morgan," Greg grumbles. "I love the winter. Minnesota's best season by far. You play nice, or I won't help you name your brew."

"Please," I grumble. "Why does it have to have one name? Why can't it be something different to everyone?"

"Sounds a little hooker-ish, doesn't it?" Rusty asks. "My name's whatever you want it to be?"

"If that's how your brain works, Morgan, you shouldn't be allowed to name it at all," Greg says. "I'm telling you, this stuff could make you a fortune. If you'd put me in charge of marketing from here on out." He lays down the bottle he's already drained.

We're all feeling drained, actually, staring out at the lake.

Rusty sighs. "I still miss Aunt Helen," she mutters.

One Year Ago

LAKE OF THE WOODS FISHING RESORT
MINNESOTA

Rusty staggers through the house, the same Earl and Helen had shared right there at Lake of the Woods. The one with the floral wallpaper and the furniture handed down from past generations. The one they built along the back of the property, so they'd never have to leave the resort they loved. Not even for the night.

She's looking for something—a knife, perhaps. A pair of scissors. Something to open a plastic package. Another one of those pre-made dinners. The kind that just needs to be thawed out in the microwave.

The house is a sty. Newspapers are strewn across chairs. Last winter's coat is still in the same wad where she'd dropped it last March. Paper plates litter the floor.

The knife or the scissors—at this point, she'd take a screwdriver, one she could stab through the plastic top—could be anywhere. The fireplace. The top drawer in the bathroom.

She tries the desk inside the front door.

And finds a note addressed to her from her Uncle Earl. Had it always been there? When did he put it there? Did she?

Rusty rubs her forehead. Everything is fuzzy. She has been either drunk or hungover for—what? Weeks?

Months.

She knows that. It has to be.

But the note. It makes her forget her dinner. She tosses the plastic container of frozen food into the top drawer of the desk.

"This way to the site of a broken heart," the note reads. On the back, he's drawn a map of the resort.

Rusty takes a deep breath and steps outside. Squints at the sun, which is bright enough to hurt.

Or maybe she has simply been inside too long.

She follows Earl's map. And stops. The trees rustle in the early spring breeze as though they're all shaking their heads at her.

Like Earl would have.

In fact, there he is, in her mind's eye. As he looked the summer she enlisted. Pointing to a crack in the earth. "Know what that is?" he'd asked her.

"Probably due to the drought—" Rusty'd started, but the chastising look Earl threw at her cut her off.

"Drought," Earl had mimicked. "'Course, folks always look to the surface of things. Easiest answers. Hasn't rained in quite some time, I'll give you that. But that's not what that is, there."

Earl squatted, running his hand along the gap.

Rusty'd squatted beside him. It was deeper than she'd initially thought.

"Nature's so human. Proof of that's all around. You know plants sleep?" he asked her.

She thought a moment. Unsure if this was true or one of Earl's wild stories, she'd said, "Well, some of them open in the morning, right? So that'd make sense."

"Plants need sleep," Earl repeated. "And the earth can get a broken heart."

She'd almost laughed out loud. "What breaks the

earth's heart?" she'd asked instead.

"Seein' what folks can do to one another."

His words sent a chill down her spine. She would be off to another land, another strip of earth, where she would witness some of those cruelties. Even then, she'd known.

"When next you come back," Earl promised, "this crack won't be here. Because if you let it, the earth can heal."

"Too bad people can't do that, huh?" Rusty'd tried to tease, nudging him with her elbow.

"You're not listenin'," he scolded. "The earth heals. Heals itself *and* anything that happens to be standin' on it. This earth does, anyway. Can't speak for other places. Just know this one."

He paused to stare right at her. "You remember that. No matter how deep the wound, this earth can heal."

The scene in Rusty's memory fades. Earl is gone. She's alone.

With the map and the note in her hand.

She squats, touches the ground. There is no crack. The broken earth has healed.

Rusty bursts into tears. "I'm so sorry, Uncle Earl," she says.

She races back to the cabin. The date. There has to be a way to find out the date. She turns on the radio as she clomps through the bedroom before circling back through the living room. She retrieves the paper delivered earlier that very morning, slipped into the rural delivery box outside her front door. Yet another paper she has not read.

"A year," Rusty mutters, collapsing onto the couch. She's lost an entire year.

She never intended to. This has never exactly been the plan. But then again, the mere word—*lost*—shows something has happened that you never intended. If you've *lost* something, it happened despite your best efforts. It was an accident. One laced with regret.

She'd simply intended to rest. Get her wits about her. Then, she assured herself, she'd be better able to rejoin the world.

But one year? Seems impossible. And yet, she knows exactly how it happened. Because every single time she stepped outside, no matter the weather or time of day, everything around her would take her back to the IED blast outside of Bagram Air Base. The flash of light. The boom that scattered the world around her. The ring screeching in her ears. The feel of her feet hitting the ground.

Once it found her, that terror hitting her with its fists all over again, it was always just *one more day of rest*. Or, *I'll get to that tomorrow*.

And now, one full year has passed. Embarrassment rushes over her. This is not what Earl had in mind when he left her the resort.

He had wanted this plot of earth—his own little bit of heaven—to heal her. He had wanted her to believe it could.

She heads into the bathroom, where she washes her face and ties her red hair into a ponytail. Throws on a pair of faded jeans and her favorite flannel shirt. Heads into the kitchen, snaps open a large black plastic trash bag, and starts to fill it, tossing in pizza boxes and beer cans. It takes all morning to pick up the trash that has accumulated during her long stretch of—what has it been? Inactivity? Hibernation?

How could she have done this to Earl? How could she have not opened the resort at all last summer?

She is crying now. In a way she hasn't cried in ages.

"Why did you think this place would fix me?" she wails. "How did you know that I would need it?" But she doesn't need to ask.

Anything ever bothers you, Rust, you just get busy. That was what he'd always told her. No amount of worry ever held a chance against a long to-do list.

"You didn't want me to wallow here. You wanted me to work. Didn't you?" Rusty blubbers. "You wanted this resort to fill my days. And by filling my days, it could mend my heart and mind."

It's always been so beautifully simplistic.

She wipes her eyes with the back of her wrist. She will open this year. She will do right by Earl.

She makes her way down the front steps and pauses. She remembers when her uncle had proudly built a kind of mini-row of cabins for the work staff. When she gains enough distance to see the employee cabins, she reluctantly turns.

And grunts.

Shaken by what she sees, she stuffs her fingers into the front pockets of her jeans and begins to make her way about the resort.

The place is overgrown. Full of wild, brown under-brush. Once-manicured paths that stretch between the main lodge and the guest cabins now seem far less distinct. The cab-ins themselves are eyesores. The launches, still sitting on the lake, look a little like cars abandoned at the side of the road.

"Oh, Uncle Earl, I'm so sorry," she moans. "This isn't what you had in mind at all when you left your pride and joy to me. You gave me a place to get my head together. To have a purpose. A reason to get out of bed. And now…"

She makes her way down one of the docks, wishing that she could toss a line into the water and reel in an idea that would erase the past year and save the coming summer.

"I wish at least Aunt Helen were still here," she groans. It would be nice to have her to talk to. She and Earl knew how to steer through any hardship. Helen would have been able to tell Rusty what to do now.

Rusty wipes a tear, thinking of the way her aunt and uncle had died within a month of each other. Unable to exist apart, it seemed. One of those love stories you read about or see on the big screen. One of those love stories that you think could never be true in the real world.

And yet—theirs was.

What if she has waited too long? What if Earl's resort is toast?

It can't be, she thinks. *It just can't.*

For the first time in months, she grabs the key to the main lodge and bursts inside. A musty odor attacks her. The floor is a lighter shade of brown now beneath a blanket of dust. A few cobwebs cling to the walls.

She stomps about the building, circling back toward the check-in counter. Wondering if anyone would ever check in again.

Opening the top drawer, she finds another envelope covered in Earl's handwriting addressed, "Rusty."

The letter inside simply says:

If you run into trouble, call these guys. I know the four of you will make me proud.

"The three musketeers!" Rusty exclaims. That's what Uncle Earl had called them, anyway. Little boys, they had seemed to her back then. What had they been—four, five years younger than her? Kids who had learned to fish and hike and love the resort. The same threesome who had given her the nickname that had followed her through the rest of her life. *Rusty*, when her real name was Rachelle. Rusty, a way to tease her about the red pigtails that bounced about her shoulders as she begged Earl to let her go whitewater rafting.

Yes, three boys who had spent their teenage summers learning the ins and outs of what it took to run a resort.

Hadn't Earl written to her about them, even when she was in the service? Told her how good it made him feel when they showed up every single summer, each year as anxious as ever for new adventures. How he'd come to think of them almost as his kids—easy to do since he and Helen had never had children of their own.

Three names, three different sets of contact info. Clint, Greg, and Todd. Three young boys who have hopefully grown into men who still feel the same way they always had about the place—and would be willing to work for…well. Not much.

She'll start with the name of the boy she remembers as being the natural leader of the three. Earl's favorite. He could help her convince the other two.

She'll start with Clint.

Today

Back to the Swing
at the Edge of the Water
Lake of the Woods Fishing Resort
Minnesota

Clint
Drag

"**Guys!**"

I jump. When I turn, Todd's full beard pops into my face. He's gone all mountain man lately. So much so, Greg's started calling him Jeremiah Johnson. His dog trots up to his side.

"Hey, Blue," I say, reaching forward to rub his ears.

"Speaking of names," Greg grumbles, "that's got to be the worst dog name of all time. *Blue.* For a Blue Heeler."

"Just—shut up for two seconds," Todd demands. "Listen. I've got news. I'm going to Alaska."

"For what? A couple of weeks?" I ask.

"Permanently. I've got a job."

This lands like a swift kick on the shin. Greg, Rusty, and I exchange worried looks. "We were kind of counting on you being here for the summer," I tell him.

"Aw, man, I've been here with you guys a year already."

True enough. The three of us jumped at the chance to be part of the place last spring, when Rusty called. Lucky enough for her, we were all getting ready to graduate, and none of us were committed to anything else yet. Help out at Earl's place? Get it back to being the place we'd all grown up loving? In a heartbeat. But all we've really managed to do so far is tread water.

"There's still a ton of stuff that needs work around here," Greg reminds him. "Can you delay it until the fall?"

"Come on, guys! I thought you'd be happy. This is what I want to do for the rest of my life. One of my instructors at Great Northern recommended me. And now—rock climbing. Big time fishing. A guide. In Alaska. It's gonna be heaven!"

"I *really* wish Aunt Helen were still around," Rusty mutters in my ear.

I know what exactly what she means. It's been an unspoken, heavy guilt inside us all, knowing we're in the midst of screwing up Earl's dream come true. And now, this thing with Todd. One less pair of hands to work the resort.

Helen would know what to do. She and Earl always knew.

"I don't leave for a whole week yet," Todd says.

A week? Rusty mouths. She's panicking.

"You guys'll find somebody to take my place," Todd

assures us. "Who wouldn't want to stay here all year long?"

"Oh, somebody with a steady, reliable nine-to-five that actually pays," Greg says. "Or somebody who wants to retire in peace. Somebody who doesn't want to fix boats day in and day out. Somebody who doesn't want to deal with the plumbing in cabin three."

I stand, slap Todd on the back. "Congrats," I tell him. "I really am happy for you."

He beams. "Come on, Blue!" he shouts, already jogging back toward our cabin. "I gotta pack."

Rusty and Greg are both staring at me with *you can't be for real* looks on their faces.

"He's right. We'll find somebody," I contend. "Just watch." But my doubts are every bit as big as the lake. Bigger, even.

Somebody else who remembers this place as fondly as we do? Who'd ditch everything else they've got going to help bring it back to life?

I can't, for the life of me, imagine who that could be.

Chelsea
Forgetting Curve

"You know, it is possible you don't remember that place exactly right," Brandon says, unlocking the trunk of my Camaro. We're not even out of town yet, and we're already having to rearrange our stuff—move some of the duffel bags around, keep the mounds from sliding into us at every single stop light.

"Mmmm-hmmm," I grunt, opening the driver side door and pushing the seat forward.

"Hey, whoa!" Brandon cries, holding his arm up. "You are not going to move Francine. She gets the back seat behind the driver. She's right where I want her."

"Are you going to make me stop to pick up a child's

seat for her, or are you going to be okay with buckling her in using the seatbelt?"

"Sure, sure, joke away. This is serious stuff. This is Francine. Francine Julianna Les Paul."

"Oh, my God. Now she's got a middle name," I say, smashing my last duffel against the floorboards. "And I'm referring to the thing as 'she,' too."

"Of course it's a 'she.' Francine has a pink pickguard."

I chuckle, remembering how we'd expected Brandon to replace the pickguard on the vintage guitar. We'd all chipped in to buy it for his high school graduation gift, right about the time he'd also announced that he wasn't going to be some run-of-the-mill garage band bass player, but a full-blown multi-instrumentalist as well-versed in classical composers as he was in stars of classic rock. Whoever had owned the guitar previously had made several of what some might call "girly" upgrades—including that pink pickguard and some floral mother-of-pearl inlay in the fretboard. Brandon had simply claimed that it meant the guitar was female—not that it needed to be played by a female. "Of course I should have a woman guitar. One that would love the touch of a man's hands," he'd said, wiggling his eyebrows as we'd all melted into belly laughter.

I'm still watching Brandon situate Francine in the back seat when he suddenly pauses, shouts, "Hey! You're bringing a yoga mat? Who's weird now?"

"You two going on a summer adventure?"

I turn and find myself staring into Gabe's face. Again. Twice in the same week.

"I—uh—" I'm at a loss. Brandon and I are headed back to the same resort where I met the guy I cheated on Gabe with. Does that even matter? We just found a kind of weird peace. Would admitting where we're going destroy it?

"Rented a cabin. My graduation gift to Chelse. Making her unplug," Brandon says.

I am constantly amazed at how the guy manages to ditch being a little brother long enough to be a pal at exactly the right moments.

"Right when I thought we'd be seeing more of you two at White Sugar," Gabe says, tugging a woman up to his side. "We came by to take a look at those wedding cakes. This is Leslie."

She's beautiful, of course. Thick brown hair that swings against her shoulders and shines in the sun like she's starring in a shampoo ad. She's wearing a strapless sundress covered in little purple flowers, and instead of clutching a purse, she's clutching Gabe's arm.

"This is Chelsea," Gabe tells her. "Old friend from high school."

She nods once and smiles. "Gabe was so insistent on getting a cake from his hometown bakery."

This gives me a strange sense of pleasure. Yet again, his visits to White Sugar seem to offer proof that he really did care. That I wasn't about status. That what we had mattered. If it hadn't, White Sugar never would have crossed his mind. "You going with the chocolate cake?" I wind up asking.

"I'm good with what Gabe decides," she says.

"What's the post-graduation plan for you?" I ask, leaning against the Camaro.

She looks at me like I'm dense. "We're getting married this summer."

"I know, but—what about you? I mean, what'd you major in? What're your own plans?"

"I was an art history major. Dad's got a job lined up for Gabe in the family business—we own a chain of sandwich shops—and I'm going to be a special events planner at one of the galleries back home in St. Louis."

"Sounds like you've got it all worked out," I say.

Leslie tugs Gabe even closer. "Gabe's been saving up for our trip to Rome," she gushes. "He's taking me to see all the works I studied in real life."

Gabe beams.

It's so perfect—Gabe gets to be the hero, and this Leslie person gets to have a hero.

And maybe, if things really are perfect, it works the other way, too. He certainly talked Leslie up back at Hill Toppers' like he thought she was some sort of superhero.

Is it ever possible? Can you be the rescuer *and* the rescuee? Can you really take turns that way? I used to believe so. And now, with the latest postcard from Lake of the Woods in the pocket of my shorts, I think I might be able to believe it again.

"You kids have fun," Dad calls through the entrance of White Sugar. It sounds like something from an old sitcom. "Need money for breakfast?"

"We've got Mom's fresh croissants and doughnuts!" Brandon shouts. "Why'd you think we stopped here first?"

Dad waves again and dips back inside the shop.

"Good luck. Seriously," Brandon says, extending a hand. Gabe shakes it. And then Leslie leans in and Brandon kisses her cheek.

I should thank him. I know I should.

Brandon knows it too. When we get situated in the car, he clears his throat in an overexaggerated way.

When I turn, his eyebrows are raised expectantly.

Instead, I say, "Listen, we wouldn't even be going at all if it wasn't for my free week. You should be thanking me."

"Thanking you?"

"Yeah. You. Francine. Peace and quiet of the resort.

Perfect setting to write songs. Even more perfect than being at home. Plenty of distractions there. All those hours you'd wind up putting in at White Sugar—"

"What's with that, anyway?" Brandon interrupts. He's dropped any hope that he'll hear any kind of gratitude from me, and now pivots toward the surprise mailing from Minnesota. "Four years, no word from the resort, and out of nowhere, a postcard? Unsigned? Congratulating you on your graduation? Telling you your free week's still good?"

I don't answer. Just chew on my bottom lip.

"*Were* you and Clint still in touch? Somehow, I didn't think you were."

I shake my head. "No. Not since spring of my sophomore year."

"Weird. Why would he—"

"Maybe Greg and Todd are still at the resort," I blurt. "You could get the band back together."

"You're evading my question."

"I don't know," I say. "I tried to look them up, but the website was down. When I called to book, I got a woman. Some girl at the desk who didn't know the place very well."

"How's that?"

"She seemed surprised about Earl's free week thing. For the biggest catch of the summer. Just said to bring the postcards with us."

"Postcards plural?"

"*Postcard*, I said. Just one."

"No, you didn't." Brandon leans against the passenger door, trying to get a better look at my face. "You still have the first one, don't you? The one that said you could claim a free week in the first place? The one Clint sent you four years ago? I mean, you couldn't have held on to it on purpose. No, that couldn't be it."

"Brandon."

"You were oh, so sad that Mom and Dad would be too busy with White Sugar to come, weren't you?"

"*Brandon.*"

"Really, Chelse," he says, going completely serious for a change. "What do you expect to find when you get up there?"

"I don't know."

"Did you Google him?"

"Clint? I couldn't. A picture wasn't going to tell me anything."

"Might tell you if he's married. Got kids. That might be a good place to start."

"If he is, I'll spend the next two weeks at a self-made yoga retreat," I say, tossing a thumb toward the mat in the back.

"Clint would be the one most likely to remember you'd be graduating."

"Yeah." Maybe it was part of why I didn't look him up. It seemed that he'd finally changed his mind—he wasn't going to wait. Not anymore, not like he'd said that day on the phone. He was giving me an invitation to come. So of course my immediate reaction was to come back with a definitive date, like we'd promised. Request a reservation. Show up on time. No excuses.

Even if I haven't gotten it exactly right, there's a reason he sent me that postcard. There has to be. And no matter what the situation is with him, I don't think the real reason could ever come out during some phone call. I have to go up there, see him in person.

After a few quiet moments, I dare to ask, "Do you mind going with me?"

"No way. Francine might, though. I'm not sure she's the outdoorsy type. You ever think of asking her?"

His phone dings. "Mom wants us to say hi to Chef Charlie," he says, reading her text. "She wants to know when she can see him winning the Beard Award." He lets out a deep sigh. "Looks like you're not the only one who has grandiose memories of Lake of the Woods. It's a ton of pressure being the only realist around."

"Here's realism for you: we've got a little over nine hundred miles to go."

He turns on the radio and fusses with the dial until he finds one playing classic rock.

"Not exactly highbrow, Mr. Music Major," I tease.

"It's my first love. You wouldn't know anything about that, though, would you, Chelse?"

Nearly Two Weeks Ago

LAKE OF THE WOODS FISHING RESORT
MINNESOTA

Greg has seen this before.

After all, he and Clint have been friends since the days of lunchboxes and spelling tests. And in the way of old friends, he knows when darkness or danger is creeping on the horizon.

He stands near the main lodge, hands on his hips, watching Clint.

The sun is staining the sky with the end of another day. And Clint is carrying a six-pack onto The Minnow, the skiff he and Todd and Greg bought together in high school. He floats off, into the center of the lake, by himself.

Greg's boyhood friend has become a solitary creature. Anyone else might think it's a phase. Or, at most, a kind of mellowing out brought by a little age. Adulthood. But Greg is afraid that this is something more, a kind of chill in the heart. And he's afraid it could become as lasting as the names of the summer flings carved into the tattooed tree, the one up by the main hiking trail.

Hurt has etched itself into Clint. And disappointment.

Greg remembers when they were younger and he could confront Clint. Call him on his b.s. Even a few years ago, when they were still in college, he could slam his elbow into his ribs when he was approached by a girl at a party. "You dead?" he could shout at him over the music. But by now, this attitude of Clint's doesn't feel like something Greg could chip away at by himself. Clint's world is the lake, the kitchen at Pike's, and a hockey rink full of teenage boys. Women don't exactly come to the resort, not anymore, not like they used to.

And he's beginning to act like that's just fine with him.

Greg knows that Clint never wanted Chelsea to be confined to a single summer. The fact that he got Earl to agree to letting her come back for a free week proved as much.

And the fact that she didn't show up? It killed Clint.

In the end, Chelsea proved to Clint that no matter how good it felt to open yourself up to somebody, it also inevitably left scars and a lingering embarrassment.

It would sound corny if he said it out loud, but Greg knows that Clint's heart is in danger of being put in sunset mode permanently.

He needs to wake the guy up.

And he has a feeling he knows what—or who—it will take.

Well, Earl knew, anyway.

Greg heads toward the main lodge. Stepping inside, a scene from his memory pops back to life. This kind of thing happens to all of them—Greg, Clint, Todd or Rusty. If the memory involves Earl, it is powerful enough to relive. They'd all loved him that much. This memory, the one Greg sees now, is a day three years ago when he'd come streaking through the lodge. He was horrifically late for his first fishing group. A whole launch of vacationers waiting on him.

He'd been sure, that day, that Earl would be furious. He ran, blubbering his excuses: "...still getting in the groove. Sleepless most of last week. Finals week..."

But Earl had only smiled at him through his steel wool beard and curled his finger. "I never did tell you the end of the waterfall story, did I?"

"The one about the girl who offed herself," Greg had said, panting.

"'Offed herself,'" Earl repeated. "And you're the more enlightened of the two friends."

"She died. Wasn't that the end of the story?" Greg didn't mean to be flippant. But he hadn't been lying about the sleep deprivation, and he couldn't understand why Earl was fine with him being so late. He had a whole boat of guests waiting to go out. Shouldn't he care about that? Any other summer, he'd be all over Greg about it.

"Nope," Earl told him. "Not the end. Not of that story. The world never ignores true love. We do all sorts of horrible things in the name of love. Dumb things. We make all kinds of selfish decisions. But when two hearts are meant to be together, the world always finds a way.

"I bet you didn't know her betrothed died shortly after her. Didja? When it happens that way, one going so quickly after their partner, it's a sure sign it was a love meant to be. A heart can't be expected to keep on beating when half of it ceases to exist, now, can it?"

"So they both died and—"

"They say the two of them were reborn," Earl told him, "only to have to find each other all over again."

"Uh-huh."

"But at least they were given a second chance."

"Yeah," Greg muttered.

"Just imagine if they could have had a second chance in the same lifetime." Earl squinted at Greg, tapping the guest book. "So far, cabin number four hasn't been rented out by any member of the Keyes family."

"Clint's old cabin," Greg agreed. "The one his family always stayed in."

"Not old," Earl said, holding up a finger. "I'm pretty sure it's always gonna be his. 'Cause it's always gonna have a special place in his heart."

"Yeah," Greg said through a grin, catching on, "and since Chelsea's free week never expires—" he paused to get Earl's nod of approval—"Clint may get to have some more good times in cabin four."

"A second chance," Earl agreed.

"Second chance," Greg repeats as the image of Earl evaporates and he finds himself standing alone in the dusty, run-down main lodge. Greg thinks, *If I can give them a push, I should.*

It was what Earl wanted, anyway. Get Chelsea back to cabin number four. Earl was a sucker for romance. All those woman-in-the-waterfall whoppers of his. He was sure that Clint's story wasn't finished.

Maybe, Greg thinks, Earl was right. Maybe, if Clint could get an ending, he'd finally be able to move past it. As it is, it's almost like part of him is still waiting. He needs to see Chelsea again. Hash it out. Whatever happens, at least a last sentence gets to be written.

It would finally let Clint begin to write chapter one of another love story, if that's what he really needs to do.

Greg veers past the old dining room toward the gift shop. He snatches a postcard—of a sunset, no less—and carries it back to the check-in counter. Scrawls a message. Tugs a piece of paper out of his pocket, the one that holds an address he'd looked up in town.

He drops the postcard into the mail slot.

And hopes he hasn't made a giant mistake.

***

Chelsea
SENSORY MEMORY

Nine hundred miles later, the crickets are all that's around to greet me and Brandon as we pry our stiff bodies out of the Camaro's bucket seats. I free my phone from my purse and let out a frustrated growl.

"What've you got, half a bar?" Brandon asks.

"No reception at all," I say. "No Wi-Fi. That's not like Kenzie."

"Ohh. Kenzie. Wonder what she looks like now."

When I shoot him a glare for fantasizing about the woman who had once been the resort's beautiful on-site tech expert, he shrugs. "What? You're not the only one up for some sightseeing." He smirks and adds in a sickening kind of sing-song tone, "Now, you can't change your mind about looking him up."

I roll my eyes. But that's exactly why I'd pulled my phone out. Curiosity'd had nine hundred miles to get to me.

Now, all I can do is listen to the crickets squeak out background music to my questions: What if Clint really is married? What if he's unrecognizable somehow? What if I made a bunch of assumptions I shouldn't have? What if our address was on a master list of everyone with outstanding free weeks or discounts, and we *all* got reminder postcards? What if Clint's long gone, playing for some sort of minor league hockey team in Canada?

I do my best to shake it all off as we grab our essentials-only bags: one duffel for me and Francine for Brandon. "We'll unpack tomorrow," I say, dragging myself through the front door of the cabin. We rely on only the moonlight filtering through the windows to stumble toward the same rooms we had last time.

I act like I can't wait to crawl between the sheets. Make a show like I'm so tired, I can't even deal with brushing my teeth.

The truth is, my heart revs like the V8 engine in my Camaro.

I pull Clint's old Boy Scout compass from my luggage. It points toward my bedroom window.

I hoist it open, closing my eyes and absorbing the sweet evening breeze. Letting the rhythm of the distant waterfall filter through my screen.

With my eyes closed, it all comes back to me: the cool, quiet peacefulness of the first night I'd arrived to the resort, those four years ago. How I'd stood in the darkness, listening to the distant waterfall, thinking that the entire night sky looked like a woman. That the black fringes of the pines were like a lacy formal gown and the moon an opal pendant at her throat. How the swaying of the trees made it seem the sky-woman was dancing to the music of the loons.

When I open my eyes, I see her again. The sky-woman. And for a moment, it seems to me that the waterfall is actually her, talking to me in a whisper. *Shhhh, shhh. Remember. Remember.*

Mist hits my face—it can't really be so, I know that, but I can feel it. And I can feel Clint in my arms. His skin on mine. How, when the two of us sought out that waterfall for a bit of seclusion, the entire world disappeared, and there was only us. How we felt.

Right then, it doesn't seem like the past. It doesn't seem like a moment that's come and gone.

It feels like forever. Something that has been going on all this time.

I pull my face away from the window. Before I crawl into bed, I touch my cheek.

It's impossible—I know it is—but my skin feels covered in misty droplets.

When the sunlight begins to seep into my room, I lunge for my duffel and pull out the extra-flattering shorts and fitted white T-shirt I'd purposefully packed on top. My day-one outfit. I grab my white canvas sneakers, slather on a little lip gloss, and let my hair go wild and wavy. I'm already flushed— no need to apply any color on my cheeks.

I'm trembling as I race through the living room, which has far less furniture than I remember. Sparse is more like it. A short sofa on one end of the room, a chair and an end table near the fireplace on the other side. It smells musty, too—like a hotel room that's been closed up for years.

My trembling explodes when I throw open the cabin door and step onto the front porch. Only—no. I'm not the one trembling. The porch is. Boards creak and bow with each step. I glance down, finding moss of some kind growing around a few of the nail heads. I try to take a step to the side, but the porch under the spot where my foot wants to land is gone. It's rotted straight away, letting me see the ground below. I gasp and lunge in the opposite direction. It's a wonder we made it inside without breaking a leg last night.

I back up, down the steps, which are soft enough to bow like hammocks under my Keds. I hadn't noticed last night—maybe it was the darkness, or maybe I was bleary-eyed from all the hours on the road. When I take a look at the front of the cabin, it's nothing like the one in my head. This looks more like a "Before" picture in *This Old House* magazine.

Brandon can't be right. I didn't build this place up in my mind. Not this much. Did I?

The trail pointing away from the front step of the cabin is dotted with wild, unruly patches of weeds.

I hurry forward, picking up the pace. I'm jogging now, elbows bent, chin wobbling with each forceful jolt. The way my heart thrashes about, you'd think I'd just hit the twenty-first mile of a marathon. I sprint down the main path, taking in the rest of the resort. The other cabins have flower boxes full of brown leaves and withered plants. Windows missing giant chunks of caulk. Hard to imagine how they could have possibly kept the mean Minnesota winds from blowing straight through the bedrooms last winter.

On to the main lodge, where still more weeds are growing up through worn-thin patches in the gravel lot. I lunge inside calling, "Earl? Earl?" but no one answers.

The doorway to the dining area is closed; I try the knob, but it only turns maybe half an inch. Locked. I look through the glass panel, finding chairs stacked on every table. "Isn't anyone here for breakfast?" I mumble. When I press my face still closer to the glass, I focus on the complete lack of decor—no paintings on the walls, no decorations on the fireplace mantel, no evidence of candles in the center of any table, no tablecloths. A few tracks of muddy footprints criss-cross the tile floor.

Confused, I race into the gift shop. But the racks of memory cards and shelves of last-minute ponchos and sunscreen and books on Minnesota wildlife are all gone. Only a single scraggly display of picked-over postcards remains. It's really no more than a bait shop offering hand-tied flies and coolers of worms. Band-Aids and beef jerky. Boxes of ammunition. And it smells like rotten fish.

"What happened?" I mutter. But there's no one to answer—because it also has a self-checkout counter. The main lodge is deserted.

I'm back out into the sunlight, running down the scraggly brown trail straight for cabin number four.

"Brandon!" I shout, hopping over the rotten porch boards like they're squares in a game of hopscotch. I race to his room, shake his shoulders. "Brandon. Come on. Get up."

"There are reasons sororicide became a thing, you know," he murmurs into his pillow.

"Brand. We were tired and we couldn't see in the dark last night, but this place has changed."

"Doubt it. I warned you that you probably wouldn't remember it right."

"No. Brand. There's no dining room. The trails are grown over. This cabin—and all the others—they're falling apart."

"What are you talking about?" He grabs his glasses from his nightstand and pulls himself from his bed. Frowning, he shuffles out of his room, still dressed in his boxers and no shirt. I follow closely, trying to work my way around to his side, so I can see his face and his first reaction to the present day Lake of the Woods resort. It'll tell me I'm not nuts. Surely, it will. My memory couldn't have shined the place up this much—could it?

Brandon runs his fingers through his hair at the sight of the living room; when we step through the front door, I grab hold of his arm. "Watch out," I warn, pointing out the rickety porch and steps.

He glances about, turning his head first one way, then another. "Whoa," he mutters.

"See? What is this?"

"Dunno." He crosses his arms over his chest, takes a deep breath. "Bet you could ask them," he says, pointing toward the dock. I shade my eyes against the glare of the morning sun. A small group of men are filing down the dock toward a launch. One of them is standing to the side, greeting each of the men boarding the boat.

I'm short of breath. And not because of dashing back and forth between the main lodge and cabin number four. Because the man standing to the side has a familiar build. And a shock of shiny black hair.

Clint.

Clint
Breaking the Surface

I glance over my shoulder, and it's like I'm staring at a mirage. Seeing the "C"s on the heels of my skates yesterday messed up my head.

I've imagined her into existence. Chelsea Keyes, making a beeline for the dock, the same way she had that morning four summers ago when I'd glanced behind my shoulder and seen her, the ex-basketball player on vacation with her family.

Only, I must have the best imagination ever. Because once she hits the dock, I can literally feel the vibrations of her every step. As she gets closer, I can see each wavy, wild hair on her head and the freckles on her arms. I've even imagined a new outfit on her. Which is weird. But not as weird as the fact that one of the resort guests actually takes a step to the side to get out of her way. Takes a step to the side to clear the way for my mirage?

She looks at me with a bewildered expression. "You have a beard," she says.

I reach up to touch my chin. I've had it long enough to forget about it. I guess Todd's not the only one who's gone all Jeremiah Johnson.

Her eyes bounce across my face, then turn up to take in my hair, which is far longer than it was four years ago. These days, it hangs down halfway over my ears.

"You—you're—don't you recognize me? It's me," she says.

Apparently, I'm not greeting a mirage in the appropriate way. I feel like telling her to give me a break—this is my first time talking to an imaginary ex-girlfriend. If that's what she even really was in the first place. Girlfriend, I mean.

"Hey, Chelsea," Greg greets as he comes down the dock carrying a tackle box and a handful of extra poles.

No more chalking her up to a vision. Chelsea Keyes is real. She's standing less than a foot away. And Greg is acting like this is no big deal. Like people go all Lazarus every day, popping up out of nowhere, coming back from the dead.

On the Dock

"I came back, Clint," Chelsea says. "I made it. I'm here. It's been a long time. Longer than it should have been, I know. But—I'm here."

"Why?" he asks. It is all he can think of. It is the only word that fills his head. The shock of it all is making his arms tingle. He can't hear right. He's drowning.

Chelsea staggers. That single word—that *why*—hurts.

"Are you angry?" she asks. "You told me…You said…it wouldn't matter how long. Two months or two years—"

"Am I *what*?"

Greg puts himself between the two. "I sent you the postcard," he tells Chelsea.

They turn to him, faces twisted. It's like the aftermath of a fender-bender. Chelsea and Clint have crashed into each other, and now, neither one knows what to do.

Greg has caused this crash by never giving either one of them any indication he was butting in. When Chelsea called to make reservations, Rusty simply took the details, with no idea what was already in motion. He figured as much when he dropped the postcard in the mail. Now that he can see the looks on their faces, though, he feels like a jerk.

"What—happened?" Chelsea asks, looking around. Nothing is the same. Not Clint. Not the resort. Her memories of the place are already growing rust. Maybe she will never think back on it the same, having seen it this way.

Clint fumes. "Earl died."

"Is that why—?"

"Why what?"

"Why everything is, well—more—rugged than it used to be?"

"Hardcore," Clint growls. "Our current clients are serious outdoors guys. They don't need a bunch of childish comforts."

He does not understand why he is attacking her. Why he is this angry. Is it only being caught off-guard? The judgmental way she's looking at his resort?

Chelsea takes a step back. She hadn't meant anything by what she said. She's confused and embarrassed. She feels unwanted. And she has no idea what to do about it.

"Who—owns it?" she manages to ask.

"Rusty," Greg starts.

But Clint interrupts, "If you want to check out now, that's perfectly fine. Full refund. Won't even charge you for one night. I can give you the phone number for Wheelers Point. They're just down the road. I'm sure they'd be glad to have you for the remainder of your vacation."

"Why would I—" She looks at Clint like he's dumping her. Breaking her heart.

Because he is.

"Sure did surprise everybody, didn't I?" Greg asks, a crooked smile on his face. He puts one hand on Chelsea's shoulder and one hand on Clint's. "Maybe we need some time to let it all settle in. What do you say we meet tonight at Pike's? Is your brother here?"

Chelsea nods, her head spinning.

"Great. We'll see the two of you tonight. Me, Clint, Todd, and Rusty."

"Rusty?" she repeats.

Clint points at an ATV bouncing along the nearby terrain. A woman steers; seeing Clint, she turns sharply, spraying mud. She speeds down the shoreline, the red hair she's pulled through the back of a ballcap flying about wildly. When she gets within earshot, she tugs her sunglasses down her nose, shouts, "You need something, Clint?"

"Nah, just pointing you out to the guests," Clint says.

"You're game for Pike's tonight, right?" Greg asks.

"Always," she says, and speeds off.

Clint turns a cold face back to Chelsea. This is nothing like she imagined. He is acting like she has stuck him in a penalty box for two years. Even though he told her it wouldn't matter how long it took, that he would be happy to see her. He said that on the phone. What happened? Shock is one thing, but this all feels cruel. Like he needs to get even.

She backs away, retreats. She doesn't know what else to do.

When she's out of earshot, Greg holds his hands up. "I know," he tells Clint.

Clint's eyes are full of fire. Isn't this what he once wanted? Dreamed of? Pined for? Hadn't he still felt a pang of sadness the other day, seeing the "C"s on his skates?

"As your friend, I had to," Greg says, hoping to calm the turbulent waters.

"Had to what?"

"You're different. Something's happened to you."

"Come on."

"I'm completely serious. I've seen this before."

"Seen *what?*"

"Seen you bury a girl."

Clint blows through his lips, making a noise of disbelief. Starts toward the fishing launch and the group of men who are waiting for him.

Greg grabs his arm. "I mean it. You buried Rosie. I

was with you. I know what that did to you. Her wreck—it wrecked *you*. You laid her to rest. You mourned. And then Chelsea came. That summer, she opened your heart back up. But you're retreating all over again. And just now, the way you were when you saw her—it looked to me like you've buried Chelsea, too."

"Buried—?"

"Buried how you felt about her. Dug a pit someplace inside you and shoved everything you felt in there and covered that hole back up. Dusted off your palms."

"You had no business." Clint's humiliated. All those years of pretending Chelsea didn't hurt him that much—Greg knew all along it wasn't true.

"Don't get mad at me yet," Greg argues as he's backing up, heading down the dock, ready to leave Clint to the only fishing group scheduled for the day. "Let the shock cool off. See her tonight. Hang out with her. Or tell her to get lost for good. It's your decision. I think you've checked out lately, man. If you're still mad when she leaves, *then* you can punch me."

That Night
BAUDETTE, MINNESOTA

Chelsea
AMYGDALA

"The Bottom Dwellers reunion gig!" Brandon shouts as I ease the Camaro into the parking space. "All right!"

The downtown area of Baudette's pretty packed, actually. And everyone seems to be heading straight for the Morgans' restaurant. We've had to park all the way down the street from Pike's, in front of a dentist with a giant smiling molar on the door. The funky white hue of the painted tooth says it promises to glow in the dark after sunset.

"You think the regulars still remember us?" Brandon asks.

"The Bottom Dwellers? A band that played a handful of gigs four years ago?"

"No, no, you don't understand. Todd, Greg, and I

weren't a band. We were magic."

I kill the engine; the sounds of chatter and laughter spill down the sidewalk to filter through my still-open window. Does the sky here look different than it did four years ago? Is it maybe a different shade of blue? What if Pike's is different—every bit as affected by the hands of time as the Lake of the Woods resort?

"You know, sis," Brandon says. "We don't have to stay. We really could spend the rest of our vacation over at Wheelers Point. Like Clint suggested."

I groan. "You heard."

"Oh, I heard."

I run a hand through my hair in frustration.

"I wouldn't say anything to Mom and Dad," Brandon offers. "If you want, we could say it wasn't the same. Tell them about the rotting cabins. Tell them the place wasn't safe anymore. That's not even really much of a lie."

I take a deep inhale, trying to decide what I think about all this.

"You don't have to go in Pike's, either. You could go back to the cabin, get all our stuff ready to head out tomorrow. Come back for me at the end of my set. Forget Wheelers Point. Who says we even need to stay in Minnesota? We could have a vacation anywhere."

But at the same moment my escape hatch opens, my entire body starts screaming out at me that it's the last thing I truly want to do. I'm not ready to cave.

"Oh, yeah," I say. "I can hear it now. All the razzing I'd get. 'You drag me to Minnesota to see your ex! And it turned out *he* was the one who wanted to put a toxic squirt in your Squirt—not Gabe!'"

"Seriously," Brandon says, his eyes shining with sympathy behind the lenses of his glasses. "We can do what you want."

"I don't want to leave," I say, my voice an even mix of softness and pure determination.

"I mean," he goes on through a crooked smile, "don't think I haven't been through my share of tangles with the opposite sex."

"Brandon."

"The ladies *love* themselves a musician."

"Brandon."

"And a smart, good-looking musician?" He purses his lips and sucks in a sharp breath. "I got sticks stashed everywhere. You know. That I gotta use for beatin' 'em all back."

We're both laughing as he pops his door and circles to the back of the car.

I pause, one hand on the door handle, the other still on the steering wheel. I need to suck up my courage. I also need to figure out what I'll do when I see Clint. "Chelsea!" Brandon shouts. "If you're comin', get your butt in gear. And by 'gear,' I do not mean neutral."

I tug my phone from my purse. *Here in 1 piece*, I text Dad. *Sorry so late. No signal @ resort.*

I reach into the back seat for Francine, but Brandon stops me. "Oh, no."

"Brand, I'm pretty sure I can get Francine to Pike's without so much as damaging a single 'E' string on her head."

"Seriously," Brand grumbles. "I get Francine. You get the Crates."

"Nooo—"

"Oh, yes. I *am* doing you a favor coming up here. Which means you're Crate girl. I carry Francine. And, being the nice guy I am, I'll take the mic stand, too."

"You brought a mic stand? You had this planned all along."

"I didn't expect. I hoped," he says. Then sings out, "If you're coming, hurry up. I told you—butt in anything but neutral gear."

The Crates are practice amps—just about a foot tall and a bit wider. My Camaro wouldn't tolerate any of his enormous Marshalls. But the Crates have to weigh at least twenty pounds apiece. And, sure, I was spotting Lady Bears in the Missouri State weight room last week. But the practice amps are bulky and awkward, with those short little handles on top. When I grab hold of them and start to make my way down the sidewalk, I'm swaying side to side with each step—like a penguin. I quickly start sweating inside the jean shirt I'd worn with my ankle-length skirt to protect against a possibly chilly Minnesota night. Yes, there I am: a penguin sweating straight through her makeup, her shirt falling off her right shoulder, her hair hanging down the left half of her face while her purse swings around wildly, like a pendulum, smacking her butt then her wrist, butt then wrist. Not exactly the grand entrance I'd hoped to make at Pike's.

As I waddle, I notice a few new businesses have moved in—an athletic store, with sneakers and yoga pants in the front window. And a new wilderness store, advertising a half-off sale on sleeping bags. A coffee shop / used bookstore—the kind of place with paperbacks and black coffee in Styrofoam cups. A small hardware store. And some sort of web development business with a kitschy name: Kode. I wonder, as I rock back and forth with each step, what's up with the "K."

"Hey, check that out," Brandon says, pointing at a store advertising records in the front window. "Man, I wish I had my turntable with me."

"I don't," I groan. "You'd probably make me carry that, too. Besides, that's a flea market, Brand. Not a music store. Something tells me you'll find few rare jazz masterpieces in there."

We pause on the sidewalk in front of Pike's; I glance up at the still-visible inscription on the gray stone, high above the Pike's Perch sign: *Bank—1906.* The smells that trickle out are one part fried food and one part pure Cecilia Morgan delicacies.

Brandon holds the door open to let me shuffle inside.

Pike's is exactly as I'd remembered: same tables and small stage area toward the back. Same former teller's booth now open and holding a cash register. Brick walls, tin ceiling. A waitress steps out of the vault with her fingers wrapped around the necks of four bottles of beer, confirming that the old vault is still being used as a kind of microbrewery. The restaurant feels as frozen in time as a photograph—in here, it could still be four years ago. I close my eyes—my melting mascara's probably going to glue my eyes shut, but I close them just the same, so I can picture Cecilia, Clint's mom, in the kitchen, taking orders.

Yes, I think with relief. *Some things refuse to change. Some things are engraved permanently—like the letters on the front of this building.*

"Can't be!" a man's voice booms in my ear.

"Gene," I say through a strained smile. Clint's dad. *Pop,* that's what Clint called him. And he still looks exactly like his son, plus thirty years. Clint, I think as I stare at his father, will always be handsome. Even with pepper gray hair and creases around his mouth from smiling.

"Sight for sore eyes," he goes on. "We need to get this girl a drink. Or food—did you come for food? Where's Clint?"

"I—really ought to get these to Brandon," I say, raising the amps at my sides.

"Oh, sure, sure. Help you with those?" He leans forward, as though to take them off my hands.

"I got it," I promise.

"Okay. *Really* good to see you, Chelsea," he says, patting my shoulder and turning to lay some menus on a crowded table.

I take a few steps and have to pause for a minute. It's hitting me all over again—the way I felt four years ago, coming to town for the first time. How similar this stretch was to Fair Grove. How standing outside of Pike's felt like standing by White Sugar. The family business. Growing up working the cash register. I swear, I could be standing in Fair Grove at that very moment.

"Chelse!" Brandon shouts. "That's neutral!"

With a sigh, I start to waddle my way through the crowd. The place is packed. More than I remember it ever being, actually. That much is different—isn't it? Did I not notice the crowds back then because I only had eyes for Clint? I do my penguin walk up to the stage, where I finally drop the two amps.

Todd's already here. Of course it's Todd. Even though his blond hair is darker than it used to be—more like wet sand now—and he's wearing sunglasses inside Pike's, I recognize him right off. It's the build, I think. He looks like a football player I worked with a couple of years ago. One who'd had a couple of concussions. Actually, the longer I stare, the more I realize Todd has a funny droopy look—kind of post-concussion himself.

He also seems pretty unsteady on the stool behind his drums. He sways slightly, concentrating on lining a few beer bottles on top of his snare. "I'm making a *xylophone*," he informs me. Puts a finger to his lips and lets out a sloshy, "Shhhhh."

Make that post-six-pack.

"Think it's going to be a short set," I tell Brandon as I

reach for the collar of my jean shirt. Sure, the nights up here had a tendency to cool off. But right now, the shirt's too hot. Period.

Across the room, the vault opens again and Clint emerges, a beer bottle in each fist. He pauses to stare at me. Somewhere in the back of my mind, I'm aware that I'm still sliding my shirt off my shoulders—seeing Clint and wondering what he's thinking has turned all of my movements slow-motion. I'm slipping that shirt off in a way that's slow enough to be considered a tease. In a way that says a long silver pole ought to be stretched from the stage behind me all the way to the ceiling. *Crap*. I hadn't meant it to come across that way.

Clint shakes his head at me, glares like I'm taunting him on purpose. I try to hurry up with pulling the rest of my arms out of the sleeves. But the strap of my purse is getting all tangled up in the material and everything is so awkward. I'm suddenly the equivalent of a stripper who can't figure out how to take off her bra.

Rusty appears, still in the same dirty T-shirt and jeans and a ball cap that's fraying along the edge of the bill. She's a knockout—in a man's woman kind of way. Long hair, worn-out hip-hugging jeans. She looks utterly capable. Not at all like someone who'd ever have a problem taking off her stupid shirt. She looks more like she could outdrink anybody in the restaurant, beat every last one of them at arm wrestling, and smile through it all in such a way that no guy in the room would mind getting his butt kicked.

My theory turns out to be right on, as I realize that Rusty hasn't just snagged Clint's attention. Men all across the restaurant are turning to look at her. Their looks turn to stares.

Clint leads Rusty across the floor to a table, and pulls a chair back. I'm so focused on that motion and the horrible ache it opens up in me that I don't realize at first that Greg is watching this scene. But there he is, his head moving slightly, back and forth between me and Clint. After a while, I become horrifically aware of the fact that I'm still standing in the center of the stage.

Face heating up, I climb down as Brandon grabs hold of his guitar case, flips it open, and gently lifts Francine. Starts attacking an assortment of black cords.

"Hey," I say, waving my hand in front of Todd's face. He's cheeks puff out, like the back-and-forth motion of my hand is making him seasick. "Is Rusty Clint's girlfriend?"

Todd shakes his head. Doesn't he? Or is he just swaying, sick, on his seat?

Brandon's squinting at me in a way that says he wants to give me some advice. I can see it floating up there in his head. Something along the lines of, *Don't push it, Chelse.* Or, *You can't force it.* Or, *He's not interested, Chelsea. What does it matter if he's got a girlfriend or not? Back in Missouri, you said it'd be fine if this turned out to be a yoga retreat, didn't you?*

Instead, Brandon waves Greg closer to the stage. "Guys!" he shouts. "Come on. The fans are hungry for a Bottom Dwellers set. They miss us. Seriously."

"You're deluded," Todd slurs.

"Oohh," Greg says. "Good word. Someone was awake in English 101. One day, at least."

I hurry off the stage, but wind up feeling like a fourteen-year-old staring at a cafeteria crammed with unfamiliar faces on the first day of high school. *Where am I going to sit?* Being alone in a crowd of people who all have dates or friends or cohorts—being the only person here with absolutely no one to laugh with, not even a foot of space near a wall where I can try to melt into the backdrop—is horrifying. My mortification only makes me feel hotter in the packed restaurant.

I want out. So I start to weave through the restaurant, feeling like a pinball, bouncing and crashing and trying desperately to angle myself in a way that will allow the crowd to whack me straight toward the back exit.

Until I collide against someone. Hard. Before I can apologize, I'm overwhelmed by the familiar feel of the person in front of me. I recognize the dark skin on the arms, react to the warmth radiating through the white T-shirt. I don't have to look up into his face to know who this is. When did Clint stand up? Leave Rusty? Did he rush to meet me, or was he going back to the vault for another round? The crowd pushes us; we act like pieces of driftwood a river current has smashed together and is carrying to the edge of the rapids.

The back door bursts open, and we gush through.

Yes—the patio. I can deal with Clint on the patio. I remember being out here, with Clint and a couple of beers and a basketball hoop. Even now, something about being near a net makes me feel tough. *Perfect*, I think. *I can tackle this awful mess I've made with Clint if I'm beside a net.*

But instead of a cracked patio and the old scuffed backboard, I'm greeted by a weathered pool table. Underneath a slanted awning that stretches out from the back of the building.

"What—?"

Clint stares, waiting for the rest of the question.

I shake my head.

Clint puts his beer bottle in the grass. He turns to rack the balls on the faded felt. Grabs a cue. Leans against the table. Stares off into the distance, his back to me.

"Are—you—I—" God, I feel stupid.

"Waiting for Rusty," Clint says, still without looking at me. "She promised me a game."

"I'll play," I offer, tugging my purse from my shoulder and tossing it into the grass. I have a hundred questions. About Rusty. About the resort. About him. *Where have you been?* I want to ask. *What have these past few years been like?* Most importantly, I wonder, *Who are you now?*

"That's okay," Clint says. "I can wait." And then falls quiet.

"Busy tonight," I blubber. "Really busy. Kind of un-usually, uh—"

"Busy?" Clint finishes.

I'm officially even more embarrassed out here than I was inside.

"Business picked up the last couple of years," he says. "Ours did, at least. Some of the areas around here, they took a bit of a downturn. But no matter how hard times get, no matter how little money you might have, at Pike's, you can come share an order of appetizers and nurse a beer. Sit around for hours and talk, know you're not going to be pressured to hurry up and leave. Mom really played into that—started advertising Pike's as a less-expensive place to go, get out for a while, hang out. She's got the best gourmet appetizers around. And large dinner plates that can be split, too."

"One plate, two forks."

"Right."

"So, Earl—" I say, because I'm still searching for the hammer that'll finally smash right through this tense, awk-ward space between us. Clint's annoyance. Most of all, I want to obliterate the ice of Clint's annoyance. It changes his face, makes his features look hard and cold, more like something carved rather than a living, breathing human being.

"Passed away. As did his wife, shortly thereafter. His *niece*, Rusty, inherited the place."

I fight a sigh of relief. Niece.

"Rusty needed a place. Somewhere to decompress after

her time in the service. She was a combat medic in the Army," Clint says. "When she got back, she didn't need a bunch of noise. She needed the birds, the lake, a place where she could clear her head. Earl made sure she had that."

"Guess the medic needed some medicine of her own, when she came back to the States."

"I'm sure that's why Earl and his wife felt she was the right person to get the place," Clint says. "They liked the idea of somebody getting the resort because it was good for them. Wanted the place to be more than just a paycheck. Anyway, Rusty reached out to me, Greg, and Todd to help her out. We've been living at the resort full-time for the past year."

"It, uh, it—"

"Took a hit. That's what you're thinking."

I shrug. "I don't mean—"

"Rusty refers to the first year she was here as her lost year. A whole year without upkeep out there at the resort. By the time she called us, damage had started to set in at the place."

"In one year?" I ask.

"Place wasn't exactly new to begin with. A year of hard weather—and a year of ignoring plumbing or electric issues— stuff really starts to snowball. But there's not much money to go around. The guys and I don't have it. And like I said, the local economy's been kind of sluggish lately. We didn't get a lot of our regular renters. Might have been the lack of money, but it also might have been because we're not Earl. Anyway, new repairs come faster than we can fix the old problems."

He reaches for another cue, hands it to me.

"Changed your mind," I say. I hold my breath as I lunge forward to snatch it. But I'm such a ball of nerves, my hand reaches farther than it needs to. My fingers accidentally drag across the inside of his wrist.

My touch makes him flinch.

Clint leans over the table. With his back turned toward me, I can let my eyes linger, get a good look at him for the first time. His body is four years older but every bit as muscular as ever—his calves flex as he positions his body, and his right tricep bulges and tightens as he pulls the cue stick back. When his shoulder moves, I remember our ATV accident four summers ago. Remember how terrifying it had been to see him fly over the handlebars during that long-ago mushroom hunt of ours. How I'd screamed when his body had come crashing down against the gnarly tree root. How contorted his shoulder had looked when he'd dislocated it. How guilty I'd instantly felt, because I shouldn't have been pushing him, racing him.

He let me help him back then, though. I'm not sure if Clint will ever let me get close enough to fix whatever this is that's out of place between us now.

Clint breaks, sending the balls flying. None land in a pocket. He steps away from the table but doesn't look at me.

"Must be—must be nice," I start. I want to act like I know what I'm doing with the cue, too. But I wind up making a circle out of my thumb and index finger and sticking the cue through it. "Like making summer vacation last all year."

He steps behind me and wraps his hand around mine. Pries my fingers loose. I hadn't been aware of how tight my hands had become, at least not until his fingers start to relax every last muscle. He shows me how to position the fingers of my left hand on the felt; he places the cue on top of my thumb. His breath is on my neck. His hair brushes my cheek.

I'm flooded with memories of our summer together. Of a drive-in theater, of Clint murmuring, *Do you care about this movie?* and the two of us taking off, to park along a secluded section of lakeshore. How I couldn't stop touching him.

How I didn't even have to think about what to do—there was no right position, no right move. And here, now, I'm feeling it again—with Clint's arms around me, there's nothing to learn. No strategy I have to memorize. The cue moves forward; without having to question what I'm doing, the balls click. Two fly into the bottom left corner pocket, one right after another.

He pulls away. When I attempt to repeat my performance, I smack the red three ball so hard, it actually flies off the table, into the grass.

"Hardly," Clint says, finally responding to my vacation-all-year comment as he fishes the three ball from the weeds. He leans over the table. His arms flex as he attacks the white cue ball. He sends a few balls bouncing against the sides of the table, but nothing lands. That's twice now. Is he bad at this? Nervous? Is he off because he's irked?

"I've got a free room and all the fish I can eat," Clint says. "But it's a lot of work, too. To make ends meet, I've got a second job."

"Oh yeah? Doing what?"

He hesitates. "Coaching, actually."

"That's fantastic!" My enthusiasm is too much, too screechy. But here it is—something we can really talk about. "Where at?"

"Youth hockey at the rink in Baudette." He shrugs it off. "The three of us—me, Greg, and Todd—we thought maybe we'd get a little breather after graduation. Before the real work started at the resort, I mean. But no such luck. We had to scramble to get our heads screwed on straight. Figure out how to pay student loans and keep the boats running. The boats are the most important thing. It is a fishing resort, after all."

"Wait," I say, as some of Clint's words finally sink in. "You, Greg, and Todd thought you'd get a break after you graduated? *Todd* graduated?"

Clint laughs. It's the kind of laughter that ripples through him, relaxes him in the same way his touch had relaxed me. "We pushed him along. He's not a dumb guy. He's just not driven. At all. Unless girls or an outdoor adventure is involved."

"Did you get your degree in geology?"

He nods. "Sports psychology? Were you still working with Durst?"

"Yeah. I was." Clint remembering this is far more important to me than Gabe remembering my favorite soda. Makes me a little brave.

"When'd this pool table get out here, anyway?" I ask.

"'Bout a year ago," Clint says.

"No, it didn't."

"It didn't? You know all about the pool table, do you?" Clint asks. His eyes twinkle in the moonlight, and a playful grin starts to transform his face.

"Judging by the wear to the felt, I'd say it got out here about four years ago," I challenge, crossing my arms over my chest.

Surprise washes his face. I have that right.

"It didn't get out here because you wanted to play pool, either. It's was never about pool. It was about the net you had to take down. So it wouldn't be here when I got back. Because you, Clint Morgan," I say, grabbing hold of his arm, "cannot stand to lose."

Clint holds my gaze. And he doesn't pull away.

Neither do I.

She's beautiful. Even more so this time around.

Sounds superficial. Even to myself.

Last time around, there was a slight shyness about her. Strength was in her, too, but it was buried under the surface. It was something that needed to be coaxed out.

This time, she's got the confidence of a woman who knows what she wants.

I swear, the way she's looking at me makes me think the thing she wants is me. It makes my head swim—even more than the beer I've already downed.

She's beautiful. And she's here. And I already know how she tastes. That part pleases me, maybe more than it should: I already know what she tastes like.

And I figure, if I want to, I could taste her again.

She raises her chin, like she's readying to meet my mouth with her own.

But something in me pulls back. Probably the sound of the back door flopping open.

"Clint!" Rusty shouts.

"Hey, Rust. Chelsea was warming up the table for you," I start.

But Rusty's pointing behind her shoulder, saying, "I'll play you some other time, Clint, sorry. Gary showed up."

I wave her off in a way that says it's okay with me.

"One of her Army buddies," I tell Chelsea.

She nods.

Something about the air out here feels a little spoiled. I toss the cue stick onto the felt. "If I remember Brandon right, I think it's safe to say he'll play till the sun rises."

"Probably," she agrees.

"I'm heading back."

"Already?"

"Place is too crowded and too noisy tonight," I say. It's an excuse. "If you want to get to the resort before dawn, this is your chance."

I could kick myself. Because clearly, Chelsea drove herself and Brandon to Pike's. She doesn't need me to get back to Lake of the Woods. It sounds like I'm trying to be alone with her.

She brightens up at my offer. "Let me go tell Brandon," she shouts, and bounds back into the restaurant.

Chelsea
No Inhibitions

"What are you doing interrupting us?" Brandon asks as he steps away from the microphone. "We'll take an official break before our second set. We'll talk then."

"Second set?" I repeat, pointing toward the back of the stage. "Brand, your drummer doesn't even know the last song is over."

Brandon turns and eyes Todd, who's still whacking at the drums, swaying back and forth, and looking a little green.

"We're off to a rough start," he admits.

"It's not just the start. You're different now. You were a kid the last time we came. You're not still somebody who happened to pick up a bass because he likes to imitate loud, classic metal bands. You're a music major now. You play jazz. The only way you can save this thing tonight is if you turn it into a solo gig."

"I don't know," he mutters. He doesn't want to admit I'm right. At least, not in front of Greg. He doesn't want to hurt the guy's feelings. But then he frowns, asks, "Hey, why're you trying to butter me up, anyway? And—why are you trying to shove your keys into my hand?"

"I trust you to get the Camaro back."

"You've never trusted me with it before." He frowns. "Why are you taking off? Why wouldn't you want to hear my sol—*oh*." His eyes land on Clint, leaning against the front entrance.

"I just..." I start, but that's all I have. A start. I don't know where the end of that thought leads.

"Okay. I get it," Brandon says. "But look, my phone's on vibrate in my pocket. You need me, I can be there in two seconds, gig or no gig."

"Now, that's love."

"You get schmaltzy on me, I'll take back my offer," he warns.

I race across the packed restaurant, weaving between a crowd that now feels like it's watching me. Every single pair of eyes.

But Clint's watching, too.

And all I want right then is to find out what he sees. Someone he used to know? Someone he'd like to get to know again? Or, like Brandon, has Clint simply moved on past that summer? Is he in a different place now, and he needs to tell me that?

Something in the way he has his hand on the door, anxious to leave, says that's not the case.

When I get close enough, he smiles at me.

That smile is like magic. Because right then, it's enough to erase four years. It's enough to make me feel like we can pick up from that last night we were together. A night out in a field. Just the wildflowers. And the fireflies.

And us.

The View from Clint's Truck

The radio is off, but there's still music in Clint's truck—made up of the engine and the jiggling of the doors and the squeaking of the dash and the bench seat and the steering wheel—as he veers off the road and into the grass.

They're closer now to the resort than they are to the restaurant. In so many ways, Chelsea and Clint both feel they're not driving to a place, but a time. To days in which the space between them swelled with a kind of heat that neither one of them had ever truly known before. When neither one could put a name on what kept drawing them together, because the words other people used weren't right for them. Theirs was a feeling all its own, one outside the usual labels. *Girlfriend, boyfriend, love, lust, right, wrong* none of it fit or was truly enough. Just as their time together never seemed like quite enough. Three weeks. It was almost cruel how short it was. Especially when every moment together was powerful enough to change the way they saw the world—and themselves.

Tonight, four years after their last night together, Clint drives over ruts and bumps, steering with one hand, his grip on the wheel loose, unworried. As though this stretch is every bit as smooth as the highway.

The glove box pops open, whacking Chelsea's shin. She yelps a bit and reaches to shut it—but scraps of paper are tumbling out. In the light from the box, she can see Clint's handwriting covers all of them. List after list. Pros and cons. He's deciding something. "Bemidji," Chelsea reads. "Finish in a semester."

Clint shoves the pages back in, slams the glove box shut again.

He pulls to a stop in a patch of tall grass. His door creaks as he pops it open.

Chelsea follows. The moon is full, casting a blue haze across the open field, enough to see it's full of swollen buds.

"This place is about to explode with color," Chelsea says. "Plenty of lady slippers, I bet. State flower of Minnesota. Isn't that what you told me?"

He nods. "Takes so long for them to bloom. Anywhere from four to sixteen years. These flowers that are here now, getting ready to open—"

"—were here during our first summer."

They're both thinking of all they had found growing wild in these green fields.

But something odd happens at that moment. They are unsure how to be here, alone with each other. There is nothing holding them back, and yet, somehow, everything is holding them back.

"Love is the flower of life. Blossoms unexpectedly and without law, must be plucked where it is found, and enjoyed for the brief hour of its duration."

"What is that?" Chelsea asks.

"Lawrence, I think. Some lit class I had to take."

"A year out of school already, and you still remember some random passage."

"Yeah," he says softly. "I remember."

124

"This field blooms in waves, though," Chelsea goes on. "All summer long. Black-eyed Susans and daisies and lilies and honeysuckle. Place looks different every time you walk through it."

"Are we going to talk in flower analogies all night?" he asks.

One of them had asked the same thing four summers ago. On that last night. Here it is again, staring up at them.

"I'm just saying," Chelsea tries, "sometimes, it's not a single bloom."

Clint chuckles, scratches at his beard. "Well. Since we're gonna keep at the whole flower thing, orchids are finicky. They don't transplant well." Even though he has no idea if that's really true.

This cuts into Chelsea. She's tougher than that—and he should know it. She wants to say something that bites. She holds back, though, offering less of an attack but still to the point: "They survive, though. Think about it. All those rough Minnesota winters they have to go through. Since it takes years to bloom."

She's nervous and doesn't quite know how to be. How to stand. If she should reach for him. The gap is widening between them. A regular sinkhole, too deep to see the bottom, both of them on opposite sides.

"Sometimes," Clint says, "Mom keeps flowers. You ever do that? Press them in the pages of a book?"

Tears spring to her eyes. "Yes," she whispers. "The important ones. Yes, I do." She is telling him that she has saved it all inside of her: every single day they spent together that summer. She wants to tell him as much outright, but struggles for the words.

"I thought the invitation came from you," she blurts. "The last postcard I got. I didn't know it was Greg."

Clint stares at her, the moonlight outlining his face. "Greg likes to get into everybody's business. Likes to think he knows what's best."

He finds it a little hard to breathe beneath his thousand angry questions. She has graduated, which means she's at yet another crossroad. Same as the summer four years ago. Does she only come to him when she needs to make a decision? Does she like to take a break from real life long enough for everything to become clear to her? Is there another guy at home this time? Is he number two again? What does she want? A little escape? Is that all he is to her?

Chelsea stares at him—the shaggy hair, the beard. And she wonders where the other Clint disappeared to. The one who worked all those jobs, who wanted to run a boot camp program at the resort. Who saw possibility in everything, including her at one time. Who showed her she was more than a broken hip.

Does he still think so? Or does she look different to him? Like someone who only takes and never gives back in return? Had she been selfish not keeping in contact? What if Clint thought it was cruel? What if he was really saying during that last phone call, *I'm leaving it to you when we get in touch. Ball's in your court. But please, please, please, Chelsea, make room for me in your life as soon as you can. If you don't, I'll assume you're through with us.*

What if her not taking time to email or text only rang like a rejection in his heart?

He'd said once she had changed him for the better. Opened up his heart. Showed him that he could love again after facing so much loss.

But did her silence only close him up again?

His face is hard and severe. Almost accusatory. In his frown, Chelsea sees a new question. She shudders against it:

What would I have done if Greg's postcard had never arrived?

Would she have returned on her own? Would she have left that entire summer behind?

Hadn't she decided she was better off without a man? Hadn't she just been thinking that, mere days ago, sitting across from Gabe in Hill Toppers'?

Why does she feel the need to stay, even when Clint is so chilly to her? Why can't she let him go? Why is she so determined to turn this around? Turn a losing situation into a winner—for her *and* Clint? What does a winning situation even look like here? Is winning possible at this point? Will she only leave another trail of hurt behind? *Is that really the kind of person you want to be, Chelsea?*

Her head swims. The answers arc eluding her, and it's an uncomfortable feeling for her, not even knowing what the goal is. The only thing that's certain is how it feels to stand so close to him. It's electric. Even with the angry look on his face. There's something magnetic about him. There always was. But this time, he's not just handsome. He's not a strong, sun-darkened body and a boyish grin. She knows him. Knows his story. Their chapters intertwine.

There's a kind of power in that.

The air here in the field is fragrant and fresh—unlike the air at the resort, which is tainted with the smell of rotting wood and musty, empty cabins. Here, among the wildflowers waiting to bloom, it smells like earth and grass and all the possibilities that have yet to bloom. Colors are about to erupt, overpowering any drabness.

Chelsea props a foot on top of the truck's back tire and hoists herself into the bed. She stretches out flat—not an easy feat. The metal bed is lined with uncomfortable ridges. But then again, this whole night feels uncomfortable to her.

"Well," Clint grumbles. "I guess no trip to Minnesota

should ever be considered complete without a little evening stargazing." His voice is soft—neither friendly nor accusatory. He grabs hold of the bed of the truck and hoists himself in, too. Reaches into a canvas bag beneath his tool box and pulls out a folded quilt. "Here," he tells her. "Use it as a pillow."

She shoves it under her neck as Clint tucks his arms behind his head.

She raises up, opens up the quilt enough for two heads.

Clint eyes her in an *exactly what are you doing here* way before finally accepting.

Chelsea stretches out beside him. So close, she can feel his chest rising and falling with breath.

"Are you going back to school?" she asks.

"What do you know about—"

"I saw the notes that fell out of the glove box."

He hesitates. "I think about it."

"A master's?"

"No—get my teaching certificate. Bemidji's got this FasTrack PostBac. Since I already have my degree, it wouldn't take much time—or money—to get my certificate."

"What would you teach?"

"High school earth science. And then I might even be able to coach the school hockey team."

"Do it."

He chuckles. "Just like that."

"What's holding you back?"

"Rusty. I promised her I'd stick around to help."

"But you said you'd only take a little while. How far is Bemidji?"

"It's after the certificate that's the problem. I mean, I promised her I'd be around to help with the resort. There's still so much to do. But if I'm going to work full-time as a teacher, I'd be deserting her, wouldn't I?"

128

The crickets sing.

"And you?" Clint finally asks. "You're done with school, aren't you?"

"Not yet. I graduated, but I'm going for my master's," Chelsea says. "Still working with Durst. I'll be able to include my one-on-one work with three injured athletes in my thesis."

"Sounds like you've got it all worked out," he says.

But she doesn't. Something is nagging at her. Once, the gym had been the only place on earth she wanted to be. But had it ever had the same impact as this place? Even rotten and falling in? The feeling that overwhelms her when she hears the distant waterfall. A peace that settles into her soul.

"I'm not shh—" she starts. But the rest of her *sure* is cut off as a firecracker erupts, tossing colors across the darkened sky.

Surprised, Chelsea points skyward toward the shower of gold.

"Wheelers Point shoots them on the weekends," Clint murmurs.

Another firecracker detonates, rattling their chests and spilling down their arms. Fire streaks, screaming as it slashes the darkness.

Clint crosses his arms over his chest in a protective manner. He asks himself, *What am I doing here? With her? Why didn't I take her back to her cabin?*

She bites her lip and asks herself again, *Why can't I let this go?*

And still, the sky explodes.

Hours later, they blink themselves awake, startled to find

they're still in the truck and still together.

The sun is shining. But the sunlight feels cold. A morning breeze draws goosebumps.

They'd rolled into each other in sleep; Chelsea's head is on his chest and her arm is draped around his waist. Their legs are tangled. Their calves are skin on skin.

The truck bed is hard beneath them.

They rub the last of the sleep from their eyes, but they don't know how to laugh at this. Or if they should. Maybe there's too much scar tissue.

Frightened, they sit up and glance out from the bed of the truck. They're surrounded by buds twisted up tight, like fists.

Chelsea
SELF-BLAME

Silence sits between us as Clint drives me back. When cabin number four comes into view, he slows down.

"I can get out here," I say. The first words either one of us has said the entire drive.

Clint doesn't answer, just stops the truck.

I get out and turn, hoping he'll say something.

"See you, Chelse," he murmurs. But it doesn't really seem like he's saying it to me. He's staring straight ahead, through the windshield.

I slam the door.

The wheels kick up dirt, and he's gone.

But I'm not exactly alone. Brandon's on the front steps of cabin number four, barefoot, his hair still mussed from sleep. Drinking a cup of coffee.

And shaking his head at me.

I'm already groaning, because I know what's coming.

"Is *that* a walk of *shame*?" he shouts at me.

I frown, try to hush him.

But he's laughing so hard, he has to clutch his stomach.

"Shut up. Move," I bark when I get to the steps.

He scoots to the side, giving me room to sit beside him.

He passes me the cup and I take a sip. "You make it too strong," I grumble.

"Talk about coming on strong—" he starts, and laughs again.

"Please stop."

"Looks like somebody's having a great vacation."

"Or not," I say. "Nothing happened."

"Seriously?"

"We drove out to one of the fields we used to hike through," I say. "Firecrackers were popping."

"Oh, man, that's not some euphemism, is it?" he jokes. His face falls as he asks, "And then nothing? Really nothing?"

I drink another sip.

"Man. What's the deal? Spark not there anymore?" He tilts his head, waiting for an answer. He's trying to hold some horrendous *warned you* back. I can tell.

His face shifts into a kind of sickeningly sympathetic look. "You were really hoping there would be."

"Why do you think I came?"

He shrugs. "I thought you were curious. I believed you when you said you'd have a yoga retreat if it wasn't the same."

"It's so weird. He kind of treats me like—like he doesn't forgive me."

"For what? Taking so long to get here?"

"I don't know. Maybe. Or maybe he's mad about—the way I stuck him in the middle of me cheating on Gabe—or something."

"He upset about it, or you are? Because you saw Gabe again, and it drudged all that stuff up?"

I flinch. "I do care about what happened. I care a lot. But—"

"He knew about Gabe at the time, and it didn't seem to matter to him," Brandon argues.

"Yeah, but now it seems like maybe he thinks I'm somebody that can't be trusted or something."

When Brandon doesn't have an immediate comeback for that, I add, "I can't blame him. I mean, he knows I'm capable of running around on somebody. Even if that was four years ago. And then I don't talk to him at all for two years, and it probably had to feel to him like I took what I wanted from him, too, and just moved on. Almost like I cheated on him, only with my job at school instead of another guy, if that makes sense. Putting more of myself into—or committing to—the athletic department, but not him. Pushing him to the side always. And then, when enough time's passed that *anybody* with a pulse would have been over it all, I show up, and—"

I grunt. Take another gulp.

"You gonna drink *all* my coffee?"

I hand the mug over. "He called me in the spring of my sophomore year. Last time we talked. Said I could come back at any time. Even if it was two years. Those exact words. Said it'd be okay."

I squint into the morning sun. "Cleaning out my dorm, I came across the first postcard, then Clint's compass. And then when you came into Hill Toppers' with the second postcard...It felt like a sign. Like the stars were aligning.

I know I said it wouldn't matter if things were different, but the reason I could say it so casually was because I knew in my heart it wouldn't happen that way. I knew this was it. Our time, mine and Clint's."

"What happened?"

"I think two full years of no contact was more than enough time to let me go."

He scrunches his mouth up into a look of disgust. Or maybe that's disagreement.

"What? You don't?"

"I think it's a little fatalistic," he says. "I mean, what do you want, Chelsea?"

I can't answer that. Why can't I?

"Maybe he's looking for you to tell him why you showed up," Brandon says. "I mean, that summer we were here before, he kind of knew where he stood. He knew about all of it. Even Gabe."

"But even Gabe—"

"—got over it. I know, I know. I'm not trying to lecture you about Gabe or whatever. The point is, you don't know where you stand with Clint, either. All you guys know is that you and I are here temporarily. Maybe, last night, you were the one being every bit as distant as Clint. Maybe what you're really afraid of is that he'll treat you every bit as selfishly as you suspect you treated both Clint and Gabe four years ago. Does he have somebody else in his life?"

"I don't know," I admit.

"Why are you tiptoeing around him? Why can't you ask him what's what?" When I don't immediately answer, he says, "You don't even really know each other."

"How can you say that?"

"Something happened between the two of you. You guys got off to a running start, that's for sure. But neither one of you really had the time to get to know each other. Not like you know a friend. That happens over a lot more time than three weeks. Maybe the reason you guys aren't clicking is you're basically strangers."

I squint at him. "You take a psych class or twelve last semester?"

"I'm telling you, I have learned from personal experience. The girls love themselves a musician. I might have found myself in a few sticky romantic situations of my own."

When my laughter winds down, all I can do is look out at the resort and say, "What happened to this place, anyway?"

"I can't tell you. It's really awful, isn't it?"

We laugh again. It's good to at least admit what a mess it really is. I smack his knee. "Were you kind to my poor Camaro?"

"Poor Camaro? How about poor Brandon? That thing's on its last tire. You put me in control of a death trap."

"Please. You never could drive. I gotta go someplace," I say, lunging from the porch.

"Hey!"

I stop midway down the steps.

Brandon holds his arms out. "You didn't even ask how our first night went. The Bottom Dwellers are *back*, baby!"

"I find that hard to believe."

"No—I'm telling you. I whipped those guys into *shape*. And maybe turned down their amps just a teensy bit." He flashes his perfect grin, courtesy of all those years of braces.

"At least Greg and Todd are glad *you're* here," I say.

He shouts something back at me. Something about only Greg being glad. I don't know what happened last night, but Todd was about as sloshed as I've ever seen. I can't really imagine Brandon even wanting to play with somebody who was that out of it.

I make my way down the dirt path. It's not like the place is completely deserted. One group is already fishing from a launch out in the middle of the lake. A couple of guys float along in rowboats. But the resort as a whole still reminds me of a worn-out pair of waders.

I step inside the main lodge. The place is eerily empty. I know Earl's long gone, but no one else has taken up the job of bellowing friendly greetings from behind the check-in counter. Not a single sign on the bulletin boards. No current photo of the summer's biggest catch.

I wonder if they're even still doing that.

I also wonder why they'd quit.

And why Greg would have remembered that I had once won.

I hear a clatter, and decide to follow it, straight into what had once been the dining room. Rusty's pulling back one of the least-dusty bentwood chairs, sitting down at a table with what appears to be a notebook and a cup of coffee.

She glances up and sees me. Waves me closer.

Last Night

Maybe, Clint will think, it was seeing the "C"s on the skates. The ones he had so recently scrubbed off. Maybe it was the shock of seeing Chelsea on the dock. Maybe it was the fact that he was lying beside her in the bed of his truck. But Clint is having a night of dreams. One after another. Each one more puzzling than the last.

The most vivid one, the dream that will still feel real long after he opens his eyes, the dream that will haunt him, is of being on the ice, in the midst of a pond tournament. A fringe of pine trees—so dark green, they appear black—surrounds the water. The sound of spectators chanting a name other than his own frightens him. A sudden chill adds a feeling of dread all its own.

That cold—it permeates everything.

For some reason, though, there are no teams. Only Clint and one opponent. And, behind his shoulder, a goalie in an unrecognizable uniform.

Clint's opponent has control of the puck.

He skates forward, but is unable to gain any momentum. He feels tied back somehow. He doesn't want to crush the opponent. He doesn't even feel the familiar need to win.

But he does want to get closer.

Why, though? What's going on?

While he's trying to figure it all out, the player suddenly changes direction and speed, a classic decoy—and skates around Clint to score a goal.

Clint swivels. The opponent pumps a fist against the sky in victory. When the still-unknown opponent tugs their helmet off, long blond hair tumbles down. It's Chelsea, Clint realizes. Smiling at him.

"Why did you do that?" Clint shouts. "That play—you faked me out."

He tries to skate toward her, but his skates won't move. The ice has swallowed his feet. He's frozen in place.

Chelsea's response is simply to ignore him. She blows kisses to the crowd as she skates off, leaving him unable to follow her and calling her name to no avail.

"You've got it all wrong," he screams. "You think I'm the one who can't stand to lose? You don't even play fair."

The cheers of the crowd grow louder, drowning him out completely. Applause and screams of, "Brava!"

She turns circles, acknowledging their approval.

Of course they approve.

After all, she has won.

That's what Chelsea does, Clint thinks. She wins.

Clint

SINKER

I'm in the gift shop, digging through the cooler in the back, when I hear her voice.

Chelsea.

I feel myself tightening up inside. Did she follow me here? Who is she talking to?

I tug out a can of Coke, crack it open, and take a sip. A poor substitute for coffee, but the hope was that if I managed to avoid seeing Greg until later in the day, he'd be too focused on whatever part had just fallen off one of the launches or whatever plumbing catastrophe had just happened in one of the cabins to remember to pester me with a bunch of questions about what happened last night. And Todd…as far as I know, Todd's still in Pike's, slobbering all over his drum set. I'd convinced myself I'd never have to talk about Chelsea at all if I managed to avoid the guys through the morning hours.

By tomorrow, well—I doubted Chelsea would still be at the resort.

Or maybe that's hoped.

I can't shake that awful dream I had the night before. *Only a dream*, I tell myself, even though I know it's more than that. It's true. Chelsea faked me out in real life. That's how it feels, anyway. She told me things—made grandiose promises—to get what she wanted. Chelsea Keyes is the one who needs to win, above all else.

"Not what you remembered, is it?" Rusty asks.

I peek through the doorway to find Rusty and Chelsea sharing the same table.

"Guess it's too much to hope that Chef Charlie's around, and could possibly whip up an omelet," Chelsea says.

"No chef." Rusty props her elbows on the table and rubs her eyes. "No eggs. No milk. No dry cereal. I can offer you a semi-warm Coke." She's trying to make light, but her tone is anything but happy.

Chelsea waves a *that's okay* as she looks about the room.

"Maybe time works its disastrous ways a little bit faster than we could ever imagine," Rusty observes.

"Maybe," Chelsea mumbles.

"You'd like to check out early," Rusty says.

"Maybe."

My stomach knots.

"Well, I don't blame you," Rusty says. "Greg should've given you a heads-up. It's not really a family vacation spot anymore. Wheelers Point took up that mantle."

140

"I heard," Chelsea squeaks.

"And it's hard to go up against them, since they charge so little." She massages her temples, like she's trying to rub away a headache.

"Okay. You're right. It's more than Wheelers," Rusty admits. "I know. It's plain old run-down. I have so much I need to get done." She kind of half-chuckles at her notebook. "This is my need-to list. Used to be a wish list. But I think we know the place has progressed past mere wishing. Good thing Earl's not around to see the way this list has exploded."

"What's keeping you from it?"

"Everything," Rusty groans. "Money. Time. The guys are free labor, but they have other jobs. And other dreams. They have a right to other dreams. Greg wants to be a full-time conservation agent. Clint—he loves that hockey team of his so much, surely he wants to do something along those lines. But he'd never tell me. Not after promising me he'd stay until this place was turned around."

I eye Chelsea for some reaction. She shows no hint of knowing about Bemidji. At least she keeps that much to herself.

"They live here rent-free," Rusty goes on, "but they've got to eat. They have insurance and college loans, too. So they're not here all day long. Other jobs, like I said. This can't go on forever. They have their own lives to get to. And it's not like I can hire somebody…"

"No," I hiss from the doorway. "Rusty. No." Because if this Chelsea is anything like the Chelsea I'd known four years ago, she'll take this bait.

Chelsea perks up, leans forward. "Why don't I help?"

Rusty laughs. "What, you have some masochistic desire to ruin your summer?"

"A burning desire to do something other than a bunch

of yoga," Chelsea corrects. "I can't stand to sit around. And my master's program doesn't kick into gear for a while and—"

"You're serious!" Rusty says.

"Absolutely. I have a free week. If I could—"

"Girl, you can stay the entire summer for free if you're willing to help around this place. I need painters and carpenters and—you wouldn't know anything about plumbing, would you? The guys keep having issues with the kitchen sink in cabin seven."

That does it. I burst through the door. "We don't need you, thanks," I announce. But apparently, I'm not just announcing it to Chelsea and Rusty. I hadn't noticed that Todd's in the back of the dining room, in sunglasses, holding his head.

"Actually," Rusty argues with me, "we do."

"Can all of you shout a little softer?" Todd croaks.

"What do you want this place to be?" Chelsea asks.

"What's that mean?" My defenses are already up. I don't need Chelsea sticking around, making me feel like a fool about the resort, too. Feeling like a fool in matters of the heart is enough.

"I mean—Wheelers Point is about family vacations. What are you?" she asks.

"A fishing resort. Like always," I say.

"Even fishermen want a place that's not falling in," she tells me.

"Fishermen do not care."

"Come on, Clint," Todd croaks. "Admit it. You need help. Especially since I'm leaving."

"Leaving?" Chelsea asks.

"Yeah. For Alaska!" he shouts, then grimaces at the noise and puts his fingers on his forehead.

"This business stuff is not my thing." Todd reaches

into his back pocket and comes up with a roll of antacids. He pops one, goes on, "It was never going to be my thing. But the longer I stay, the more it's feeling like I'm in prison, man. *Spreadsheets*. Uuugh."

"When we get someone to take Todd's place, it should be permanent," I argue. "And besides, we should take someone on who has the same vision."

Chelsea lets out a bark of a laugh. "If you call rotten cabins and molded fish guts a vision."

"Listen, just because it isn't your thing doesn't make it bad. We've got plenty of guys coming to stay with us. You're not the only guest right now, are you? Didn't you happen to notice there were other guys out on the lake this morning?"

"This place is far emptier than it used to be. You know that."

"Dave," I blurt. "One of my tried-and-true regulars. He's here. Ask him. He's a little over thirty, single. An MD in need of time away from the high-stress gig of literally having somebody's life in his hands every single time he clocks in. Works the regional hospital in Baudette. Shows up at the resort on his days off. Nearly *all* his days off."

"You think an MD isn't bothered at all by rotting guts? Someone who disinfects and washes his hands and kills germs at every turn? At what point do guys like Dave stop coming completely?" she counters. "At what point do they decide some other resort is better, because at least it isn't raining on them through the hole in the roof all night? There are plenty of other fishing spots nearby, you know."

"Clint, we need her," Rusty insists.

"Sure do," Todd says, even though he's got his head on the table at this point, and looks on the verge of unconsciousness.

"And Brandon!" Chelsea adds.

"You think he'll want to stay?" Rusty asks.

"I can convince him. Especially if he's got a gig at Pike's. He'll do anything for a chance to play in front of a crowd."

I'm not prepared for this. I'm standing on the ice with no protective gear. I'm about to lose all my teeth. Get an eye knocked out. I know I am. I'd just about convinced myself I could have stood to have Chelsea around a couple of weeks, if she insisted on staying. I could have avoided her. I could have volunteered to help more at Pike's. I could have spent any minute I wasn't on the lake over at the rink. Couple of weeks, a guy can hold his breath.

But all summer? Is that really what Chelsea is considering?

"We need a little more time," I try to tell Rusty. "If you'd wait—"

"Wait?" Rusty repeats. "You know what my Uncle Earl would have said to that? 'Oh, I'd rather get a whoopin'.'" She pauses to chuckle. "And so would I. He spent his entire work life building a reputation. He was proud of what he'd done. He was proud he had a place you and Greg and Todd loved enough to come back to time and time again. Was proud I had a place to come home to." She sighs. "I can't tell you how bad I feel about really screwing up Earl's place. You know we've done him a disservice, Clint."

"I can do this," Chelsea says. "I can help you get back on track. I remember exactly—"

"I don't want to go back," I tell her. And in that moment, I mean it in every way possible. I don't want to go back to the way the resort was four years ago, when she was here. And I know, right then, that she and I are not going to happen. Not this summer, and not any other summer, either. Greg made a mistake. I really am going to punch the guy.

"Then don't," Chelsea says. "Don't go back. Make this place more. Make it your own."

"My own? My own what, Chelsea? This is a fishing resort. *Make it my own.* You don't have the slightest idea—"

I stop when Chelsea juts her chin forward and tells me, "As I remember, you appreciate a good competition."

"So?"

"So—you against me. Your idea for a rotgut fishing resort against my new and improved idea."

"Rotgut? That word doesn't apply to resorts. That's how much you know."

"Inferior and unpalatable seems to describe this place fine," she smirks.

"Oh, really? You haven't even said what this idea of yours—"

"Afraid?" she asks.

"Of what? Someone out of her league who doesn't even have the hint of a plan to stand on? Who doesn't understand the economics of the area?"

"*I* don't understand the economics of the area," Todd insists.

"We cater to a certain clientele. These guys want the excitement of pulling in a ten-pounder—cooking it over an open campfire while nursing a sunburn—then dropping into bed exhausted as the sun goes down, ready for another day on the lake."

"So you say." She crosses her arms over her chest.

"So I know. Prepare to be beaten. And completely, totally embarrassed."

"It's on, then," Chelsea maintains, her eyes glistening.

"Good! Now, if I just knew what I was going to do about Blue, I'd be set," Todd grumbles.

"What's Blue?" Chelsea asks.

"It's a who," Todd slurs. "My dog. I love that guy, but what am I going to do with him in Alaska? When I'm on a climb? Doesn't really seem fair to him, does it?"

Chelsea sticks her bottom lip out, thinking. "I'll take him."

"You?" Todd laughs. "You on some sort of rescue binge, Chelse? Why don't you adopt twelve kids and volunteer at the food bank while you're at it? Ooh! And run for mayor!"

"I had a cat forever," Chelsea tells him. "He got old and…I've missed having an animal around. I'd be happy to have him. I'll take good care of him. I promise."

Todd's smile fades as it becomes clear this is a real offer. He stands, stumbles across the dining room, and they shake on it.

She and Rusty shake on their summer plans, too.

And then she turns to me. She's so tall, we can look each other square in the eye.

I accept her handshake; the pressure nearly crushes my fingers.

I don't let her get by with that. I narrow my eyes, squeeze right back.

My wordless acknowledgment that I'm in this not just to win but to thoroughly destroy Chelsea makes her face relax into a pleased smile.

Chelsea
Substitution

"**What** do you mean, you're not going to be here for camps?" Durst asks in a familiar unhappy tone, the wrinkles in his forehead growing deeper as he leans into his webcam.

"Who's not going to be here?" I can hear from another area of Durst's office. "Chelsea? Chelsea won't be here?" Makayla sticks her own head into Durst's laptop.

"It'll only be for camps," I assure him. "I'm visiting an old friend. Turns out, he needs my help." I'm still thinking about how inaccurate that statement is (*Old friend? Who needs me? Ha!*) as I go on, "Summer camps don't have anything to do with what I've planned for my thesis—" Instantly, I regret such a ridiculous statement. "But I know you were counting on my help with some of those incoming freshmen—"

"Not like you, Keyes," Durst says. "Not like you at all."

I clear my throat as I shift uncomfortably in the Camaro's front seat. "It was totally unexpected."

"Where are you?" Makayla asks, flashing a frown of her own.

"Minnesota." I hold my phone up to my window. "I'm in the town of Baudette so I can pick up Wi-Fi. Just outside this restaurant where my brother plays music." This immediately also sounds foolish. I'm here to work, but Brandon's playing music at some bar and grill? I scramble to offer a better explanation. "I mean, we're friends of the family. Their son is the one who needs—"

"*What?*" Makayla cuts me off. "You didn't say anything about this. What about—"

Durst holds up a hand to quiet her. "Listen, Keyes, you've worked hard for me. You've never once not shown up before, and I know that you wouldn't be calling now if this wasn't important. But I have to warn you I can't hold your position in the fall." It's apparent Durst is attempting to sound accepting of my excuse. I'm not sure he really is, though.

"Oh, that's not—this isn't—it's for the next few weeks."

"How many is a few? Two? Three?" he asks.

"Three."

"Three?"

"Maybe four."

"Doesn't sound definitive."

"It's four, tops," I insist. In truth, I have no idea how many weeks it's going to take. But I did promise Durst I'd be back. And now, I've promised Rusty—and the memory of Earl, it feels like—that I'd stay here. And my heart feels like it's being pulled in two different directions.

"I have a feeling I'm going to get another one of these calls," Durst grumbles. He shifts, and even though I can't see below the collar of his shirt, I figure he's crossed his arms over his chest in a disgusted way.

"I can't say for sure when I'll get through here," I admit. "But I will definitely be there this fall." Even as I form the words, I'm not sure I believe it.

"Fall now, is it?" Durst growls.

He glances at Makayla. "You," he says. "You need a summer job?"

"Do I," Makayla says.

"You're filling in for Chelsea this summer. With my camps."

"Yes," she hisses. "You bet. Thank you. This is perfect. Rescued me again, Chelse." She flashes a broad smile as Durst ends our call.

Before I can so much as toss my phone into the passenger seat, my mind fills with the image of Hill Toppers' back in Fair Grove. All those newspaper articles plastered to the walls. My picture first growing yellow, then being plastered over with pictures of the shooting guard Jana Gleeson, who took my place as Fair Grove High's homegrown star.

The Tug of War

Four years ago, Chelsea and Clint headed out to Willie Walleye Day, Baudette's official birthday party for the giant sculptural fish that served as the town mascot. Willie had never been a small marker or what anyone would reasonably call a subtle welcome to town. *Used to be two tons of concrete,* Clint was sure to point out to Chelsea as they drove past it. When it started looking shabby, it got a fiberglass update, he told her. Wasn't retired. Not Willie. Not something that important.

So many things were like that—too important to end.

And yet, Chelsea and Clint had already been forced to suffer through the end of some of the most important parts of their own lives. Basketball. Hockey. First love. No upgrades or do-overs for them.

I should have said something different, done something different, it's all on me. My fault.

That was the kind of thing the two of them had spent months thinking.

But it was different at Willie Walleye Day. There, at something as silly as a town-wide birthday party for a giant fiberglass fish, complete with funnel cakes and lumberjack competitions and homemade crafts for sale, they both found a kind of new starting place.

With light hearts and newfound smiles, they wandered the streets and the booths and the carnival rides, Chelsea looking pretty in her sundress and Clint cleaned up and handsome, having showered and changed after a day on the lake. They were at a beginning. That was the way it felt between the two of them, anyway. Two strangers with an undeniable attraction. The initial spark. The kind of spark that could ignite something powerful.

And for two people who had done nothing but deal with endings for months on end, a beginning was something they couldn't turn away from. They couldn't keep their hands off of it. Something new. Something only just starting. It was electric and undeniable.

The tug of war competition on Main Street—guys against girls—drew them in. Clint found himself at the front of one line, Chelsea at the other. Two young, strong people pulled out as likely leaders.

A few weeks earlier, each one of them might have backed out. But that day? Neither one would show such faint-heartedness, not in front of the other.

It was something neither had done in ages. Something for fun. But it was also a little scary, maybe even a touch dangerous. As they dug their feet into the ground and pulled along with the rest of their teams, they began challenging each other. Daring each other. Pushing each other. Asking each other for more.

Sure, it was play. Seeing Clint's eyes crinkle as he smiled. Hearing Chelsea's laugh. But because of what they'd both been through, it was more.

And that felt good, too.

Now, four years later, there is no silly celebration. No jugs of frozen root beer, no street dance. There is only the Lake of the Woods resort and a ton of work. A less-than-civil Clint and a Chelsea consumed with doubt. Her decision to stay and work at the resort feels about as sturdy to her as the rotten boards she discovered on her first morning.

Shortly after telling a shocked Brandon, Chelsea finds a note attached to the screen door of cabin number four: *If you're going to insist on this, do your own cabin. After that, you get cabins #2, 6, and 8. —Clint.*

"He's actually playing along?" Brandon asks, squinting into the midday sun that hits their cabin's porch.

"I'm not sure," Chelsea admits. *It can't be this easy.* "Why don't I take the first look?"

Brandon nods, determined to give her space on this. "I'll be here with Francine," he says. And slips back inside.

"Cabins two, six, and eight," she mutters to herself as she grabs one of the granola bars she and Brandon found in their bags, surely stuffed in by their mother. "Two, six, and eight," she chants, hurrying to the closest cabin—number six—wanting to take a plan of action back to Brandon.

But when she steps inside, she finds a giant hole where the floor should be, near the soot-stained old wood stove.

"No floor?" she bellows.

Heart thundering, she turns and races to cabin number eight, where dark rot and mold surround the windows in the living room.

She dips back out, sprinting to cabin number two. She stands in the center of the living room and takes a deep breath. *Not bad*, she thinks, until she picks up on the sounds of animals scurrying about overhead.

"*Morgan*," she growls. "You gave me the worst cabins."

She knows, even without a drumroll or starter pistol explosion, that another round of tug of war has begun.

Chelsea
FIXATION

"**All** summer?" Brandon grumbles as I shake him awake the next morning. "We're seriously going to be here all summer?"

"May I remind you that when we initially discussed the idea, you were all in?"

"Yeah, but I'm clarifying: *all* summer?"

"For the eightieth time, Brand, I don't know how long. I told Rusty we'd help out. I didn't sign our whole summers away, exactly. I do have to get back to Durst. You've got songs to write to take back to the Mizzou music department. Maybe we find out we have a special talent for cabin renovation and finish in five days. Improvise! You know how to do that." When he doesn't answer, I shout, "Come on. I'll buy you breakfast in town."

He moans as he pulls himself out of bed. Moans again as I push a cup of coffee into his hands. Moans as he hops through the living room on one foot while struggling to cram his other foot into a sandal.

I push him into the passenger seat of the Camaro, slam the door behind him.

I glance up as I'm about to circle toward the driver's side, and see a flash of color zipping through the trees up on a distant hill overlooking the lake. The red streak moves along at an even, quick pace. At a small clearing, a jogger emerges, dressed in red running shorts and a black T-shirt. It's Clint. I want to call his name, let my voice dance across the water like the dramatic song of a lake loon.

But yesterday, Clint already thought I was being one-hundred-percent loony. Chelsea Keyes working at a fishing resort? The voice in my head starts mimicking Durst's forceful bellow: *What are you doing here, Chelsea? Why did you jump in that way? Just to get Clint's attention? To prove a point? What point?*

I have no answers.

Once Brandon and I are on the dirt road heading back to the highway, I grumble, "Man, this stretch seems long. Maybe I should have let you show off some of your bat-out-of-hell driving."

"Mmm-hmm," Brandon grunts. "Don't butter me up, sis. So where are we going, anyway? *After* breakfast, that is?"

"To get started."

"On what? You already have an idea?"

He straightens up, trying to get a look at his hair in the rearview. "Jeez. I think if I stuck my head out the window all the way from here to wherever we're going, it'd be an improvement. Do you have a comb?"

He lunges forward, rifling around the floorboards. He lets out a triumphant whelp when he finds my purse. "So?" he asks, pulling a comb from an interior pocket. He straightens back up again as I flip the visor. Even early in the morning, the sun feels harsh. "What's your idea?"

I toss a folded-up sheet of notebook paper into his lap.

"This is Rusty's list," Brandon complains. "Everything *she* needs done. What's *your* idea?"

"Don't give me grief. We have to start someplace. Those cabins need help. Regardless of what else we come up with, we have to fix them. You and I both know we do. We'll already be ahead of Clint if our cabins don't look like they've been through ten tornadoes and a forty-day-and-forty-night flood."

"Ahh, the plagues and the pestilence. Getting biblical now, are we, sis?"

I grunt.

"You know, you don't have to do this."

"You keep reminding me of the whole cut-your-losses-and-leave option," I say. "Do *you* think I ought to leave?"

"I think sometimes we all need to be reminded we don't have to prove anything to anybody. People get wrapped up and say stuff in the spur of the moment all the time."

"I know. But I want to. I mean, when I woke up, I still really wanted to."

"Clint's single. I asked Greg."

"Yeah, I suspected."

"Did you know he asked if you were?"

"He did?" This lifts my spirits a surprising amount.

"Yeah. Didn't seem to help you much, knowing you didn't have a boyfriend."

I don't know what to say to that.

"Come on, sis. You're a big girl, here. Think about it. What happens if he doesn't get any less pissed? That's what you're counting on, right? If Gabe can stop being pissed, surely Clint can?"

I wiggle my jaw.

"You want in with Clint," Brandon goes on. "You want to get the Morgan seal of approval."

"Look, I don't know about Clint. At all. But I do know I wasn't the best person last time around. I don't want to be a jerk. I don't want him to remember me as a jerk. If I never see him after this summer, I'll at least be someone who helped when the resort needed it."

"Right. You want Clint to stop being mad, so you jumped in with Rusty, offering something that you thought would make him like you again."

"That's not exactly…I think I could deal better with you blaring your jazz fusion than I can with your chestnuts of wisdom," I grumble.

Which brings a smirk to Brandon's face. He wears it all the way to Baudette. It finally disappears when I pull into a McDonald's drive-thru. "I knew it. You still owe me a real breakfast," he warns as we unwrap our sandwiches and drive for the hardware store Rusty told me about, the one down the street from Pike's.

When I slip into a parking space and kill the engine, the air fills with cackles. Only, it's not coming from Brandon—it's coming instead from three guys sitting out front, sipping coffee from white Styrofoam cups and surely swapping their own tall tales. One of them leans forward, says, "You're not from around here."

The hairs on my arm instantly go all porcupine needle. Do I look especially inept to him? Like someone who could never survive anywhere but indoors—tucked safely away from the blistering lake sun? The kind of girl who would wind up rolling around naked in patches of poison ivy or pile the world's most poisonous mushrooms on her oh-so-healthy salad?

"That car," he explains, pointing. "You can't be from around here. That thing wouldn't make it to the end of the driveway, not in the middle of January."

They're not talking about the resort? About my competition with Clint? I sigh with relief, pull myself out from behind the steering wheel. *Quit being paranoid, Chelsea. How could they know?*

I reach for the front door of the hardware store only to run headlong into a man leaving, a gallon of primer in each hand. He's dressed in jeans and a gray T-shirt and ball cap, all of which are coated in various stains—paint, tar, even what looks like dried concrete. He nods in greeting as we untangle ourselves and he pushes the door once with his shoulder, forcing it all the way open for us. I offer a quick thanks as I hurry inside, Brandon on my heels.

The interior of Rogers & Sons Hardware is completely old school. Small wooden bins of screws and nails line the wall near the checkout counter. And it smells like sawdust and glue and paint remover.

"Hey," I say, leaning over the counter.

The man behind the cash register raises his head from the slick pages of a home improvement magazine. He's forty-ish—the perfect age for the skin across his forehead to have a few shallow indentions. The wrinkles deepen, though, when he meets my eyes. "Hello?" he says.

I offer my hand to shake, making his forehead lines turn as deep as ditches. "Chelsea Keyes," I say. "I'm over at camp Lake of the Woods, starting some serious improvements. For—"

"Rusty!" he finishes. The lines disappear from his forehead, a smile appears, and his handshake firms. "You know, I used to love it out there—we went every summer when I was growing up. Me and my folks. And my brother. Sean. Who just left, right when you were walking in. I know Rusty's been wanting to get that place back to looking like its better days. She even had me and Sean tour the resort, tell her where we'd get started on the cabins. She hasn't been back in, though, and I was getting scared maybe she'd found some new hardware store she liked better—or had started going to that big-box store off the highway." He pauses to grimace. "Mike," he finally introduces himself.

"Brandon," I say, pointing. "He's *my* brother. And we have our own fond memories of Earl's old place."

Brandon shoots me a look.

"Electrician?" Mike asks Brandon.

"Jazz musician," he corrects.

"That's right," Mike says. "Think I caught you at Pike's. Not bad. But we'd better start with the basics."

Slowly, Mike starts walking through his aisles. "If I remember," he says, "some of those cabins need some fairly extensive repairs. I'm assuming you don't want to tackle carpentry work or plumbing."

"You would assume right," Brandon says.

"Maybe the best place to start is with a deep clean," Mike says.

"And paint," I add. "We can paint."

Brandon grabs a large wheeled shopping cart, which I fill (at Mike's suggestion) with wood cleaner and a few cans of paint. And brushes. And mixing trays. And caulk. And painter's tape.

"Earth to Chelsea," Brandon mutters, once Mike dips into the back to look for some additional tarps. "This is serious cash you're dropping here." When I turn, he's shaking his head at me. I swear, even the picture of Miles Davis on his T-shirt seems to be shaking his head.

"Rusty gave me a resort credit card."

"An emergency card."

I shrug an agreement.

"That she clearly hasn't wanted to use."

"Until now."

"And you're going to fill it up," he hisses through clenched teeth.

"She thought I might. She gave me the go-ahead. Said

Earl also left her a little cash. Not much. Which is why we'll need the card."

"Why now?" Brandon asks. "She's had all this time to start charging away."

"Because she's getting some real help and momentum. Now or never, she said. Told me she was betting on an increase in interest as a result of the cleanup. More renters to help pay for the charges. Told me to buy whatever Mike said we needed."

"Got your tarps!" Mike shouts from the back.

"Meet you at the checkout counter," I answer.

"Finally," Brandon mutters. "I was beginning to think we were going to buy out the entire store."

Mike hums, punching the rubbed-blank buttons on his cash register. His own work area around the front counter is cluttered with Post-it reminders and family photos on 4x6 card stock, all of them curling around the edges. Warped by the Minnesota heat, I figure. A few of his bulletin board papers—about auctions or fishing tournaments—flap in the breeze of a nearby oscillating fan.

As he reaches to pull a few more items from the cart, his T-shirt rides up his arm to reveal his tan line. A pronounced bicep. A wicked silver scar right above the elbow. This Mike person is Minnesota tough. But he hasn't once "sweetheart"ed me, not even as I pummeled him with what had surely been ridiculous questions (as in: *oh, sweetheart, you don't have it in you to renovate a dollhouse, let alone a half-dozen or so resort cabins*). Which in itself means that I have his vote of confidence—don't I? He doesn't think it's odd that I, Chelsea Keyes, am purchasing this weird, forked nozzle thing. Of course I look like the kind of gal who could talk nozzles all day.

"Jeez," Brandon groans as the numbers click higher

and higher on the cash register.

Mike tugs the long scroll off of the top of the register and hands it to me. When I see the total at the bottom, I literally feel my gag reflex kicking in. It's far more than I anticipated. I reach into my purse, pull out Rusty's card, and try to get control over my racing heart.

"Tell Rusty if you guys have any questions, be sure to call," Mike says, picking up the tail of the receipt and clicking his pen before scrawling a phone number. "My brother Sean's a contractor, so if there's something I don't know right off, I'm sure he will."

I nod gratefully and fold the long curly scroll into my pocket.

Outside, the sun offers the same kind of pleasantly scorching heat that fills saunas or blankets beaches. The kind of hot that makes the sweat droplets racing down your sides feel good—far more like relief than torture.

"Why don't you load the car?" I say, fishing my phone from my purse. "I ought to call home."

"I knew you'd figure out a way to get me back for the Crates," Brandon shouts as he steers the overloaded shopping cart. "This isn't over. You just wait!"

I hurry down the sidewalk as Dad's business tone fills my ear. "White Sugar."

"Hey, Dad."

"Chelsea! I was worried about you two. Some measly text is not enough to put a father's mind at rest, you know."

"Things have changed."

"What's changed?"

"How long we're staying."

Dad pauses. He knew—all those summers ago, he knew exactly what was going on with me and Clint. And he also knew that it was the opposite of the way I'd felt about

Gabe. *Love has different shades*, he'd said back then. My love for Gabe was more like friendship. Puppy love, maybe. Clint, he understood, was a completely different story.

"You're coming back sooner?" The question's loaded. Dad's asking about Clint. He's asking what's happened between the two of us—without using Clint's name.

"No. Staying longer."

"Longer," he repeats. "How much longer?"

"I'm not sure."

Silence.

Followed by more silence.

And still more silence.

"Dad?"

"What about school—getting your master's degree?"

"No, I'll be back in the fall. It's just, see, the place isn't the same, and I want to help fix it up because—"

"Chelse, this is coming from a place of pure, one-hundred-percent love—but I'm a little afraid you're getting derailed here."

"Derailed?"

"After your accident, when you couldn't play ball anymore, you seemed kind of lost. And then—these last four years, you were back to being the old Chelsea. So driven, so focused. The no-excuses-allowed Chelsea. You really excelled in college—and I know Clint's a big part of that. I'm grateful that you two found each other when you desperately needed someone your own age who understood some of what you were going through. But now I'm worried. The one thing I've learned these past few years is that time doesn't go on forever. You've got one life. One chance to do what you love. To go after what makes you *you*.

"I know this guy's still important to you, but what about all that talk about loving being back in the gym—even if it's not playing? What about working with the Lady Bears, the soccer players, the wrestlers, the track team? How many hours have you talked my ear off about how you thought you'd never get back in a gym again after you broke your hip? About how cool it is that you get to spend so much time working with so many different athletes? You'd give all that up for this guy?"

"It isn't like that. I'm coming back. Like I said."

It happens again: Silence.

Followed by more silence.

And more silence after that.

"What if you don't?" he asks.

I don't have an answer. Why would he ask me that? He saw the truth of the matter before—what does he see now?

"I don't like this, Chelsea. I can't help it. The voice in my head says you're grown and I have to let you decide what you're going to do, but this whole thing is out of character and it scares me. Would you talk to your mother? Please? She's just taken some sheet cakes out of the oven and—"

"I really can't. I only came to town for a little while to shop. I need to get back to the resort."

"Wait, Chelse. She's right here."

"Really, Dad. Got to go. Talk later."

I hang up and turn the phone off. Because he'll try to call me right back. He'll try to talk sense into me. Do I want to hear the voice of reason? What *is* reason here? "Sense" is subjective, right?

Only, the doubts are back yet again, and I'm suddenly feeling every bit as out of place as my Camaro looks parked under a Minnesota sky.

Brandon's putting the last plastic sack of supplies in the trunk by the time I get back to the car. As I stare into the packed-tight trunk, a new feeling starts to find me, tamping

162

out any fires of panic. This is a new challenge. I'm daring my-self to take this task on—the same way I used to dare myself to shoot five hundred lay-ups in one day. Or run an extra mile at the exact point I thought my legs were going to give out underneath me. Or score three points more than I did the last game.

Brandon refuses to give the keys over when I hold my hand out. "I know that look," he grumbles. "That's the focused Chelsea Keyes I'm-about-to-whip-your-butt look. If we don't get back pronto, you're going to unleash on somebody—most likely, me. Since I'm the closest person around. You'd better let me drive."

I figure Brandon could actually give street racers a few pointers as we careen down the highway, then down an off-ramp. This time, we approach the camp in the daylight—and now that I'm not driving and don't have to keep my eyes glued to the dirt road, I can let myself take in the rugged, heavy woods that surround the place. Minnesota's not for the weak of heart or mushy calf muscles. The wooded areas near Fair Grove seem like the minor leagues compared to these rocky, pine scented, heavily wooded sections.

We have to pause at the main lodge to allow for an enormous SUV to pull onto the dirt trail.

"That's a monster," Brandon says, pointing at the boat attached to its bumper.

I nod. It is. And there are maybe five guys inside the car.

Clint wasn't lying. There really are guys who prefer this place as-is. Who want to put on a pair of hip waders, grow another inch on the end of their unruly beard, and get some unidentified black gunk under their fingernails. Sun and stars and mud.

The SUV rolls forward; Brandon steers my Camaro

along behind it. He slows at cabin number four. But the SUV continues on, rocks popping under its tires as it heads toward a cabin farther down the path.

As Brandon and I start to unload the trunk, I feel it all over again—that half-frightened-but-mostly-determined burn.

"Hey," I call after him. He turns, a gallon of paint hanging from each hand. All he'd wanted to do was write songs, not scrub floors and remove mold. But here he is, helping me just the same.

"Yeah," he says. "I know. You owe me. Big! And don't think I'm not coming to collect."

"I would expect nothing less," I confess, smiling as I grab a few plastic bags and rush to beat Brandon to our front porch.

Time to get too busy to doubt.

I attach a hose to the faucet on the side of the cabin. It's like the last few seconds before the jump ball is launched into the air. *Can I do this?* I ask myself. *I don't know*, I answer right back, *but I'm going to give it everything I've got and then some.*

I glance up in time to see Clint on the dock, ushering a new group onto his launch. He pauses as he looks my way.

I square my shoulders, acting like I know exactly what I'm doing as I attach the two-part nozzle thing first to the cleaner attachment, then to the hose. "Turn the water on," I tell Brandon.

"Why don't you—"

"Just turn it on," I growl through gritted teeth.

"You're about to regret that move," Brandon warns. I only roll my eyes at him.

While Clint is staring, I aim the hose on the side of the cabin. Start at the top, near the roof, and slowly begin to

164

work my way down. I look every bit the expert—that is, until I get halfway down, and realize I've sprayed through an open window, straight into the living room.

I cringe as Brandon shouts, "Nice move!"

I swear Clint's laughing as he steers away, toward the deeper part of the lake.

I'm covered in gunk by the time Clint's launch putters back up to the dock: water and window caulk and some primer and even the fresh red paint I've slathered on the cabin door.

Brush still in hand, I back up a few steps to get a good look at the impact the cleaning job and the caulk and some fresh paint have all made. But the porch boards creak dangerously beneath me. I race down the unsteady front steps, which actually start to splinter beneath my weight.

"Brand," I call, "we're going to have to go back and talk to Mike about some replacement boards for the porch." I say it loud enough for Clint to hear, my voice going decidedly construction worker—gruff and abrupt. "And a hammer," I add. "Couple of saws." This whole renovation thing is really adding up moneywise. No wonder Clint and the guys let so much go unfixed.

I toss my paint-covered brush into the nearby scraggly grass, wondering how big the job of replacing a few rotten boards will turn out to be. How hard it will be to pry the old ones loose. Curious, I squat down, wrap my fingers around the edge of the bottom step, and tug upward.

The wood has no fight left in it; removing it's as easy as picking a book up off a table. Enough sun has made its way through that the hollow bottom step has become something of a tiny greenhouse. Grass grows here, as does a single orchid. A lady slipper—the same kind of beautiful wild orchid that Clint had refused to let me pick in what's beginning to feel like a lifetime ago, claiming they were protected. The state flower of Minnesota. *Do not pick under penalty of law.* It's kind of amazing that she's grown here, though—hidden away from the world, thriving only on strips of light and precious few drops of water that have dripped down through the rotten holes. Unseen by anyone...until now.

I smile, gently replace the step, and carry my brush and my paint tray over to the side of the cabin to clean them.

I turn the faucet on; a stream splashes into the tray, spraying watery red paint all over my face and across my shirt and shorts. I hold my hand up to block the stream, but it flies up my nose and into an eye and all over my chest.

I growl and frantically turn the knob all the way off, pretending not to hear the deep-throated laughter trickling up toward me.

I tug a rag from my back pocket, wipe my face. Clint's still laughing when he gets to the side of the cabin.

I'm sure he's waiting for me to say something. But I'm too busy for chitchat. At least, that's what I tell myself. I tighten my lips, clear my throat, and reach for the faucet. I'll turn it on gently this time. No more crazy spraying. But it's stuck. It won't turn back on. At all. I try to get a better grip using my rag, but that doesn't help, either.

I use two hands, clench my stomach, try it again.

Clint squats beside me, reaches for the faucet himself.

"Don't bother," I grunt. "I can get it. Besides, I wouldn't want you to break the rules."

"What rules?"

"We're in a competition, remember? Your cabins are your cabins, and my cabins are numbers two, four, six, and eight, right?"

Clint offers an easy smile. "Don't worry. Nobody's looking."

He twists the faucet, and the water gushes a second time, splashing across the front of my face. This time, though, I squeal and giggle instead of letting out a frustrated growl.

Clint turns the faucet down rather than off. It still flows hard enough to send tiny droplets across my forearms and across Clint's hands as he reaches forward to slide my brush from my fingers, drop it into the tray.

Without thinking, I offer him a no-strings-attached thank-you kiss on the cheek.

Water droplets that have gathered on my lips break the moment my mouth touches the side of his face, high on his cheek above his beard. The cold locked inside the water is sharp; it stings. But there's heat beneath, radiating from Clint's skin. I feel myself relaxing into it, absorbing it. The warmth is soothing, but as it lingers, it begins to open up a familiar desire. One I haven't felt since I was with him—not once. Not like this. It's heating me from the inside out, opening me up like petals at the first touch of sun.

Clint doesn't move. He's not pulling away.

My thank-you kiss lingers; I inhale, finding that he smells exactly the same. Like summer sun and pine and the fragrant sections of earth that grow fleshy orchids. I inhale again, savoring this—a favorite memory come back to life.

He clears his throat and stands. Without a word, he pivots and heads toward his side of the property. But he's a bit unsteady on his feet, as if his knees don't want to hold him. He pretends he's stumbled on a rock. But I know that underneath the prickly overgrowth of his beard, the prickly outer exterior he wears when he sees me, he feels the same way I do: loose and wobbly and flushed. I touch my lips.

It's still alive—I know it is. Everything we had—lust and attraction and maybe even full-blown love—it's still here. Buried, just as the beauty of the resort is now buried under weeds and weathered wood.

Like that lady slipper, what lies between Clint and I still grows underneath the rot.

Later That Night
Just Outside of Pike's Perch
Baudette, Minnesota

Clint
Turnover

"So you're heading out," I say. I'm standing on the sidewalk near Pike's front door. And Todd's Jeep is so crammed full of his stuff, I swear the vehicle's actually changed shape. Kind of like how an overfilled stocking looks on Christmas morning.

"Heading out," Todd agrees as he ties a bandanna around his head. He's got on an enormous pair of cargo shorts with pockets that also have the Christmas-morning-stocking look.

"What about the drums?" I ask, pointing a thumb over my shoulder.

Todd shrugs. "Leavin' 'em. No room. Besides, it gives

me an excuse to visit."

"Oh, the drums. You come back to visit the drums. Not like you have any—oh—family here. No lifelong friends or anything."

Todd finishes the knot on the back of his head. Takes a breath. Nods. "Those are nice drums, man. Zildjian cymbals."

We chuckle like this isn't killing both of us. When the quiet starts getting brutally awkward, I hold up my six-pack.

"Ah-ha. Clint's Ice-Cold Icin' Brew. Or is it Rink? Icin' Rinky Brew? Or Rinky Dink? Or…What was it that you were calling it these days?"

"Doesn't have an official name," I remind him, handing the six-pack over.

"Jeez. It's not a human being. It's beer. Just pick a name, already."

"Be nice. Or I'll put it back. Maybe you don't have room?"

"Oh, I have room. I got room for Clint's Kickin' Cold Ones."

"If you wait, I'm sure Greg'll be here soon—"

"I already saw Greg." Todd feeds my bottles through the open passenger side window.

"And Blue?"

"Dropped him off at Chelsea's cabin earlier today." He acts like it was a library book he had to return, not like something he thought was going to be his forever. But I know better. He's surely shed more than a few tears over giving up his dog. He's just not the type to shed those tears in front of me—or anyone else, for that matter, including Blue.

He straightens back up, turns toward me. He wants to stick his hands in his pockets, but there's no room.

"I'm jealous," I say. "You're off for the adventure of a lifetime."

"Nope. Think that's you. Adventure came right back to you, didn't it?"

"Gimme a break. That's not it at all."

He slaps me on the back. That slap is as sentimental as he'll ever get. He climbs into his Jeep, starts the engine, and takes off. Decades of camping trips and bare feet and learning to swim and learning to drive the launch and learning to drink. With one last wave through the driver side window and a flick of the turn signal, it's all gone. A giant chunk of my childhood. Or my childhood period. There's a change happening here. The lake is turning over.

I drag myself back into Pike's. It's not only humming—it's so busy the restaurant sounds like a hundred chainsaws attacking tree trunks all at once.

Pop's jumping back and forth between punching buttons on the cash register and handing out menus. "Free small appetizer for your wait," he promises the guests clustered near the entrance.

"How 'bout a free beer instead?" I shout. The free appetizer bit drives Mom nuts. That's where most of our money comes from these days. And besides, they're impossible to hold while waiting for a table. I dip back into the vault, grabbing as many bottles of my own brew as I can safely carry without dropping any. I figure, since we're not officially selling the stuff, it's perfect for giveaways.

I weave through the crowd to bring the bottles to those lined up by the door. Once they're all taken care of, I carry two more bottles toward the stage, place one on Todd's drum. Clink my own bottle against the neck, like I'm toasting my already long-lost friend. Greg's still nowhere in sight, and I'm beginning to suspect he's off somewhere doing his own letting go in private. Because the fracturing off of Todd—it's the end of something big. Can't deny that. Life presses forward.

Maybe that's what I should call the brew: Time March-es On. When I take my first sip, it tastes like things ending. Or like things turning out in a way you'd never imagined.

I'm still staring at the bottle when footsteps hit the stage behind me. I glance over my shoulder. It's Brandon.

"Todd's gone," I say. Actually, I have to say it twice so Brandon can hear me over the shouts and laughter and plates clanking.

Brandon nods. "Yeah."

"Greg's probably not going to be in tonight."

"That's okay," he says, tugging his guitar out of the instrument case. "*You* okay?"

He says it in a funny way. Or it hits me funny. Like the two of us are close enough to share a camping tent.

But it doesn't happen like that, does it? I mean, the sound of a door clicking shut can't still be echoing through the air when it flies back open and another person steps through. Right? Still, I'm staring at him. And he's not some kid any-more. Something in me thinks I could hang out with him. If he weren't related to the enemy, anyway.

"Dunno," I finally answer. "I mean—yeah. I'm okay. It'll be good for him. He wants this."

Brandon snorts. "Sometimes, people want wacky things."

I choose not to acknowledge that he's obviously talking about his sister. "You gonna play here alone?"

"Sure. I've been playing with the jazz band at school. I could improvise for hours. Not sure anybody else'll appreciate it."

"'Course they will."

"You sound like Earl. With the ''course' stuff. He used to say that all the time." Brandon laughs before his face clouds. It seems to hit him: Earl's gone. So many changes. One after another.

I laugh, too, mostly to be polite, then step inside the kitchen as Mom tugs a wire basket from the fryer. The phone rings, surely with an order for takeout. When she rushes to answer, I put my beer down and step closer to the basket. Start eating the jumbo shrimp like potato chips.

Until Mom slaps my hand, anyway.

"Owww," I pout.

She grabs the whiskers on my chin. "When are you going to shave that thing?" she asks, pushing her face so close to mine our foreheads touch for a second.

Before I can answer, a familiar voice calls out, "So, how do I light the pilot in the—"

Chelsea.

Of all people to see right now. And she's wearing a sundress. She's built for sundresses—for skinny straps on her sun-kissed shoulders. And suddenly, I'm thinking about the way she'd kissed my face. Out by her cabin. Over wet paint-brushes.

Todd's leaving had been the first thing to make me stop thinking about that kiss all day. And now, here it is all over again.

A kiss on the cheek is usually something reserved for great aunts or second grade teachers. But Chelsea's had rattled every cell in my body. Reliving it makes the cells rattle all over again. In the midst of all the rattling, I'm also pummeled by the same instant urge to touch her that had hit me out there by her cabin. Touch any part of her. The ponytail swinging from high on her head. Her fingertips. The side of her arm. Damn it—why did she have to do that, kiss my cheek that way? I can't let her in. Not one more time. Because judging by the way that kiss on the cheek hit me, I could fall. And then what? What happens when she's done playing her game?

When summer ends?

I don't have summer breaks anymore. They got traded in for the real world.

"Don't worry about any of that," Chef Charlie bellows as he plates one of his masterpieces—trout with watercress, roe, and herb broth. It's common knowledge that the right word whispered to a server unlocks one of Charlie's off-the-menu specialties, the same way a whispered password had once given a person access to a prohibition-era speakeasy. He wipes the edge of the plate, sends it off to be delivered by a waitress, and tells Chelsea, "I'll be in to turn the equipment on. You clean up the dining room—"

"Whoa," I say, holding my hands up. "What is this? What are you talking about?"

"I'm going to be cooking at the main lodge again," Charlie says. A grin spreads into his sweaty, red face as he leans against a counter and picks up a glass of water, chugs it down.

"We closed the dining room," I remind him.

"Chelsea's opening it up," Mom says, wiping her hands on her apron.

Charlie smiles again as he lowers the water glass. He suddenly looks twenty years younger. His gray hair doesn't even look as gray.

"What for? You haven't finished fixing up any of the cabins. Getting ahead of yourself, aren't you?"

"Not at all," Chelsea says calmly. "It's going to take a while to get the lodge and the kitchen back up and running, too. Why would I only do the cabins, and then have to wait for the lodge to get cleaned up? This way, once the cabins are ready, the kitchen will be, too."

"No way," I tell Chelsea. "You don't get to do that. You shouldn't get that kind of advantage."

"But you're not using it."

"Hands off the gift shop. That's mine. I'm using it." I'm desperate. Did that sound desperate?

"Believe me, you can have the gift shop," Chelsea tells me. "Bait shop. Whatever you're calling it. But make sure that the fumes don't leak over onto my side. Smells like guts."

"No, it doesn't."

"Wanna bet? Another bet you'll lose."

"You're going to let Charlie go?" I ask Mom. "That's asking a lot of you, don't you think? Leaving you in a regular lurch. People come from all over to hang out at Pike's!"

"Clint," Mom sighs, exasperated. "It's not like Charlie's the only other person in the kitchen. Yes, he's invaluable. Yes, the two of us are constantly coming up with new twists on our appetizer menu. But it's not as though I'll be doing it all on my own. You know I hired two line cooks a year before you fired Charlie."

"I didn't *fire*—"

"Technically, you did," Charlie says. "I miss it. I want to come back. No offense, Mrs. Morgan."

Mom waves him off as she answers the phone, jots down another order.

"All that fresh fish—pulled right out of the lake," Charlie says, already writing new recipes in his head. "Chelsea and I were discussing an herb garden."

"A *what*? Who's paying for all this?"

Charlie laughs. "We're talking a few seeds. A little water. Sunlight's free."

"No—who's paying for you, Charlie?"

"I can donate a few meals," Charlie says. "Got to start somewhere."

"Got to start," I mutter, running a hand through my hair. I'd tear it all out if I could.

Pop hurries into the kitchen, pausing to watch me fill my fists with my hair. "You found out about Charlie, I'm assuming."

I back out of the kitchen, pushing my way through the crowd as I head toward the back exit. This isn't a game. Why is everyone—even my folks, even Charlie—treating it like one? This is my whole life. Lake of the Woods is home. It's my business. It's my past and my future.

Before I can get to the back door, a hand wraps around my arm. I'm being hauled through a "Staff Only" door, down a hall, straight toward an office. Actually, I recognized the hand the instant it touched my arm. And I knew I shouldn't argue.

It's Mom.

She pushes me into the office chair. Looms over me, her arms crossed over her chest.

"What?" I finally ask.

"You can't do this pissed," she says.

"Can't do what?"

"Run the resort. Do right by Earl. You can't do it pissed."

"I'm not," I insist, instantly defensive.

She gives me the same look I got when I tried to lie about getting in a fight on my second grade playground.

"I'm not," I repeat.

"There's a big difference between eighteen and twenty-two, you know," Mom says. "Don't you think Chelsea's grown over the past few years? Don't you think she's a different person in some ways? Don't you think it's a possibility that she came up here to make things right between the two of you?"

"Speaking of change," I say, deciding to skate around this comment, "one of my oldest friends pulled away ten min-

176

utes ago. He's gone for good. A guy might be expected to be a little upset about that, too. Doesn't all have to be about some girl." I stand, lunge for the door.

"It's not some girl," Mom corrects, before I can make it through the doorway. "Chelsea was never just some girl."

I finish stomping out of the office, down the short hall, and back into Pike's dining area. There she is, all over again, sitting with Rusty at a table in *my* family's restaurant, drinking one of *my* beers as she scribbles something on her ridiculous check sheet. Behind me, her brother spits, "Testing, testing…" into his mic.

Rusty leans forward and says something to Chelsea. She nods and scribbles some new revelation into her notebook.

They're talking. Scheming is probably more like it. With Chelsea's eyes on me, I burst through the front door onto the sidewalk outside.

"Lovely night, isn't it?" an older man's voice calls out to me.

I grunt a response.

"'Course, twilight always was my favorite."

The '*course* is what gets my attention. I turn, and there he is: Earl, in a lawn chair, his legs stretched out in front of him, crossed at the ankles, one of my beers in his hand.

"Don't look so surprised," Earl says. "You've been imagining meetings with me out at the resort for about a year now. Always at the end of the day."

That much is true. Mostly because when he was still alive, I used to meet up with him at that swing by the lake to enjoy a sunset with him.

"Twilight," Earl goes on, "now, that's when a man can soak in what he managed to accomplish that day. Red sky's the glow of success."

I shake my head. "No success here."

"Well, you don't know that, do you?" Earl asks. "I know you think Chelsea's gainin' on you, but—"

"Gaining?" I interrupt. "She's slaughtering me. Those cabins I gave her should have sent her running. Instead, she's got ideas coming out everywhere and I've got—"

"—the fishing tournament," Earl finishes.

"What tournament?"

"Well, you said you want a fishing resort. What's a fishing resort without a tournament?"

"A tournament!" Of course. It's perfect.

"Only thing you got to work on is gettin' the word out. And I think you got somebody who can help you with that." Earl points at a neon sign down the street from Pike's: Kode.

"You're right. It's about time for me to get in the game." With a pang in my heart, I admit, "Miss you, old man," like I always do every time I imagine him back into existence. Kind of a way of talking to myself, really. "Wish you were around to tell me one of your whoppers."

"You need a story?" Earl asks. "Aw, Clint, you know exactly where you can find every story that ever played out at the resort," he reminds me before fading away completely.

Twelve Years Ago

LAKE OF THE WOODS FISHING RESORT
MINNESOTA

Clint is the last one still on the launch. Even his father has gotten off the boat.

"Son," Earl tells him, "I know what you're doing."

Clint's eyes go wide, like it surprises him that Earl has used the tone reserved for boys who are about to act up, cause trouble. "I wasn't—"

"Oh, I know. You're not lookin' to cause harm. You think I'm gonna take another group out on the lake, and you could come right along with all of us. But son, if I let you go out a second time, there won't be a single fish left in this lake. Your pop's got a whole mess to cook tonight as it is."

"Oh—I didn't want to fish again."

"Then what?"

"I want to know about the tattooed tree." Clint has such a seriousness about him.

Earl nods. "'Course, you're a little young for all that. What are you, twelve? Eleven?"

"Why am I too young? How can a tree be tattooed? What does it mean?"

"Where'd you hear about it, anyway?"

"Some of the guys—" he starts.

"Some of the guys," Earl repeats. His eyes wander out

toward the teenage boys he's hired for the summer. They like to talk big. Mostly, their mouths are bigger even than their brains. Earl thinks that when Clint is their age, things will be different. He'll have someone working for him who really does know what he's doing.

"Why're you listening to 'em at all?" Earl asks. "I bet none 'a those boys could tell you what that tree started out being. What kind of tree. Beech, black walnut, river birch. Not a one could tell the difference. Why do you give any credence to anything they say? How do you know they're not all pullin' your leg?"

Clint keeps looking right at him. Waiting.

"All right," Earl concedes. "You ain't gonna let up, I can see."

He clomps down the dock, Clint on his heels. They walk, the two of them, down one of the many fingers of hiking trails.

"The tree," Earl starts, "is a place where love stories are written."

Clint's feet skid to a stop, kicking up dirt. "Oh," he says with disappointment. At his age, he was still hoping for an adventure story.

"Now, you wanted to know. So come on," Earl urges.

After a pause, Clint trudges along behind him.

"Been that way for decades. Generations!" Earl shouts. "Long before I even opened this resort, when hikers came to the area around the lake to enjoy pristine wilderness. Back then, sweethearts chose the tree for its complete seclusion. Nobody would come scare 'em off while they were carvin'."

"Aw, man," Clint grumbles.

"You don't realize this now," Earl says, "but you have not yet lived long enough for fear to raise its ugly head. You and your friends, you grab that frayin' rope attached to that tree limb hangin' over there, and you expect it to hold you as you swing from the shore out over the lake. You don't think it'd do anything else.

"Love is the same way, when you're young," Earl goes on. "When you've never jumped before, you trust it. Never know that sometimes, it's nothin' more than a fraying rope."

He points. "There it is. The tree the boys've told you all about. Carved all over with initials. Proof that *John loves Katie now and always.*"

Earl snorts. "Those boys out there—the ones I hired, who take families on hikes and fishing trips on the lake— they're all hot to trot about that tree because they're havin' their own love stories. Right now."

"How do you know?"

"'Cause it always happens that way. Every summer, another batch. 'Course, the guests have a few love stories, too. Sometimes, they fall for the guides. Sometimes with somebody else also stayin' at the resort. Maybe somebody they meet in town. Or with each other. Inevitably, some of 'em make their way to this here tree. Really does look tattooed, don't it?"

Clint nods, stepping closer to read some of the inscriptions.

"I guess carving initials is kinda like preserving it. Recording it for everyone to see means it happened. Even if it was short-lived, it was important. That's what they're all saying."

"Why short?" Clint asks.

"'Cause summer love stories are always too short."

"Except for that one," Clint says knowingly as he locates the carving that started it all. *Earl + Helen.*

"Yeah," Earl says. "'Cept for that one."

Earl pats him on the shoulder and leaves him to read

the crudely carved initials, the same way he often reads comic books in the back of the old Baudette mom-and-pop country store, zipping through the pages before he can be caught.

Earl glances over his shoulder once, in time to see Clint run his fingers across the rough carvings and giggle. At his age, too young to fully understand romantic love, the tree might even seem a little lewd. Like something he shouldn't be touching at all.

A few days later, something calls out to Earl. Tickles the back of his neck. He follows the trail toward the tattooed tree, almost like folks with binoculars follow after birds' songs.

And there, near the roots, he sees the newest addition to the tree: bright red shiny paint. Model paint, Earl figures. And the crooked letters: *Clint & Rosie.*

Earl smiles. "Well, well, well," he says. "What do you know?"

A first girlfriend. Her name painted by a young man—the first time Earl truly thinks of Clint as such—to show everyone how deep his love goes.

Rosie sure is some lucky girl, Earl figures. He knows Clint is the kind of boy who loves with everything he has. Clint's heart is a place you never could escape. Not once he set you up inside it.

Chelsea
ACCOMMODATION

"This beats painting any day," Brandon mutters as he screws a mic into the stand at the front of the dining room. He points to the stone fireplace. "You think there's any way we could build a fire in that thing without it getting so hot in here, we'd send the guests running?"

"Dunno," I say, wiping forehead sweat with the back of my wrist. At this point, a little over a week into our efforts to fix up the resort, I'm pretty much sweating pure dirt. I could always turn the air conditioning on, build a fire for ambiance. But we opened the windows all through the main lodge immediately after snagging Chef Charlie's help, with the intention of airing the place out. And the early summer breezes through the screens are as sweet as Mom's secret honey icing recipe. I'd kind of fallen in love with the idea of that delicious Minnesota air dancing across the faces of the guests as they ate one of Charlie's gourmet meals. I figure his first menu back at the resort is destined to make the culinary history books.

"Do you have your set planned out yet?"

"Chelse, as I've now told you eleven billion times, I am a semi-almost-professional jazz musician. I do not need a set list. I am going to improvise. You never know what the crowd's going to respond to. Maybe Francine and I will even play a few originals."

I gasp. "Originals? But don't you think you ought to play something that's recognizable to everyone?"

"I said at the beginning that I was going to be playing jazz. What about jazz is recognizable to most people?"

"I was hoping you'd include some of the old standards, too. Especially for our opening night. You know—Pink Floyd, Led Zeppelin…"

"That stuff used to drive you crazy. Wait a minute. Opening night? When is it, exactly? Which cabins could we possibly rent out? Ours isn't even in such great shape yet. Who have you told about the place? Did somebody actually make reservations?"

"Tip jar," I announce, sidestepping his questions, none of which I have an answer for. "I'm putting it on my shopping list. We need to get you a tip jar. Extra deep."

"Awwww, sis, you're getting soft in your old age."

"Watch it," I warn.

But at that moment, with the sweet summer air filtering through the dining room, with the linen table cloths I'd found in storage on every table, with tiny vases in the center of every one of those tables (just waiting for the wildflowers I'll pick for our first official dinner), with the tile floor mopped and the walls dusted and the wooden fireplace mantel polished, running the resort seems kind of easy, actually. This job is like the joy of a playground swing—completely and perfectly uncomplicated.

There's another reason I feel a light happiness in my heart: Blue's favorite walking path goes right by the old tattooed tree. And earlier that morning, while he was sniffing around the base, I saw it: a weathered but still clearly visible *CM + CK*. It was us. I knew it was.

I also knew I wasn't the one who had carved it.

"Chelsea," Rusty shouts from a back table, tapping her wrist to remind me of the time before curling back over her calculator and ledger. Not only is Rusty unfazed by the balance on her emergency credit card, she keeps pushing me for more. More shopping trips, more paint, more, more, more. *Now or ne-ver, now or ne-ver!* She keeps chanting it, almost like a military running cadence.

"Think you could watch Blue for me while I head to town?" I ask. He's stretched out on his side, taking up nearly half of the dining room, snoring. Worn out from that morning hike of ours, the one that took us by the tattooed tree.

"Only reason that dog would let you out of his sight is if he's asleep," Brandon says. "You'd better hurry up and slip out now."

I cringe against a clatter that explodes from the other side of the dining room door. Apparently, Charlie's finding that getting a professional kitchen back in working order after months of sitting dormant is far from completely and perfectly uncomplicated.

"What do you want to wear? For your performance?" I ask. "Since I'm about to make another one of my fifty-thousand daily runs to town."

Brandon tiptoes past Blue into the center of the room, takes a deep breath, and squints at our small makeshift stage area. "I see—a white shirt. Narrow black tie."

"Aw, man," I grumble.

"Sunglasses. A fedora."

"A fedora?"

"Yeah. Or a Panama. What's more jazzy? A fedora or a Panama?"

"What's the difference?"

"Not a clue." He offers a grin wider even than his glasses.

"Fine, Slim."

"Slim?"

"Don't jazz musicians all have nicknames? You need one. Sonny. Cool Cat. Or Fingers!"

"Fingers?"

"Yeah. For your nimble playing ability."

"Needs some serious work. But the intention's good, at least. 'A' for effort." He's already back on the stage, his hand gripping Francine's neck when he shouts, "Don't forget the Panama!"

I'm still laughing as I stick my head into the kitchen. But my smile quickly evaporates. Charlie's hair has fallen limp over his decidedly sweaty face; he's attacking a grill with a wire brush, but Charlie looks like the one worked into a lather.

"I cleaned that already," I offer timidly. Except, the hours I've spent working in Mom's bakery have taught me that when you do a good job of cleaning anything up, you don't have to broadcast it. Clean speaks for itself.

"I have a list," Charlie barks, sliding a piece of notebook paper down the stainless steel counter. Even as he pauses his scrubbing job to hand it over, his face is still crinkled in pure concentration. At least, I hope it's concentration—and not annoyance. I promised I'd do the cleaning, get everything ready for him. All he'd have to do is just step inside, turn the ovens on, and start cooking. It's a job I appear to have completely bungled.

"I—"

Charlie sighs, raising his head from the grill. "Yes?"

I read volumes into that single syllable—and it's all about my inability. I back out of the kitchen, suddenly feeling like running this place isn't easy at all. I feel like I'm messing everything up. How is that possible? I know the resort, and I've worked in a kitchen. What else have I missed? What details have I overlooked?

To make matters even worse, I have a bit of an owner-of-a-sweatshop feeling as I leave for a shopping trip with Charlie and Brandon both still working in the lodge. I was always the last one off the court when I was playing ball—the last one to leave any gym when I was working for Durst—and that work ethic never really dies, does it? I can't help thinking I should be in there sweating right alongside both of them.

I'm still fishing the keys from my pocket when I glance into one of the Camaro's rolled-up windows and see myself— wild wavy hair secured with a headband, and a completely wrecked T-shirt covered in dirt and various paint stains. Not a drop of makeup. But I'm flushed and I'm smiling.

Hard to believe that hard physical work has put the smile there.

Six Years Ago

Driveway of the Keyes House
Fair Grove, Missouri

My body is on fire.

Everything hurts.

I'm home, finally. After a five mile run, my legs are jelly. But turning into the driveway doesn't feel like relief. As much as I'd like to veer off into the front yard, collapse into the grass, let the blades tickle my hot, sticky, flushed skin, I can't.

I have rules against that sort of thing.

Here, when fatigue has gripped me, it's time to practice shooting.

I retrieve the ball from the garage and start to dribble.

She loves it so much, the neighbors all say, tilting their heads in admiration.

But that's my secret: I don't. The training is hell. Pure torture.

It's the win that feels good. The glory of the win.

It's the winning that gives me my claim to fame. Puts a smile on everyone's face when they see me. Gives Fair Grove its bragging rights. The rest of it? The working toward the win?

I hate it.

As I send the ball into the sky, toward the rim, I want

to be anywhere else.

But I'll take the agony. It's what I have to do.

It's all about the win.

Today
BAUDETTE, MINNESOTA

Chelsea
CURIOSITY

"Chelsea!" Mike exclaims, before the bell on the Rogers & Sons entrance has a chance to stop jingling. "My favorite cabin restorer. How goes it?"

"Know any good exterminators?"

"That well, eh?"

"I should have asked when Brandon and I were here earlier. I got a little—"

"—inundated with the finer points of mold removal?" he jokes.

"Something like that," I admit. "Oh, and what do you recommend for floor replacement?"

"Cabin six!" Mike says. "Decided to tackle some bigger jobs, did you? Impressive." He tugs on the bill of his ball cap. "First thing's first. The exterminator. Let's see. You got carpenter ants? Bees?"

"Unseen critters with feet."

"Random rodents. I'd call Jerry," Mike says. "Got his number right over here."

He reaches for an old yellow pages, rattling, "You know, I bet they got in the attic. Most cabins don't even have attics. Just vaulted ceilings. But I'm sure Earl wanted to insulate against the winter..."

His voice fades in my ears as I notice Clint running out of Pike's, rushing to getting in his truck.

"Hey, Mike—listen, I've got to check on something first," I say, heading for the door. "Be back in a little while."

"You sure? I found him right here in the book. Betcha he could be there this afternoon…"

I hurry out of the store, launching myself into my Camaro. I can see, in my rearview, that I've gotten in my car faster than Clint got in his truck.

"Score one for Chelsea," I mutter.

Clint's too consumed with where he's headed to glance my way.

I back out of my space and follow him.

A few blocks away, I steer into a parking lot and kill the engine. The enormous building ahead of me proclaims, "Community Arena."

"Youth hockey," I mutter. "I gotta see this."

I lunge into the back seat, grabbing up my jean shirt and throwing it on over my awful T-shirt. I tuck every last blond strand up into the plain black ball cap I'd once used to shade my eyes while accompanying Durst on the soccer field. I slip on a pair of sunglasses.

Inside, I glance around to get my bearings. And I try to make myself as inconspicuous as possible.

I can hear Brandon's voice in my head: "So, you'd like Clint to know you recognize that you haven't exactly shown him the best version of Chelsea Keyes. You want to do more than apologize. You want to do right by him. But you do that by…telling him his resort is a rotten mess, by betting him that you can do a better job than he can? And then by following him and eavesdropping on his team? Oh, yeah, Chelse. That has 'forgiveness' written all over it."

A few girls have already clustered in the stands. I find a seat on a bleacher several rows behind them all. A row that's still close enough to the penalty box to hear the voice of the coach.

After all, he's the one I've come to see.

"*Life's* not worth living if it's away from the water," I tell Luke.

"You say that all the time," he whispers. He has no patience today for my pseudo-poetry.

"Look at this," he orders, shoving a mayonnaise jar into my face. "I caught them last night." He's got some twigs and grass and a little piece of pine inside his jar. And crickets. Tons of crickets all bouncing around. Poor guys. They're probably panicked.

My eyes turn back to the rink in time to see a puck hit the boards so hard that it ricochets, flying back to hit the blade of another player's skate. The player does a clumsy somersault, his helmet whacking the ice.

"Hey!" I shout. I'm angry. My voice makes no mistake about it. Luke flinches, sticks his fingers in his mouth. Gets that *uh-oh* look that says he's afraid for what's about to happen to his brother.

"I missed," Ryan tells me, skating away. Only, he doesn't get far before two of the older guys skate up to his side, their blades slicing viciously against the ice.

Before I can say anything, they send Ryan flying. His body strikes the boards with a thud that sounds more like the detonation of a bomb.

They're not done, though. Fists start flying as I hit the ice.

"Hey!" I shout again, grabbing the backs of jerseys and pulling them away from each other. One is still swinging his fist as I yank him free.

"I missed! I didn't mean to knock him down," Ryan shouts.

"You want to tell me that again?" I roar. "Nothing worse than a lie told three times."

"I'm serious," he swears between pants. "I missed."

I drag him to the penalty box, hand him a Kleenex for his bleeding nose. "You were mad. You were frustrated. So you hit that puck as hard as you could. Like some little kid throwing a tantrum, hurling his toy against the wall."

He ignores me, pinching his nose shut with the Kleenex.

"You're gonna kill somebody with your attitude. Or make somebody mad enough that they turn right back around and kill you. You'd have deserved that much a minute ago."

"Are you okay?" Luke asks. "You're bleeding."

Ryan rolls his eyes. He's so fifteen. I want to smack all the fifteen right out of him.

I swivel back toward the ice to let the rest of the players know we're done for today. My watch is telling me I have less than ten minutes till my appointment.

But I stop when I realize they're laughing. My goalie has his mask off, and he's pantomiming Ryan's response, the way he cupped his bleeding nose.

The laughter carries through the arena. Even the girls in the stands are giggling now.

"That's it!" I bellow. "You're all going to be here on Saturday."

"Saturday?" "Why?" my players begin to whine.

"No, coach, it's fine," Ryan pleads.

But I'm on my feet, skating back out into the middle of the rink. Ryan's on my heels.

"You owe me," I tell them all.

"For what?" Ryan asks. With his bleeding nose still pinched shut, it sounds more like: *Fah whud?*

"You for saving your hide out there. And the rest of you for not kicking you all off youth hockey right now."

They stare back at me. They don't really take me seriously. Not like they would if I were one of their own regular high school coaches. But I'm about to make them. Because I know they want to keep working all summer, in the off season. They want to come back to their high school coaches harder and tougher and better than they were last year.

I know, because I wanted the same thing when I was their age.

The giggling from the stands begins to trickle off. And I get this strange feeling of being watched. Not in a bad way—just paid attention to, like I haven't been in ages. In another lifetime, my own high school girlfriend, my Rosie, used to watch my practices. And I always had this sensation of knowing what I did mattered. That it had the ability to impress someone I cared about immensely.

I have that sensation now. And I'm not sure why.

"Call yourselves players? You call yourselves a team?"

"Technically," Ryan says, "we're not an actual team. You divide us into new teams every time we come—"

"Enough," I growl. "You don't know anything about being on a team."

Ryan frowns, confused. "How's that?" *Ow's dat?*

"This isn't working. Even Luke can see that. Without his magnifying lens."

I glance behind my shoulder. In the penalty box, Luke's

got his fingers in his mouth again.

"You guys aren't getting better this summer. That's the point, isn't it? All this blame and dysfunction…it's ridiculous. None of you are going to learn a thing if you don't get your heads screwed on, decide that whoever you're paired up with is your teammate and not someone to crush." I slam my hands on my hips. "Saturday. Bright and early. You'll be here. All day, if that's what it takes. We need to work through this."

I hear a shout from the stands. The girlfriend section. They're probably protesting. Kind of a knee-jerk thing. I'm taking their guys away on a weekend.

For what? I don't have a shred of a clue.

I check my watch. I'm already late to my appointment.

"Look, I can't get into it now," I say. "Saturday."

I skate away.

Four Years Ago

Lake of the Woods Fishing Resort
Minnesota

Kenzie is under a tree, sitting cross-legged, her laptop perched between her knees.

She's something of a sightseeing draw herself these days, with her long wavy hair and her classically attractive figure—tall and strong and healthy looking. It hadn't always been so. But the on-site techie, who keeps the cabins connected to the outside world and maintains the resort website, gave up her glasses years ago. Along with her baggy sweaters.

It's a cliché, she knows, the things that get so many boys' attention. And yet, here they are, tripping over their own feet when they see her.

Todd is the one who vies for her attention most frequently. This afternoon, he's sitting close enough that their knees touch. Unaware he smells like fish guts and soured lake water, he leans still closer to her as he weaves some wild, embellished lie meant to impress.

Like girls who came of age being overlooked, Kenzie has no patience for boys like Todd. Boys who treat her like something they could win, something that would make the rest of the world envy them. She is interested in kindness, and men who know how to love deeply.

Like Clint.

At least, she *had* been interested in Clint. For years, he'd made her heart ache. Going all the way back to their elementary school days, when she was the bookworm with the big glasses and he was pining for their classmate, Rosaline Johnson. But that was then. Earlier that very summer, he'd had a fling with a resort guest, proving his period of mourning for Rosie had reached its sunset. Once Chelsea was gone, he'd relented, told Kenzie he finally was ready.

But their one and only date had been a disaster.

She shades her eyes with her hand to watch him wave from the dock. He's especially friendly to her these days. Trying to save face, it seems. Or save their friendship, at least.

"Can you watch this for a minute?" Kenzie asks Todd, pushing her computer off her lap. "Make it worth your while."

She means that she'll buy him a beer at Pike's. But the look on his face makes her think he interpreted her offer in a completely different way.

"I don't—" she starts. When Todd turns his hopeful eyes her way, she smiles. "Never mind. I'll be right back."

She races up the hill. There it is—the legendary tattooed tree. The one that offers a place to record every summer love story. Decade after decade. By now, there really should be no space left. But the sun and rain and ice have a tendency to take their toll, tugging at the muddy bark. Occasionally, pieces fall away completely, causing a few couples' names to disappear. A fresh blank space shows up where new names can be carved. One love replaced by another.

Having seen it before, Kenzie easily finds Clint's original heart—painted with model paint—the red childlike letters slightly faded.

She circles the tree, searching for her own message.

She finds it, the simple, hopeful *C + K* she'd carved. The letters are shallow, making them easy to flick off with her own pocketknife.

As she reaches down to pick up the chunk of bark, she sees it: a new message, with two sets of initials. Chelsea's and Clint's. Kenzie's face flames with embarrassment.

If only she had seen it before carving her initial beside Clint's, like some sort of heartsick little girl. Why hadn't she seen his carving earlier? Was it new? Had it been the glare of the sun that blinded her? Or had her own blinding hope kept her from seeing it, a message of love carved after a summer of unexpected heat?

All she knows, as she places that bit of bark in the pocket of her shorts, is that her name and Clint's were never meant to be carved inside the same heart.

Today
BAUDETTE, MINNESOTA

Clint
BRACKISH

I'm late for my appointment, thanks to the fight on the ice. To make up for it, I stop by an old hole-in-the-wall coffee shop, picking up two coffees. But I can't, for the life of me, remember how she took it. Black? Fancy flavored cream? I grab a couple of sugars and different creamers before racing to the tiny new shop down the street from Pike's: Kode.

I stomp inside, sloshing a bit of coffee on my T-shirt.

"Hey, Clint," comes a call from behind a desk.

Her chestnut hair is shorter than it used to be—it kind of swings above her shoulders now, looking all sleek and perfect. Professional, I guess is the right word. Instead of a Lake of the Woods Fishing Resort T-shirt, she's wearing a blouse and a suit jacket. But I recognize the face.

"Kenzie," I greet. Earl's favorite bookworm. The young

girl who sat beneath the resort trees reading or typing into her laptop, now a full-grown business owner. A friend who'd given me space after Rosie's accident, then (at the exact same moment she'd decided I'd had enough time to grieve) driven me crazy chasing after me. Flirting. Coming up with reasons for the two of us to be alone in a dimly lit main lodge dining room.

She'd hated Chelsea the summer she'd shown up. So much, she'd even tried to warn her I'd never fall for her. Told her I was damaged goods. Too hurt to want another relationship.

But how times change.

Now, I'm the one that's chased Kenzie down. Made an appointment. Asked for her attention. Here we are, me feeling suddenly underdressed in my shorts and stained T-shirt and grubby sneakers. On the opposite side of the desk, Kenzie looks completely together and exactly like the accomplished woman she's become.

She grins. "Thanks for texting me."

"Rusty had your number," I say, placing a cup in front of Kenzie. But there's already a cup on her desk. A ceramic cup. With a perfect dollop of foam on top and…is that cinnamon?

I glance behind me. She has a cappuccino machine.

And I bought her crummy black coffee. I try to lay a sugar packet on her desk, but it's all wrinkled up from where I'd smashed it in my hand.

"Sorry—I was at the arena."

"Oh yeah?" she asks, typing away on her keyboard. "Heard you were coaching."

"Did you?"

She nods, pauses in her typing just long enough to flash me a knowing look. "So what was it like seeing Chelsea again? After all this time?"

I flop back in my chair. "How'd you know?"

She lets out a belly laugh. "It's so obvious. Why else would you text me?"

"Because I—"

She raises her eyebrow.

"I'm messing this up. This meeting."

"About as bad as you messed up our one and only date."

Four years ago? The awful tangled mess in my truck? The single evening that had her pushing me away, telling me it was clear that we were never going to work? *I hoped you'd fall in love again*, she'd told me, meaning after Rosie. *And you did. Just not with me.*

She still remembers all that?

She laughs at my horrified expression. "It's ancient history. I'm seeing someone—it's getting serious—and besides, I promise you, you look at me the same way you look at Rusty."

"I look at Rusty in a bad way?"

"Oh, come on," Kenzie says. "I just mean we're a couple of old buddies." She wipes a laugher-induced tear from her eye before taking a sip of her cappuccino. When she puts the cup back down, it's got a red lipstick stain on the rim—kind of makes the cup look like its smiling. But I feel about as far from smiling as I can get.

"I wish she'd go home," I say quietly. "I can't wait for her to turn around and head back to Missouri."

She squints at me, flashing a skeptical look.

"So I need your help. You're part of my plan. To get rid of her."

I can't stand the way Kenzie's looking at me, so I stare down into my own Styrofoam cup. The cream's made the coffee look muddy—like a lake after a rain. "You think I'm egging her on."

"Aren't you?" she asks. "In fact, I'd say the reason you got in touch with me is because the two of you have some sort of one-upmanship going."

"Why—"

"Once a competitor, always a competitor. You two push each other. Challenge each other. Always did. Had to be some sort of contest."

All I can think about is how wild and exciting everything feels when Chelsea and I are together. Even now. Even though I'd wanted to cut myself off from her. Being near her brings with it the strongest déjà vu. I feel all of our first summer—the thrill of pushing her to rebuild her confidence and strength, and knowing she'd push right back. Knowing I'd have to up my game when I was around her. The back and forth—at the lake and Willie Walleye Day and bowling. The laughter that came even when I was far behind.

"The thing is," I start, "I need to prove to her she doesn't belong here. Then life can get back to normal."

She points at some figures on her screen as I catch sight of Chelsea through Kenzie's front window.

"I've looked into Wheelers Point, which is your main competition," Kenzie admits.

But Chelsea's out there on the street, coming out of Rogers & Sons.

"…considering how much they charge, their occupancy rate, the fact that they're only open five months…I think you're on the right track with…"

Chelsea's filling up her Camaro with two-gallon cans of—

"Clint."

"Yeah." I swivel to give Kenzie my attention.

She sees what I'm looking at. "Back to normal, eh?"

she repeats.

"I have to know what she's up to. What she has planned."

"Mmm-hmm."

"I don't think this is fun, okay?"

She taps her desktop, thinking. "Clint, you're riding the line."

"Of what?"

"Of being a jerk."

"Please."

Her stare turns hard. After a moment, she turns the screen toward me.

I can't believe what I'm seeing. "That's the resort," I stammer. "But how did you know—I didn't even ask you to build me a new site—"

"I knew."

"Is that a social media feed down there?" I ask, pointing.

"It is. I'm handling that as well. Don't forget I was one of Earl's crew, too. I remember the place fondly. I can probably sell its best features better than you. Mind getting me some of your striking photos?" She reaches into a drawer and hands me a point and shoot. "Bring the camera back by when you're in town. I know you don't have Wi-Fi out there these days. Makes emailing photos a bit tricky."

"I can't believe you already did all this. Is it too much to ask you to add something about a fishing tournament?"

"Of course not. If you have email addresses for your regulars, I can do a marketing campaign. Can't wait to hear all the details."

"I can pay—it'll take a while—"

"I'm doing this whole promotion thing pro bono. You'll get free web design and graphic work and social media maintenance from yours truly."

"But—why?"

"For Earl," she explains as her face softens.

"Besides," she adds, "I take matters of the heart seriously."

Chelsea
INCENTIVE

*C*lint and the rink and his teams keep circling through my thoughts as I return to the resort. As Brandon and I continue to paint. As I seek out Rusty's approval for each new additional improvement. As I head yet again into town—to make a purchase of my own (rather than for the cabins for once).

I'm still in the outdoor supplies store when my phone goes off.

"What's this your father's been telling me about your staying in Minnesota?" Mom asks.

"Look, I'm not planning to be here forever…" My voice trails. Wait a minute. She didn't sound mad. Was that excitement? "Are you—happy—that I'm up here?"

"I want to help," she announces.

"From two states away?"

"Yes! Sure. Why not? Your voice sounds weird. You okay?"

I grunt, wiggling my foot back and forth. "I'm trying on hiking boots."

"Hiking boots!" Mom's laughter explodes in my ear.

"What's so funny?"

"The idea of you sitting in some outdoor store, surrounded by open shoeboxes, wondering why hiking boots have to be so uncomfortable. Why they can't feel more like your sneakers."

I survey the shoeboxes spread out on the floor, containing the roughly twenty different pairs I'd tried on. Every single one of them feeling like they'd been made from concrete.

"Please tell me you'll get a pair with red laces." She laughs again.

"I've already got Brandon here to give me grief. I don't need your long-distance ribbing."

"Oh, Chelse. You always go all-in on everything. Before you know it, you'll be wearing waders and a fishing vest and a sunbleached hat with lures hanging off of it. One of my favorite things about you, kid."

I suddenly feel a little foolish there in the midst of a sea of boots.

"Do you think you could get a delivery up there?" Mom asks. "I'd love to ship you some White Sugar gourmet cookies for your first guests. Might be nice if you put some kind of welcome basket in the cabins."

"Sounds perfect," I say. "I'm getting Charlie back in the kitchen, but you and I both know he's an incredible chef but not a baker."

"Done. I have some new recipes I'm trying out. I'll shoot you a bunch of samples and you can tell me which you'd like. Hang on a sec. Did you say 'back in the kitchen'? Why wasn't he still in the kitchen?"

"Long story."

"You can tell it to me some other time. Sounds like a good excuse for me to call you later. And Chelse?"

"Yeah?"

"I'm rooting for you, hon."

My eyes actually start to prickle. "I think you're the

first person in this family who sees me being here as a positive thing."

"That's not true. Brandon's backing you. Besides, either way—go or stay—it's good."

"Dad doesn't think so. Wait—what does that even mean, either way, it's good?"

"I figure, if this works, you might very well stay and be happy. If not, you just get in the car and come home and be happy. Everything settled. Your dad had a moment of fear because 'fishing resort' isn't exactly synonymous with 'Chelsea Keyes.' He thought all of this was about—"

"Clint."

"Right."

"And you don't?"

"Oh, Chelsea, you have to experience the good and bad of life. Things don't always turn out like you'd hope, but you have to be willing to give it a shot. You never know. Celery might make an incredible cupcake flavor. And it's not like you're a complete novice at running a business. You kept my books up here at White Sugar the summer your dad had his heart attack. I think you'll be great at running the resort."

"I'm not exactly running the show," I correct her. "Rusty's—"

"And, you know," Mom interrupts, "the way you apparently jumped in—almost like a knee-jerk...that sounds exactly like my girl. That's the way she played ball. That's the way she went after Durst. You jump first, then find out how to make it work when you're there."

"I'm not sure if that's a compliment," I say through a laugh. "Aren't you supposed to look before you leap?"

I glance through the plate glass window, where Blue is waiting. I've attached his leash to a bike rack near the door, well within reach of the shadiest tree around. He's stretched out beneath it, next to his water bowl, wagging his tail at any head-scratchers who enter or leave the store.

I haven't yet told Mom about Blue. But not because I have doubts about him. The very first night, I cracked open an eye around midnight to find him standing right there beside my bed, staring at me. I wiggled backward, making room for him. And we've been together ever since.

According to Brandon, he cries when he realizes I've gone to town without him. So I decided to bring him today. But the thing is, I want him with me, right there in the passenger seat. I like his wide-eyed, joyful company. And the boy has taught me the finer points of enjoying a good faceful of car-window wind.

I'm gearing up to tell Mom about Blue, finally, when she says, "Oh, just because that's how everybody else does it, that doesn't mean it's right for you. Looking before leaping, that is. You'll figure it out. And like I said, if it's not right—"

"—no harm, no foul," I finish.

"Exactly."

"Thanks, Mom," I say, and drop my phone back into my purse.

I'm still feeling a little off-center, though. Part of me thinks that if I don't do something drastic, I'll never have a chance to get close to Clint. He won't listen to me. No matter how many cabins I paint or front doors I unstick or holes I patch, he may very well bide his time until I'm gone.

And then what?

Could be that the paint I've slathered on crackles in the weather, right along with his very last memory of me.

I let things go between us these last two years. Same as Clint has been letting the resort go a little. We're kind of guilty of the same thing—I wish I could get him to see it that way.

I scramble after my phone again and pull up the picture of the orchid I found under cabin number four's front step.

Ten minutes later, I'm tossing the hiking boots I've bought for me (and the hat I finally found for Brandon at a men's clothing store) into the empty back seat.

Blue and I drive toward the resort, but I wind up stopping in the middle of a dirt road, staring at the Wheelers Point sign. I chew my lip for a while. *Either way, it's good*, I hear Mom's voice telling me. But that still doesn't ring true.

I squint at the sign. "There's a third competitor here, actually," I tell Blue, rubbing the fur on the back of his neck. "One that's going up against me and Clint both. I should know what we're up against, shouldn't I?" I take a deep breath, finally whipping my steering wheel to the right.

I travel down a new dirt road toward Wheelers Point. But even before it comes into focus, I can hear it. It sounds like an amusement park—shouting, laughing, hums of motors. And when I slow at the edge of the property, the place looks like some sort of elaborate wind-up toy: all spinning, whirling, moving parts.

No—not an amusement park. Not a toy. That's not right, either.

I've driven right into the past.

Boats and Sea-Doos zip across the lake—so many of them, the lake almost looks like it needs traffic lanes and stop signals. And guests are everywhere—jumping into a roped-off swimming area, whipping out their phones to take pictures. Obviously using the Wi-Fi to post those photos. Resort workers in Wheelers Point T-shirts herd the tourists into various group activities. Hikes, surely. Kayaking.

Blue whines, like he aches to join them.

"So do I, buddy," I murmur.

Staring through my windshield—which has picked up another couple of nicks and cracks—I begin to realize that not all of the Wheelers Point differences are advantages. To start with, Wheelers Point doesn't have any cabins. Just one giant towering lodge, filled with rooms to rent and covered in some sort of faux wood. And the feel of the place isn't right. But I can't quite put my finger on why. It's so—

"Are you checking in?"

Blue barks and I jump, turning toward the face hovering beyond my driver side window. It's Clint. As he was four years ago. Smiling. Happy to see me. The sunlight making silver streaks in his black hair. Finally.

You're back, I start to say.

Until I blink and the image clears. It's not Clint at all. This man has brown hair and light blue eyes and the build is all wrong and even that smile—it's too crooked, too awkward. Why had I made such a mistake?

"Ma'am?" the man at my window presses.

"N-no," I say. "Not checking in. I'm sorry; I took a wrong turn." I slam the Camaro in reverse. The engine lets out a few grunts and screeches as I turn it around, take the outer dirt road back to Earl's place. Which is decidedly quieter. Far less traffic. This section of the lake is still and serene.

As soon as I cut the engine, Blue flashes me a mischievous doggy look, and makes a run for it, straight out the rolled-down passenger window.

"Blue!" I shout. I scramble to head him off, but he's too fast. "Come back! No! Stop! Heel!"

My eyes bounce about the resort, but there's no sign of a dog. Not one. No footprint. No rustling weeds. No squawking ducks announcing Blue's interrupted their peaceful afternoon.

How could I have lost Todd's dog? He trusted me; he

left me with the creature he loved. His hands shook and his eyes watered as he handed me the leash. What happens when he calls, asking how Blue's doing? And I have to tell him?

More than that—how will I ever be able to sleep tonight knowing that Blue's wandering around out here alone? What kind of wild animals are out there in the trees? Bears? Do bears attack dogs? I officially want to throw up.

"Blue!" I shout frantically, making my way closer to the lake. "Blue!"

I'm panicked. And trying to keep the panic in check. *You'll never find him if you're frenzied,* I tell myself. But I can't help it. Once something becomes important to you—once it's wormed its way in and it wanders off, *panic* is basically an automatic response. I pick up the pace, jogging down the lakeshore. Mud keeps sucking at the soles of my sneakers, trying to tug me back. "Blue!"

"Chelsea!" The voice comes from a wooden swing. When a hand raises to wave, I do a double take. Clint. This time, when I blink, he doesn't disappear—or morph into another person. It's Clint.

And he's rubbing Blue's ears.

"Oh, my God," I breathe, rushing toward them. I drop down to my knees to wrap my arms around Blue's neck and bury my nose in the fur at the side of his face. He lets out a short growl of protest.

"Shut up," I grumble back.

I plop into the swing beside Clint. "Thanks for snagging him for me. He's kind of a troublemaker. Todd never told me that."

"No problem."

We fall quiet, and my breathing deepens and my thoughts slow down. I go quiet inside. My eyes close. An unexpected calm invades me. All I want to do is drink in the serenity I've suddenly found sitting here in the swing, with Blue's fur tickling my feet and Clint's thigh brushing my own. With the gentle breeze pushing my hair across my shoulders in a soothing way. The cool kiss of shade dancing across my face. Leaves rustling musically overhead while the lake harmonizes, sloshing around the dock.

"This is fantastic," I say softly. And finally open my eyes. "I think," I add, squinting out at the sparkling lake, "that this might be my favorite spot at the entire resort. Here under the tree, in this swing."

When I glance to the side, Clint's staring with a wide-eyed expression. "Yeah," he says, just as softly. "Mine, too."

We hold each other's eyes—and without even trying, here it is. A bridge. A closeness. It's such a small thing to share, to agree on. But for the first time since I got here, there's a peacefulness between us.

It matches the peace of the resort—which is completely unlike the feel of Wheelers Point. And suddenly, out of the fertile ground of peacefulness, an idea blooms.

"I want your boys." I blurt it before I realize I've made up my mind to do it. There I go again, just jumping in.

"Who—Greg? Todd's already left, remember?"

"No—the teams. Your hockey kids."

"My—what do you know about the kids?"

"I saw you yesterday. In town. I went to the rink."

He grins. "A little spying, eh, Chelsea?"

"No—just—I never saw you on the rink."

Surprise washes over his face.

"Oh, come on. You never looked up any of my old clips online?"

He shrugs. "What'd you think?" He shakes his head a little, clears his throat. "That probably wasn't the best day to see us on the ice."

"I've been thinking about your star. Or the player who could be a star. The one everyone's ganging up on right now."

"Ryan. Hey—how'd you even know—?"

"I've watched so many practices."

He nods. "Durst."

"Right."

He stares at me a long time. "There shouldn't be a star. That's what you're thinking."

I offer a crooked grin. "Reading my mind, Morgan. Look, I'm not saying anything about what you've got going on in there—I mean, hockey's pretty much a foreign language to me. But I know how being the star messes with a person's head."

He nods. "I remember. You used to write to me to complain about Durst. How he gave you the worst grunt work going. But I could tell it was a relief, too. To not be the one that people were looking at all the time. To be the one working behind the scenes. You liked it."

He tilts his head. "So what do you want my players for?"

"This might sound loopy," I admit.

"Loopy can be good."

"I want them for the resort."

"Come again?"

"Hear me out. I got the impression—based on what you shouted at the rink—"

"Said," he corrects. "Based on what I said."

"Based on what you said very loudly and with a high degree of annoyance," I go on, which gets him to shoot me a *watch it* kind of stare, "you've been having a few ongoing problems. With Ryan especially. Maybe he's the target right now, but—"

"—if the teams were really functioning like they

should, no one would be ganging up on him."

"Right." I take a deep breath. "I'm sure you've been trying to do some basic team building stuff—"

"Mostly, I've been trying to work with Ryan on his temper."

We stop talking to stare at each other for a moment.

"What?" he asks. "You think that's a bad idea."

"I'm not their coach. And I don't want to barge in, do something that you think is going to send your players back fifty steps, undo any progress."

"But—" He motions with his hand in a *get to it* way.

"But I think team building with everyone might also help. Makes everyone feel like they've got to fix their attitudes, not just Ryan. That everyone could improve if they could get it together. Then, it sort of shows you don't think Ryan's the only player with potential, and they don't feel like they have to act out to get your attention."

"Makes sure he's no longer the target," Clint says with a nod.

"I've got to admit," I say, "I get it with these cabins. I mean, I've barely spent any time on them at all, and they're more than just a little work. I know what you guys have been going through. Peel back one layer of paint, and find five additional jobs. I totally understand how overwhelming this place must have been the past year."

"So?"

"So," I say. "You have a group of kids who need to learn to work together. And a resort full of cabins that need some additional hands."

"Huh." He twists to look behind him at the row of guest cabins. He thinks for a minute. "Okay," he finally says. Turning a smirk my way, he adds, "But only if I get the girls."

"What girls?"

"The *girls*—the girlfriends. Surely you saw them in the stands at the rink."

"What do you want them for?"

"To work on my cabins. We're in a competition here, remember?"

"Oh, really?" I cross my arms over my chest. "Coming around to cleaning this place up?"

"I always knew we needed to do some repairs. That's not exactly some lightbulb moment you had, Chelse. I just didn't want to be stuck with yellow front doors and fluffy welcome mats. My renters were never going to go for that. Not even my MD."

"And you don't think the girls would decorate that way?"

"Trust me. Minnesota-raised girls know how to put a cabin together. Besides, I'm betting those girls will work harder for me than the boys will for you."

"And how is that, *Morgan*?"

"It's me. Come on. The same guy Earl said all the girls at the resort used to make eyes at."

"Is that right?" I ask through a laugh.

"Ye of little faith. Those girls don't come to the rink to watch their boyfriends."

"They don't."

"Absolutely not." He puffs his chest out and tosses his overgrown hair from his eyes.

"I think you've spent too much time around Brandon," I tell him.

He laughs hard enough that Blue barks back at him.

"I've got to get at it, Morgan," I say, standing. "After all, I do have the worst cabins."

"Watch out, Keyes," Clint says. "Closin' in on you. Wait till I get my girls."

And here it is—the push and pull. It feels familiar. And addictive. Wasn't the need to feel this all over again a big part of what brought me out here in the first place? Once Clint bubbled back up to the surface, didn't I want this? The challenge, the play? Isn't this what I'm afraid I'll be missing if I choose MSU and Durst without giving my time here a real shot?

I flinch a little at this thought. I slap my thigh. Blue's tags jingle as he hurries to keep up with me.

But Blue's not the only thing that follows me. That sense of peace comes along, too.

I glance over my shoulder, at a distant treeline in the direction of Wheelers Point. *Hotel.* The word pops into my head without warning. That's how the place felt. But with its quaint individual cabins, the Lake of the Woods Fishing Resort feels like home.

Which, I start to realize, is why Mom's words had made me feel a little strange. Lake of the Woods already seems like mine somehow. Winning or losing here at the resort could never be no harm, no foul. No more than losing at basketball was ever okay. No more than losing Brandon or my parents or White Sugar or anything else I truly love could ever be okay. Actually, the mere idea of losing out at Lake of the Woods— losing everything here, including Clint—shoots a burst of panic through me. Just like the one I felt when I thought I'd lost Blue.

Four Years Ago

Lake of the Woods Fishing Resort
Minnesota

Chelsea sits outside the main lodge, on a concrete parking block.

Earl knows it's her. Even though, at this angle, he mostly sees her from behind. The blond hair, the familiar T-shirt. She just keeps sitting there, on one of the blocks he'd had installed along the parking spaces closest to the main lodge. Kind of a buffer to keep cars from sliding into the building during rain or snow showers. She's turned one into a seat. And since it's only about six inches tall, her knees are jutting up toward the sky. Her arms are balanced on the tops of those knees, and her shoulders move slightly, like she's got some sort of object in her hands she keeps turning over.

Every once in a while, she raises her head and looks around. Like she's wondering when she'll be joined.

Only, Clint's not around. A couple days off, on doctor's orders.

Earl has insisted he take them. A dislocated shoulder is no small injury, and Earl doesn't want him reinjuring himself.

Again, Chelsea glances behind her.

But Earl is the only person who spends so much time at the check-in counter. Is she waiting for him?

He steps outside, grunts as he lowers himself onto

218

the block beside her. "These things are murder," he tells her, which makes her smile.

"Whatcha got there?" he asks, reaching for the object in her hand. "A compass?"

"It's Clint's. Some old Boy Scout thing."

"Why do you have it?"

"I used it. In the field behind Pike's."

"Ah, yes. The ATV crash. Glad it wasn't worse."

"He was going to take me out morel mushroom hunting. And I started racing him. I don't know why I did that."

"Sure you do."

She glances up at Earl, her eyes swollen. "I wasn't trying to hurt him."

"Oh, I know you were playing."

"His tire hit a downed tree. He got launched off his four-wheeler. Flew over the handlebars. It was—" She shakes her head. "It was awful."

"Worse seein' somebody else get hurt than it is gettin' hurt yourself, isn't it?"

She clenches her jaw and nods.

"It's a sign 'a how much you care that it hurts you like that."

She clutches the compass. "I should give this back."

"Well, now," Earl says, leaning closer. "It's up to you. But I can't say for sure how good of an idea it is."

"It's not mine."

"Didn't you say it rescued you?"

"Well, rescued me and Clint both."

"In my experience," Earl says, "the things that rescue you once can rescue you again."

Today
LAKE OF THE WOODS FISHING RESORT
MINNESOTA

Clint
CAST

Chelsea paces near the main lodge, her hand in the pocket of her shorts as if she's protecting something.

"Whatcha got?" I ask, nodding toward her hidden hand. Mostly to break the silence. This particular Saturday morning finds the resort especially still.

She flinches.

"Bet you got all your fingers crossed. That it?"

She shrugs but clutches tighter to whatever it is. Clearly wants to keep it a secret.

Blue flops on the ground next to Chelsea. He props himself on his elbows, panting like crazy.

I suddenly feel like panting, too. Because cars are starting to spray gravel as they pull into the resort. Engines are going quiet beneath the early morning sky.

Boys drag themselves out of driver's seats. Typical, grumpy boys, yawning and grumbling. As they begin to look around, though, I can almost smell their curiosity.

And then, as though on cue—an additional round of cars arrives, each vehicle filled with girls who emerge smiling and chattering.

"Hey!" the boys shout, pointing. "What…?"

The girls, dressed in faded jeans and old shirts, have come to work. Not flirt.

"What is this, coach?" Ryan wants to know.

His father, who has driven him and is standing on the fringes holding Luke's hand, wears an expression that seems to imply he'd like to know, too.

I hug a clipboard to my chest. The boys edge closer to me.

I stand frozen in place as they make a semi-circle around me and Chelsea and Blue.

"All right," I say, starting to pace back and forth. My pulse beats with the intensity of a crowd pounding their feet against the bleachers.

Blue watches from his place at Chelsea's side. No barking. No jumping around excitedly. Maybe he feels my nerves.

"You guys aren't functioning as a team," I start. "No matter how I divide you up. No matter what team you're on. Our sessions seem, for the most part, to end up the same way."

A few roll their eyes.

A short screech of my whistle startles them. I don't mean to go all drill sergeant on them, but I need their attention. A pause for effect lets me search for the right words.

"That's never one person's doing," I say. I make a point not to look directly at Ryan here. I'm talking to all of them.

"Everyone on the team is responsible for the team. No one person wins or loses all by himself. Since you can't seem to figure out how to function on the ice, maybe it's best that we go for a little change of scenery. Change of tasks. It's why I asked you to come here today instead of the rink."

I use my clipboard to point. "This is Chelsea, my fellow trainer-slash-resort renovator. And, boys, your team captain. Maybe it'll help if you have to report to someone other than me for a bit. We're starting today by randomly dividing you up." She removes a stack of pages from her own clipboard and hands a page to each of my players. "On these sheets, you'll find a number. That corresponds to a cabin number. We've got three teams of four, one team of three. Your team number is your cabin number. You will report to your cabin. You will find the supplies for your team task inside the cabin."

"What task?" Ryan asks sheepishly. He's still afraid the guys he's partnered with will punish him for being the reason behind whatever torture I have in mind.

"You're all working on the cabins. Cleaning, painting, minor repairs. Numbers two, four, six, and eight." Chelsea's cabins.

"Looks like number four's already painted," Ryan says, pointing.

"It's gotten started. The porch has been repaired, and the white paint on the walls is primer."

"So—the rest of us are going to be behind," Travis, my goalie, complains.

"No, no, you'll all have different jobs. It doesn't matter that four's already had some work done. Chelsea accomplished that much with only one assistant, so we know we're not asking you to do anything impossible. Especially since you'll be working in teams."

"One of us won't have four members," observes Nick,

a six-foot-three wall of muscle who most frequently tries to smear Ryan's brains on the boards during practice.

"True enough. But do you think that should stop you?"

He shrugs.

"It's up to you how to divide up your jobs."

"How do we know what jobs we're supposed to do, exactly?" he presses. "You never said."

"Cabin two needs painting. Cabin six has a missing living room floor."

"Missing floor!" Ryan shouts.

"Only part of it," I assure him.

He makes a coughing noise and puts his hands on top of his head, kind of in a duck-and-cover style.

"Cabin eight has leaky windows," I add.

"What—how're we—"

"Rusty, the resort owner, has consulted a contractor and the owner of Rogers & Sons Hardware about the cabins."

When Nick lets out this kind of snort of disgust, I tell him, "Chelsea and Rusty got mold removed and had an exterminator out here before you guys showed up. Believe me, you should be thanking both of them."

That shuts him up long enough for me to say, "You'll find all the supplies you need inside your cabins. The same way a team is divided up into positions—goalie, defensemen, center—you'll have to decide who does what. If you're painting, for example, you'll have to figure out who primes, who cuts in, who tapes off the area."

"We're supposed to do all this stuff?" Travis asks, getting a sick look on his face as he stares down the row of cabins.

"Only if you want to win," Chelsea says.

"Win what?" Ryan asks.

"The girls will be working on their own sets of cabins. Clint's their team captain," she says as I hand the girls each a sheet of paper to randomly divide them.

The boys erupt into a slew of "Whoa!"s and "Hey!"s and "What's the big idea?"s.

"Who do you think is going to win?" I ask, ignoring all the complaining.

Nick stares me down. "Who gets done first," he grumbles.

"Wrong. Who overcomes the most."

"What does *that* mean?" he groans.

"I'm not looking for quickness. I don't want to see paint slopped everywhere. Caulk spewing out crazily. Each cabin has its own challenges. Every team's going to encounter a different set of problems. You'll all have to come together in your own ways to tackle them. *And,* I want clean work."

"So—it's a single cabin that wins?"

"The tournament is boys against girls," Chelsea says. "We'll be awarding a special prize to the best cabin on the winning side. Kind of an MVP award."

"Boys against girls?" Ryan screeches. "How are we supposed to keep up with what the rest of the guys're doing if everybody's off in their own cabin?"

The rest of the boys glance at each other. The girls are already huddled up, making plans.

My players turn to stare at me, too surprised or confused to even really know what they think of all this. But let a bunch of girls get the best of them? Never.

"What are you waiting for? Go on, go on!" I wave my hands.

Chelsea and I exchange looks. I wonder if I seem as worried about what we've set in motion as she does.

Chelsea
EXTRINSIC MOTIVATION

An hour later, cabin number four is in full-on argument mode, shouting accusations about who spilled some white paint on the porch. Cabin number six is sitting on the steps in protest, and cabin number two has yet to finish screwing the paint rollers onto their long wooden handles. Cabin number eight seems to be convinced they can get a Wi-Fi signal if they manage to find the right position. They almost look like beachcombers with metal detectors, walking and waving their phones.

The girls are organized and working away. Which is not at all what I'd hoped would happen.

"I thought the girls would kick them into gear," I tell Clint.

He grunts in agreement. Manages, "Yeah, looks bad."

"I mean, I think they see this as having nothing to do with hockey. Even after what you said. It's all about learning to work together," I say.

"Play," he corrects me. "Learning to *play* together."

"Right."

"Right?"

"You act like that wasn't really what I meant."

"I don't think it was," Clint says, eyeing me skeptically. "There's a reason they call it *playing* ball, isn't there?"

I stare at him.

"Look at that," he says, nodding toward Luke. His dad is still here with him, letting him squat beside the edge of the lake, magnifying lens against his eye. "He'll do anything for a little bit of fun. Don't have to coax him into that. Don't have to bark at him and screech whistles. He just—wants to. I wanted to and I bet you did, too."

It comes back to me—the driveway, the practice sessions. The way I attacked it like a job I needed to push through. *It was all about the win.* But we're asking the boys to feel differently, aren't we? We're asking them to befriend each other. To figure out a way to turn a job they could never actually want to do into something to laugh through. Isn't that how people get close? Through laughter? By learning to turn challenges into something resembling a good time?

"I might have a surprise for you," Clint says. "Think you can get the boys up to the main lodge? That includes Brandon."

I survey the resort, Blue jumping excitedly at my heels. I catch sight of Brandon on the edge of the dock closest to cabin number four, sitting among the currently-quiet smudge pots, scribbling some new verse down in his notebook. He pauses, cradles an imaginary guitar, and works an invisible fretboard. Then scribbles those notes down as well.

"Sure thing," I call out, already mid-bolt.

"Francine!" I shout, my feet and Blue's thunking against the boards in the dock.

Brandon swivels to look my way. "She's back in the cabin."

"I need her," I say.

"This is serious if you're calling her by name," he agrees.

"Main lodge. Now."

"Aye aye, captain. Or coach. Or—never mind," he

says, sprinting in the direction of our cabin.

I blow my own whistle, and Blue throws his head back to howl.

The boys turn to scowl at me.

"How about we all head up to the lodge?"

The girls have stopped working at this point.

"You too," I insist, waving my arm in a way that asks them to join us.

Slowly, they follow.

The moment we filter in through the lodge entrance, Clint's hockey players all begin to search out their girlfriends. Talking and shouting—but is it good? Are they happy? Are they complaining? It's hard to tell.

Clint smirks at me as Brandon pushes past us.

"What?" I ask.

He leads me into the dining room as Brandon's guitar notes fill the air.

"What smells so good?" I ask.

He shrugs. "You can thank me later."

"Is Charlie in the kitchen?"

"I might've worked something out to get him here," he admits.

"You knew we were going to need to feed those boys."

"I was a teenager once. Teenage boys are bottomless pits."

"Thanks," I say.

"Thanks for suggesting getting the boys out here," he says. "And for fixing up the lodge, prepping the kitchen."

When I pause, he leans in to say, "This is where you thank me for bringing the girls."

"Whether or not it's a good idea still remains to be seen," I remind him.

"I got faith," he says, and squeezes my arm.

The Next Two Weeks

If Earl were still around, he would snap open a lawn chair and place it between the main lodge and the row of guest cabins. He would tell you this story, his voice echoing through the trees:

Time's a funny thing 'round places like this. Some folks—mostly the real young ones who don't like fishing much—they think time just stops. Doesn't matter how much fun Dad tries to make fishing. Seems to them like they're stuck in a moment that refuses to pass.

For the rest of us—well, time passes too fast. Seems the sun's always stainin' the sky orange for some reason. Sunup. Sundown. No more than a blink between the two.

Oh, how I relish the two weeks that bring Clint's group of young people to the resort. If I could 'a lassoed time to hold it back, slow it down, I would have. Girls with hammers. Boys with paint cans. Pointing out their own successes. Taunting the other team. Teasing.

Fun. They're having fun. It's a great sound. Better even than the songs of birds. The sound of summer. Of games. Of having a good time. Happiness is the whole point. Always was, far as I'm concerned.

Doesn't take long for the girls to discover Rusty's warehouse. The one where my three musketeers—Greg, Todd, and Clint—decided to store the nicest cabin furniture. Couldn't let a bunch of muddy, wet guys sit on upholstered chairs, after all. And the girls begin to haul it back out. All those pieces my

Helen had picked out special.

Turns out to be a bit of a struggle for the girls to carry the heaviest stuff. So Rusty directs them toward the ATVs parked beside the lodge. Shows them how to hook up small trailers. And they drive by the boys, like a parade, waving and shouting and carrying on.

Which means the boys are suddenly heading for the warehouse, determined to do their own decorating.

'Course, my niece, she's always been one to find it easy to get the boys' attention. And these boys are no exception. They do plenty 'a work to get her to turn her head their way. Askin' her to come by their cabins, see 'em for herself. Workin' for her approval as much as to win the competition.

"You don't watch it, you're going to ruffle plenty of feathers," Rusty winds up tellin' 'em, which gets the boys to put on innocent faces while their girlfriends kid them about their pathetic crushes. Chelsea and Clint elbow each other— and my niece—about it.

"Yeah, well, we only wanted your furniture, anyway," one of the boys shouts, which gets him picked up off his feet and carried by Rusty all the way to the edge of the closest dock. He's still kicking and begging when she tosses him into the lake.

With the ATVs officially out from their parking slots beside the lodge, the boys decide they can score extra points by mowing around the cabins themselves. Pruning shears emerge, too. String trimmers. Even some weed killer for the trails.

But I'm no fool. And there's no sense in telling some fish tale here. Those teenagers don't leave behind perfect cabins. There's plenty 'a mishaps and some spilled paint and even a broken window or two. But they give it their all.

And through it all, they're smiling. Giggling. Playing.

Funny thing about that crack in the earth I showed Rusty years ago. When a crack like that disappears, it doesn't seem like it gets filled in as much as it seems like the two sides kinda smash closer together.

There's another crack here at the resort—between two people. And during these two weeks, the space between Chelsea and Clint is startin' to get increasingly smaller, tuggin' the two of them a little bit closer together.

Sure, Clint likes to tell Kenzie he doesn't want Chelsea around. But anytime he's outside, he looks for her.

There's laughter between them, too. The sharing of tools and ideas. Trips in Clint's truck to Rogers & Sons. Evenings at the swing, two beers and a dog and talks about the boys. Peeking through cabin windows. Chelsea warning Clint, "I'm telling you, my boys are going to annihilate your girls," and Clint insisting, "You wait, Keyes. You just wait," with a lightness that hasn't been in his voice for ages.

"Do you remember bowling?" Chelsea challenges, asking him to recall an evening they'd spent together during another summer.

"Right. Guy versus girl," Clint says. "Girl won. Who's got the girls now, Keyes?" And winks at her before taking a pull from his beer.

Maybe there are no nights out behind Pike's, not like two people who are dating. Openly falling for one another. No drive-ins, no sneaking off to find seclusion under the trees.

But as much as Chelsea and Clint are goin' up against each other, they're workin' toward the same end goal. Fixin' my old place up. And somethin' happens when two people work together. Chelsea was right about that. Maybe that was why the girl suggested his hockey players come. Maybe it was about her and Clint as much as those boys. Smart, that one.

Yessir, any other time, in order to tell a story about

my resort, I might try to spout a bit about the woman in the waterfall. Tell some tale about that tattooed tree and how names carved into it are regular magic. Maybe some crazy notion about the power of a compass, of knowin' a soul's right direction.

But this part of the story needs no exaggeration. No wild embellishments.

What's happenin' here—the love these kids all show an old man's place, and the simple way Chelsea and Clint keep inching closer together—why, that's really magic enough.

Clint

NIGHTCRAWLER

"**W**e need to figure out how to get people up here."

It's Nick's girlfriend who says it. At least, I think she's Nick's. I do know that her name is Rachel and she's on her school's track team.

I've learned lots about these girls over the past couple of weeks. Frankie the debater and Heather who works at the local animal shelter and shy, quiet Emma who can recite the dialogue of every Monty Python movie ever made.

The second after Rachel says it—*need to figure out*—everybody starts chiming in, and there are suddenly more voices than smoke out here.

It's a barbecue behind the lodge. All of us gathered around the cluster of picnic tables we've dragged out from Rusty's warehouse. If I remember right, when I was a kid, Earl had a picnic table next to each one of the guest cabins.

"We need more *stuff*," Travis insists.

"There is nothing left to go in those cabins, trust me," Rachel tells him, tossing her long black braid behind her shoulder.

"No, I mean to do."

"Fishing and hiking and birdwatching and kayaking isn't enough for you?" Frankie asks.

"You're just upset about you guys coming in second to

us," Rachel taunts.

"No, no," Ryan says. "It was a tie. Wasn't it? Didn't we say it was a tie?"

"We need fresh eyes," Frankie insists. "Let renters rate the cabins. And then whoever gets the best rating is the winner. How about that?"

"Hey, now," Brandon says. "I worked on some of the girls' cabins, too. And I heard some of that decorating advice the guys got from Chelsea."

"I'm their captain—" she tries, but Brandon shakes his head.

"If it's supposed to be guys versus girls," Brandon says, " I think the water's officially too muddied for a contest. I think it's a tie, too." Somehow, when Chelsea's little brother speaks, everyone listens.

"Come on," Nick finally offers. "Really. We can't be done here, can we? What about people that don't really want to fish? I mean, we could have a zipline, or a disc golf course. Maybe lawn darts or something."

"Or croquet," Emma adds in a high-pitched, faux British accent, which starts everyone laughing.

"Whoa, whoa," Chelsea tells them all, "I think Nick's onto something. What if we…"

Suddenly, it's a flurry of new ideas fighting to be heard. All about the resort. I can't quit thinking that none of this would have ever been put into motion without Chelsea. She's got both teams acting as if they own the place.

They love it. Like Greg and Todd and I loved it. In a way, the resort really does belong to them. Because they've put pieces of themselves into it. We share that. Because of her.

Chelsea looks right at me, her skin kissed a shade darker by the sun. Her blond hair swirls in the evening breeze.

I need to cool off.

I slip away from the group, knowing there's really only one place where I can cool off unseen. Knowing, too, I'll never be missed. Not once the Wheelers Point fireworks start going off.

I can hardly believe it, but I'm leaving the string of cabins behind and climbing the hill. Straight toward the waterfall. The same place where Chelsea and I made love on a long-ago summer evening, covered in mist—our hearts beating in time to the pulse of the water. The same place I've avoided every year since. Now, here I am, suddenly racing toward it.

I'm in such a rush to get to the water's edge, I plop down at the top of the hill. Slide down against the rough earth. Slide hard enough that the ground starts burning against my thigh. When I get to the bottom, I hoist myself back to my feet, tear off my shirt, shuck my shorts, and kick off my sneakers. I jump in. All at once. No easing myself into the cool shock of the water.

The water stings, sending a surge of coldness between my legs. My hair floats out from the top of my head. I open my eyes as the glow of distant fireworks dances across the top of the water. I exhale in a long stream of bubbles. The surface continues to slip farther away the deeper I sink. I don't stop until my backside hits the earth at the bottom.

I stay submerged as long as I can, letting the underwater world of fish and plants surround every inch of me.

Lungs ready to burst, I shove off, kicking to propel myself upward. I gasp as I break the surface. Shake the water from my hair, rub my face. God, I love the water. Always have. To me, it's alive; it's a best friend that can change everything just by being nearby. Water can instantly heal. Make everything better. Soothe. In a single splash.

Above, the sky erupts again. Orange and gold flashes wash over my skin, coloring the frothy edge of the waterfall.

There's something about the orange stain that makes the water look hot—while the droplets hitting my face feel sharp and cold. But that's exactly what I'm feeling at that moment: a mix of cold shock and familiar internal heat.

Chelsea

OBSESSIONS

I'm still outside the main lodge, seated at a picnic table, flanked by Rusty and Brandon and surrounded by Clint's teams and their girlfriends, when the Wheelers Point fireworks start going off.

I close my eyes as pops and colors fill the sky over the lake. I remember, in an overwhelming *whoosh*, that was how I'd once felt kissing Clint. When my arms were locked around his neck and he'd stopped nibbling an earlobe or grazing my cheek to bring his mouth against mine. Kissing him felt like an entire package of Black Cats exploding behind the zipper on my shorts.

My cheeks flush. I'm unbearably hot. Embarrassed, too—am I being transparent? Are the things I've just thought written all over me?

I need to get away from Brandon's constant strumming and the unending prattle and squeals of laughter. Life seems easy for every one of them.

Meanwhile, I'm the girl who doesn't even want to turn my phone on in town because I'm sure to find new texts from Makayla, asking when I'll be coming home. It's disorienting to read those texts in Baudette—how do I *come home* when this small town feels more and more like an extension of home already?

And Clint. I've had two weeks with Clint. Two weeks of flirting and smiling and working the resort. It's been simple. And sweet. And wonderful. And I can't help hoping it's the promise of something more.

Maybe eighteen-year-old me would have rolled her eyes at that one. Back then, that young girl seemed pretty convinced that love and lust were kind of all tangled together, two shoots of the same vine.

But right now, we're marking the end to yet another day. Another sunset. Time's flowing faster and harder than the whitewater sections of the Rainy River.

What happens now that the cabins are mostly restored? Clint doesn't need me to put up a zipline. There's not exactly more competition to keep us going, is there? Especially since the cabin competition itself ended in a tie. What have I done here? Why doesn't it feel like enough?

I'm prickly and unsure, and before I know what I'm doing, I'm racing up a hill. My feet throb, rubbing uncomfortably against my sneakers as I finally admit to myself where I'm headed: to the waterfall. For the first time since my return.

The place where everything was once so perfect with Clint.

I gasp at the top of the hill; the waterfall is as gorgeous as ever. Beneath the moonlight and firework explosions, I can make out the pale pink and orange petals of wildflowers that have grown in the spaces near my feet. The night sky is pushing them to curl shyly inward, their petals preparing for sleep. It's too late in the day for many birds to be singing, but the pounding of the water makes up for their absence—it's rhythmic, musical. Soothing.

I close my eyes, allowing mist to collect on my lids.

Before I can second-guess myself, I'm tugging my shirt off. Walking closer to the small pool at the base of the cascading water. I'm loosening the button of my shorts. At the water's edge, I treat the laces of my sneakers so roughly, you'd think I was exacting revenge. Drop my shorts and shirt. Unfasten my bra.

The shock of cold water attacks my every pore, every inch of skin.

I let the air in my lungs carry me up to the surface. I flip face-up, floating on my back. Letting the tops of my breasts soak up the moon glow. Wishing Clint were here. Trying to imagine what he'd do if he saw me. I know how the Clint of four years ago would react…

Above me, yellow flashes eclipse the stars; sparkling bits of light trickle down the black sky like water down a naked body. My chest rattles against every explosion.

I swim closer to the rushing waterfall. The white foamy water becomes a kaleidoscope of changing colors—orange—green—red.

A nearby splash makes me swallow a yelp. I try to duck, concealing most of my body beneath the surface of the pond. I'm not alone. I want to scramble for additional cover, but where would I go? I tread water, my eyes darting back and forth through the darkness, trying to make use of the pulsing bursts of light. Trying to zone in on who or what is with me, here in the midst of the rocks and the plants and the never-ending forceful stream.

I see him—actually, I hear him first. Hear a gush of water that comes between bursts of firecrackers. My eyes follow the sound in time to see a figure pulling himself from the water. Clint. Unaware he has company.

I gasp again—deeper than I had at the sight of the waterfall. He's beautiful; but then, he was always beautiful. All sleek lines as he stands on a rock, shaking drops from his hair. When silver and blue lights burst overhead, he looks as if he's constructed of chrome. As gold tones explode, his image softens. Shadows trace the curve of his back, the lines of his legs. He turns to pick up his T-shirt, highlighting the contours of his arms, the ripples in his stomach. The "v" shape his muscles form where his abs meet his hips.

I become an utterly mesmerized voyeur, unable to peel my eyes away. I watch as he dresses, not sure if the bubbles dancing around me are coming from the force of the pounding waterfall or the heat bleeding out from my skin.

At the Waterfall

He knows she is watching him.

And he lets her.

He stands on the edge of the water, letting her drink him in as the mist dances on his skin.

He wants her to see him.

She does—but not just this version of him. Their ghosts are here, too. The ghosts of who they were four years ago. They are still there, behind the waterfall. Tangled together in timeless memory. It is always that way when love is powerful. It remains within reach of an awakening heart.

It is knowing he wants her to see him that hits her most powerfully. It is as good as calling her name, asking her to stay.

Clint knows that the tale Earl had spun ages ago was mere fantasy. He knows there was never any legend, never any woman in the waterfall who died because of a broken heart.

And yet, when Chelsea climbs out, all he can think of is the way he can still see every inch of her, even through the thick waterfall mist.

That, according to Earl's tale, was the sign that their love was true.

I know Chelsea's nearby when I can hear Blue pant.

I swivel to see she's being joined by Rusty. And Brandon. And Greg.

Chelsea holds up the note I placed on her screen door.

"We all appear to have gotten one of those," Rusty says. "Meeting at the swing?"

"Best place to have a business meeting, if you ask me," Greg says. "I brought these, too, at your request," he tells me, plopping down our Igloo cooler. He begins to distribute beer bottles as Rusty takes a seat beside me and Chelsea sits on the far end of the swing. Brandon plops onto the ground next to Blue.

"Ah," Rusty says, "Clint's Bubblin' Brewski."

"Brewski?" Brandon says with a grimace. "That's a frat boy word." Finding no label on the bottle, he asks, "Did you really make this?"

"You bet, he did," Greg tells him.

"You could sell this!" Brandon shouts, as though he's the first person to ever think of it.

Rusty and Greg both burst out laughing. "We keep trying to tell him," Greg says. "He won't name it."

"How hard can that be?" Brandon asks. He tilts his head to the side and says, "Boogie Woogie Brew."

"No," I tell him.

"Chillin' Chops."

"Chops?" I repeat.

"Yeah—you know, when you got what it takes."

"Brandon," Chelsea breaks in, "I don't think Clint wants jazz terms on his beer."

Now that she's said something, I have an excuse to look right at her. Walking shorts, white T-shirt. Tan and strong. When she sees me looking, she rolls her blue eyes in a kind of silent apology about Brandon jumping in to name my beer. It's a shared joke, a slice of a moment of togetherness.

And suddenly, I'm thinking of the last time we were together. Out by the waterfall. Is she thinking of it, too?

"Chops is universal," Brandon argues, taking my attention away from her for a moment. "Isn't it?"

"Maybe we should get to why you called us all out here," Rusty suggests, tugging on the fraying bill of her ball cap.

"Right," I say. "First, I want to thank you guys—Brandon, you and Chelsea—"

Greg raises an eyebrow and sits on the Igloo in a kind of *this is going to be good* manner.

"—without you, these cabins would still be in a bad way," I say. "I think Greg and Rusty join me in raising a glass to the two of you." I hold my bottle up.

"To Chelsea and Brandon," Greg says.

"No, no—this was Chelsea's idea," Brandon tries, but Chelsea breaks in, saying, "You were right there working with everybody else. Keeping them in good spirits up there at the lodge. Keeping them laughing so much they didn't have time to fight."

Brandon shrugs. "Well, yes, I was *instrumental* at that."

"Is that a pun?" Greg asks. "It's pitiful any way you

look at it."

"It's probably only the beginning," Chelsea warns. "We better hurry up and toast him before his head starts swelling."

We all clink our bottles.

"There's more, though," Greg says. "I can tell."

"I want us to have a tournament," I say. "A fishing tournament. I've offered massive discounts and free weekends to the families of the kids who worked on the place. And I've already asked Kenzie to help spread the word. She's been doing some social media stuff and an email campaign with our regulars."

"Any takers?" Chelsea asks, leaning around Rusty to meet my eye.

"Yeah. A good number of the regulars have reserved spots."

"Bet your MD's coming," Greg says.

"MD?" Brandon parrots.

"He's got a guy who comes to get away from the stress of the job," Greg says.

"Got him convinced it was healthier than a flight of beers at Pike's," I say. "And yeah, he's signed up. So has Ryan's family. Got a few more father-son duos who are interested, looking into whether they can make it that particular weekend—some boys from hockey are anxious to use their discounts and show off the work they've done. A few of our semi-regulars have said they want to bring their kids for a change. But with the cabins looking so good now, I wish we could expand on it. Get new guests to check the place out."

"I've got it," Rusty says. "My guys. Going down to the meeting hall for poker and conversation gets old. They'd be up for anything that involves beer and a good time."

"The vets?" Chelsea asks.

"Yeah. Uncle Earl always said this place was powerful enough to get anyone out of their head and back in the game..."

I think I see Chelsea's eyes go a little distant on that one. Like she's thinking about the healing that took place for her—and me—that first summer.

"It's good for Clint's MD, and it'd be good for my guys," Rusty says. "With the cabins shined up, and with an added tournament to give them something to do, this would be the perfect time to get them all down here. Bet some of them would like to bring their kids, too."

"You could almost do it in teams," Brandon suggests, pointing to Chelsea. "Like the cabins. Boys versus girls."

"Military versus civilian," she corrects. "Rusty and I will be the captains of the military team. You guys get the civilians."

"Absolutely," Rusty exclaims.

We toast to it.

"How much time till this tournament, anyway?" Chelsea asks.

"This weekend," I say.

"Way to give us the heads-up," Greg grumbles.

"It's plenty of time," Chelsea says. And I think, at that moment, she winks at me.

Chelsea

REWARD

I'm stepping out of Kode the next day when I run into him. Black hair glimmering right along with his crooked smile.

"Did I see you walk out that door?" he asks, pointing to the entrance to Kenzie's business.

I shrug. "Maybe."

"What were you doing in there?"

"None of your business."

"Actually," he says, leaning a little closer, "it is literally my business."

"It's Rusty's business," I correct. When I raise a finger to point at him, I realize there's less than two inches of space between us. "Besides," I add, "we're in a competition."

"We are?" He's enjoying this.

"Don't play coy. You haven't forgotten. You're not a man who forgets. Reciting quotes out there in the wildflower field."

"So are you going to do something to my tournament?" He almost asks like he's hoping I will.

"Absolutely not, Morgan. I'm not into sabotage. But there will be no tie this time. Those vets will slaughter your civilians."

"Mmm-hmm." He leans away from me. "You're up to something."

He keeps staring at me.

"You want something."

"I want to *show* you something," he corrects. "I did, anyway. It was why I came across the street. But now that I realize you were with Kenzie plotting something, I'm not so sure." He angles his jaw to the side like he's trying not to laugh.

"You know leaving me dangling is going to drive me nuts."

"Yes."

"You think you can use that to your advantage. You'll show me, but only if I tell you what I was just doing."

"Awww," he groans. "Come on. Me?" He feigns innocence.

"I got you on the ropes."

"You think so."

"Know so. Face it, Morgan. You needed me."

His face gets a little serious. I get a funny twist in my stomach as I wonder if I've pushed this banter too far.

"Seriously," he says, pulling away. "Come on." He tosses his head in the direction of his truck.

I follow, climb into the passenger's side.

"Are you humming?" I ask as he steers through the Baudette streets.

"A little trust, Chelsea," he says. But he doesn't stop smiling. Not even when he pulls into the parking lot at the ice rink.

He picks up a long-sleeved shirt and tosses it into my lap.

I'm still shoving my arms into it as we step inside.

Clint leads me to the penalty box.

I shiver, and not only because it's so cold. I was completely honest when I told Clint that ice hockey's one of the sports I'm less than familiar with. I don't exactly have the rule book memorized; I never had to, not at MSU, where there was no such thing as a hockey team. If you want to know the proper height for a basketball rim (ten feet), or how heavy a shot put should be (eight pounds for women), I'm your girl. But if you need to know what constitutes a foul in hockey (wait—are there fouls in hockey? Surely...), I'm obviously not the one to ask. My idea of working with the team had nothing to do with the fundamentals of the game.

I fidget, feeling out of place and wondering what could be up.

"It's where I've been all summer," he explains of the penalty box. "Me and Luke the scientist."

As I settle in beside Luke, he puts his magnifying lens up to his eye and asks, "Where's Blue?"

"He's at the resort helping Brandon. Kinda miss my buddy."

"I'll be your buddy," Luke offers.

From the rink, Ryan sees me. And waves. And smiles beneath his padded helmet when I wave back.

It's suddenly a flurry of sticks and skates. The puck slides toward Ryan and is promptly stolen.

Ryan flinches. I watch as anger socks him square in the stomach. But instead of acting on it, he merely raises his hand to touch the side of his head, then grips the stick and skates forward again. In another flurry of sticks and skates, he gets possession of the puck. He flies across the ice, shoots, and scores.

The boys on his team cheer, slapping his shoulder to congratulate him.

"All right, all right," Clint's calling, clapping his hands.

My heart stomps up my throat, plays my tonsils like drums as the puck is put into play again. A teammate sees

Ryan on the opposite side of the rink and passes. Ryan shoots, but misses. Calmly regains possession, shoots, and scores.

I clench my fist with every last bit of strength I have so my hand won't shake as I offer him a thumbs up. He smiles back, holding his hockey stick up in victory.

At this point, the rest of his team turns my way. They raise their sticks in greeting—or maybe that's even a thanks.

The practice continues; for Ryan, it's a mixed bag of nailed shots and missed opportunities. But he never loses his cool—or his focus. I feel an entire tsunami of pride as Ryan smacks the puck into the net one last time. He skates toward me, pulls off his glove, and offers me a high five. He gives one to Luke, too, who's now more interested in the way my shoelace looks beneath his magnifying lens than in his hockey-star brother's triumph.

The rest of the guys are still lumped together on the ice. They seem to be avoiding the *hurry up* waves from the girls who have begun to pace along the fringes of the rink.

Ryan skates toward them—helmet off, shoulders squared—and they surround him, like gnats around a shoo-fly pie. They keep looking at me. Waving. Letting go with lots of happy shouts.

"Looks like you've acquired Baudette's largest teenage boy fan club," Clint says, skating to a stop in front of the box. "And it's well deserved. Your team building exercise has clearly worked. I told the guys it was your idea. I wanted you to see it for yourself."

He waves as Luke's dad carries him off just before pushing himself from the penalty box. With two long strides, he eases himself off the ice. His movements are fluid and effortless. I bet watching him play in one of his tournaments was something. I'm still trying to imagine it when he returns—holding two white skates by the laces. "You've gotta be about a nine, right?"

"No way. I can't skate. I'll be terrible. Embarrassingly awful."

"Give it a shot." He jerks his head backward a couple of times, urging me to get a move on.

My heart throbs—what does this mean?

He pushes the skates toward me, saying, "I really botched things up with Ryan. Was beginning to think I was ruining hockey for him, which is the last thing I'd want to do with any of my kids—but the most talented one?" Shaking his head at himself, he confesses, "I pushed him too hard. But you turned it around. You fixed my mess."

"Wasn't anything."

"Wasn't anything," he repeats. "Who do you think you're talking to? False humility is nothing I remember being part of the Chelsea Keyes repertoire."

I'm fighting to keep from laughing.

"I just want to skate with you. Are you afraid of leaving your own comfort zone? Isn't that what you did to my hockey players? Besides, you wouldn't exactly be trying to figure it out on your own. I happen to have put in a quite a few hours as a private skating instructor."

"Are you bragging that I'd be in the hands of the best?"

"No excuses. Lace 'em up, Keyes."

The grin on his face is incredibly delicious. There's no way I can turn him down. I trade my shoes for the skates. But it's impossible to stay upright on the crazy things as I inch onto the ice. I'm in a constant state of wobble. Pathetic.

Instead of feeling embarrassed, I throw my head back and laugh. Clint wraps his arms around my waist as his laughter mingles with mine.

That Night
Pike's Perch
Baudette, Minnesota

Clint
CHUMMING

"Got a pretty young lady waiting for you out back," Pop shouts at me over the voices and the laughing and the clanking of dishes.

And the cheering. The cheering is a surprise.

"What's the deal?" I ask. "There can't be some game on TV, can there?" I haven't heard shouting like this in Pike's since the Super Bowl.

Pop grins, steps to the side to reveal Brandon standing on our makeshift stage.

"That's for Brandon?"

"It's not for Greg, I can tell you that," he says.

But this also isn't a bunch of screeching twelve-year-olds, bored by the outdoor setting, looking for something to interest them for a week or two. He has the attention of the entire restaurant, and they're shouting out requests. He attacks Francine's strings, and groups clustered around tables let out howls of approval.

"He's really something," Pop says.

"Too bad he's not here all year," I agree.

Pop gives me a look.

"Brandon," I repeat, loud enough for him to hear. "Too bad *Brandon's* not going to be here the rest of the year."

"Uh-huh. You better get out back."

I lunge forward, but Pop grabs hold of my arm. "Don't go out there empty-handed. Bring that girl something to eat and drink. Good grief. Did I teach you nothing? It's a wonder you ever had a girlfriend at all." He ruffles the top of my hair like I'm eight.

"Yeah, yeah," I grumble, before dipping into the kitchen.

"Charlie!" I shout, pointing. "Just the man I want to see."

"Too late, my friend."

"Too late for what?"

"Chelsea already came to talk to me. About doing some extra cooking for your tournament."

"I have a sneaking suspicion you may have helped with the timing of all this," I tell Mom. "Making sure Chelsea got to Charlie first."

She flashes a bewildered look as I start to put together a Clint special—fried appetizer sampler, barbecue, and pickles. I grab a couple of beers before heading out the back door.

Chelsea's completely invaded my thoughts at this point. I'm so focused on the ways Chelsea's edging deeper and deeper into my tournament—and trying to figure out how I really feel about it—that I expect her to somehow materialize, the same way she did out at the dock that first morning. The sight of the girl who's actually behind Pike's shocks me. Even though I'd already agreed to meet her here.

Her jacket is draped on the pool table. Her heels kicked off on the cracked patio. Her shoulder-length chestnut hair tugged into a short ponytail. A few strands blow around her face.

"Hey, Kenz," I say, offering her a beer.

"Ah. The Clint Special," she says, glancing at my plate. She hoists herself onto the pool table, using it as a bench. I sit beside her, putting the plate between us. She immediately picks up a piece of fried shrimp.

"Been a while since we shared one of these," I say.

"Yep."

She eyes me.

"You had something you want to show me," I remind her.

"Yep."

"I'm assuming this involves the Wi-Fi here in town, and that's why you couldn't come down to the resort."

"Yep. Although..."

"Here it comes. The lecture. I've been waiting for it. We need Wi-Fi back at the resort."

"It really is standard for a place your size."

I stare her down.

She reaches for her tablet.

"I still think that looks like you're conjuring up some magical spell," I tell her as she wiggles her fingers over the screen.

She smiles. "Sounds like the beginning of one of Earl's whoppers."

"Nobody could tell 'em as good as he could," I say as

she shoves the screen under my nose.

"Where'd you get these new pictures for the site?" I ask.

She doesn't answer right away, just picks up more of my fried tidbits. Cheese and filled peppers. "These are great," she says around a mouthful. As she chews, she points toward her tablet. "Looks like they were taken by someone who really loves that place, doesn't it?"

"And knows it," I add. These aren't photos of the cabins and the docks. These are areas you only come to know after being at the resort for some time. It's the winding brown trails, the fields of wildflowers. It's shots overlooking the resort from some of the highest cliffs. It's sections of the Rainy River where the water froths white. It's shots from the middle of the lake, where the water is clear and the sunlight dances delicately on the surface.

When I finally quit scrolling, I glance up to find Kenzie's giving me one of those all-knowing female looks.

"What—you going to tell me Chelsea took these?"

"Doesn't look like I need to."

"I don't know what this means," I admit.

"You're a smarter guy than that," Kenzie says. "You still being a jerk?"

"To Chelsea?"

She opens her eyes wide in a comical way, almost to imply, *Duh*.

"I invited her to the rink yesterday, for your information. Showed her how an idea of hers was making an impact on my players."

"That's something."

"But it's not everything. I can tell. You're holding back."

Kenzie shrugs. "Might be."

It's my turn to open my eyes wide in the same way, this time to imply, *Well?*

"She did something for you," she says.

"More than these images?"

"Yes."

"Why do you know about it?"

"I might have helped her."

"Kenzie," I moan.

"Oh, shut up. It's nice, what she's done. I'm warning you about it ahead of time so you can do everybody a favor and not play stupid."

"Don't be stupid. That's your advice."

"No, don't *play* stupid. Big difference. To act like you don't know what Chelsea's trying to tell you with everything she's done at the resort—well, now, that's a bigger whopper than Earl ever tried to tell."

The Morning of the Fishing Tournament
Lake of the Woods Fishing Resort
Minnesota

The sun seems to want to sleep in.

Stars continue to fill the sky, but Clint and Chelsea are both already awake, both pacing. They have been for hours.

Blue's toenails click on the cabin floor as he follows Chelsea into the kitchen. He cocks his head with curiosity as she puts on a pot of coffee.

"You want to go outside, don't you?" she asks, opening the door. She steps onto the porch, leaving the door open behind her. The air fills with the slightly bitter smell of the coffee she's brewing as she leans against the railing, watches Blue gallop toward a tree.

In one of the staff cabins, Clint decides he can't take lying in bed sleepless anymore. He slams his feet into his sneakers, steps out into the darkness, walks to the edge of the lake.

Behind him, he hears a rustle. Blue. He squats, holds out his hand, expects Blue to run to him.

Blue sees him, but turns, races back up to cabin four.

"He sure loves her," Clint hears. "Already."

He turns to find Earl standing with him on the dock.

"Must be an easy person to love," Earl goes on.

"What do you know about it?" Clint challenges.

Earl smiles at Clint before he fades away.

"Miss you, old man," Clint murmurs.

The lights are beginning to pop in the rest of the cabins. The tournament is calling to the guests.

Turns out, hearts are rustling everyone awake at Lake of the Woods. Maybe because hearts cast their own lights. The kind that even the sun could envy.

"**E**verything okay?" one of my guests asks.

"Better than I thought it would be," I admit. "I mean, the place isn't perfect, but it's all looking so much better. And *Ryan*. You should see this kid on the ice now—"

"Come again?"

I flinch, remember I'm talking to my MD, Dave. The one who shows up to de-stress. The first one who signed up for my tournament. He has no idea what I'm talking about. No idea how Chelsea is managing to wiggle her way in.

The other five guys on my launch (well, actually, four guys and one woman) are staring at me now, too. Half of the civilian team. Greg and Brandon are taking the other half— which includes Ryan and Luke and their dad—on another launch.

Yeah, Clint. Fishing. Remember that?

"Sure you're okay," Dave repeats.

"Perfect!" I call. And start the motor.

I kill the engine in an excellent spot, well-populated by walleye. But I'm still so consumed by thoughts of Chelsea— and all she's managed to help us accomplish—I don't actually remember cutting the engine. On autopilot, I walk around the deck. See if anyone needs more bait. Offer a few words of encouragement. Let my eyes wander toward the line of guest cabins. Think again about how great they look. Almost like new.

I fail to notice one of the poles balanced next to the railing begin to slip. The line has come loose and the hook at the end of it whips forward, sinks in low on my cheek.

I let out a bellow that dances across the top of the lake. And suddenly, Dave's in my face.

"Shit," Dave mutters, as my finger slides around in the blood on my jaw. "Must not have secured that stupid hook. That's my extra pole…"

I wave him away. "Forget it. My head was someplace else."

"The hook's not still in there, is it?" he asks, trying to pry my hand away.

"No—nothing that bad. Need a little pressure to stop the bleeding, that's all."

I pull away from him, heading straight to the just-in-case junk Greg and I keep piled near the steering wheel. Grab a T-shirt and clamp it against my face. Hope I don't look as much like the complete idiot I feel I am.

It won't quit bleeding.

"You sure you're okay, Clint?" Dave calls. He squints at me from under his ball cap. Refuses to leave, even though the rest of the guests are already clomping down the dock.

"It's not bad," I say. But I knew better. My mind was wandering. I had no business being on this boat. Even the eleven-year-old me would've known that. I should have let this group go out on our motorboats. No—encouraged it.

Should have sold them on the idea. Or maybe I should have put some kind of protective guard on all the unused poles.

"It's tapering off," I insist. Only, when Dave pulls the T-shirt away from my jawline, it's completely soaked with blood. The dark kind that says at least part of the gash is deep.

"Hate to tell you," Dave says, "but you probably ought to get a stitch or two. I'll drive you to the emergency room. Get you fixed pronto."

"No, no," I say, waving him off. Only, I am kind of worried about it. And because I'm worried, everything feels uncomfortable. The sun bouncing off the lake is too hot. The shirt I've worn is too tight. The main lodge is too far away.

"I don't know how that even happened," Dave apologizes yet again.

"I'm telling you, it was me." Earl would have never let me live it down.

"Listen," Dave says, following along behind me as I step onto the dock. "I'll take you straight to my friend who's working the ER today. Let me fix it."

"It's nothing." I say it loud enough to get Greg's attention. He hurries to scrawl the weight of Ryan's catch into his tournament scorecard and jogs straight toward me, a worried expression on his face.

"You can score these catches and clean up the launch, tie it down, right?" I ask. "Need to get a Band-Aid." Slowly, I peel the T-shirt back enough for him to see what's happened.

"Jeez," he whispers. "You look like the guy in that *Fargo* movie who got his jaw shot off."

I frown in a way that says he needs to keep his trap shut. Roll my eyes over at Dave to show him why.

"Tell him," Dave instructs Greg. "Tell him I need to take him to the ER. Get him stitched up."

"Good luck," Greg grumbles. "It'd be as easy to stitch

up a bear who's decided to tango with a hunter's trap."

"Why?" Dave asks.

Greg lets out a wheezy laugh. "This is the guy who once played through half a hockey tournament with a cracked rib."

Which is true. I did that. And it was kind of badass. And the memory of it fuels me with a surge of *I can fix this.*

"No big deal," I dismiss. "Just a scratch."

"Clint!" Dave shouts. "I'm a doctor. If you won't go to the hospital, let me fix it."

I wave goodbye, turn and walk toward the main lodge. Walk, even though I'm dying to sprint up there, grab some antiseptic, and race to my cabin, where I can finally get a good look at the damage.

I burst into the gift shop—*bait shop*, as Chelsea calls it—ready to look for some bandages. I need gauze. Something to clean the cut. Surely Rusty's made sure we still have some of this stuff lying around the shop.

I start to reach for the nearest rack, muttering, "Gauze, gauze, something, come on, please," when I stop, realizing what I'm looking at.

Postcards. Not the generic kind, either.

They're all shots I took. Every single one.

"Where'd these come from?" I ask, as though there's anyone around to answer.

When I go back to my search, I realize the place is stocked. Not fully, not by any stretch of the imagination. But I'm surrounded by new displays of road maps and Minnesota-shaped souvenirs and even a few Lake of the Woods Fishing Resort shirts, the kind Greg and Todd and I used to wear to signal we were employees.

One rack holds a small assortment of toiletries—toothpaste and sunscreen—and as I'm searching for Band-Aids, I send the entire thing tumbling to the floor. The display falls like a pile of bricks.

Footsteps thunder into the shop. "What's going on in here? Who's tearing this place apart?"

It's Chelsea's voice. "Hey. Ryan. Is that you—"

She takes one look at me and the hard angles of her annoyance soften into the droopy lines of concern. "What happened to you?"

"I'm okay." I turn toward the boxes on the floor. "I just need some gauze."

Her hand is on my arm—the one I'm using to hold the T-shirt to my face.

"I'm fine."

But she keeps tugging. Why does she want to poke at my sore spot? Why can't she leave me alone to bleed in peace? The thing will heal on its own. All I need to do is cover it up.

She pulls at one of my fingers; it feels like coarse grit sandpaper as it drags across the cut. I flinch, relax my hold.

"Jeez, Morgan," she says as she gets a look at the wound. "Did someone try to fillet you?"

"Fishhook," I mutter.

"You probably should get a tetanus shot," she says.

"Got one four years ago," I grumble. And immediately realize I shouldn't have. *Clint, you moron—you got the shot in the emergency room after the ATV accident.* As a precaution. Because I'd gotten scratched up in the fall pretty good, too.

Now we're both thinking about it. That summer four years ago.

Chelsea presses my hand back against my face. The T-shirt's got so much blood on it, it actually squishes.

"I've got a first aid kit in my cabin," she says. "Courtesy of my dad. Come on. We'll clean this mess up later."

I hesitate.

"Morgan," she snaps from the gift shop doorway. "You have relatively few other options."

Reluctantly, I follow her outside. Maybe the sun is dancing with the clouds. Maybe flowers are blooming. Maybe guests are laughing on a front porch. Maybe birds are flittering from branch to branch. I wouldn't know—not with Chelsea walking in front of me. All I can see are her shoulders, exposed around the thin straps of her tank top. Strong, bronze-colored. Her arms swing with every step, making those shoulders flex and relax, flex and relax. It's hypnotic, actually.

She leads me inside her cabin, straight into the bathroom. I lean against the wall as she flips open the lid of the plastic box with a red cross on the top. I don't want to stare at her anymore. Trying to avert my eyes, they land on the shower instead.

And suddenly, all I can think of is an afternoon four years ago when I'd returned from a full day on the lake, blistered by the sun, and she was leading me in here. Tugging my clothes off—and hers—and turning on the water. God, it's still so clear, it's like my clothes are all piled on the bathroom floor and I'm standing in that shower right now. The water was the kind of cold that tugged goosebumps out all over her body, turned her nipples hard. But no amount of cold could squelch the heat I was feeling.

My skin tingles at the memory. Every muscle in my body throbs. It's so forceful I have to grip the edge of the sink to stay upright.

Chelsea wrenches my hand away from my jaw again. She's got a bottle of wound wash. Tips it into a cotton ball, presses the cool, wet cotton against my jaw. It stings worse, even, than being hit with the hook in the first place. I flinch, gasp.

"Oh, quit—buck up," she mutters.

"Don't I get a little sympathy?"

She glances up from the cut. We lock eyes. And I suddenly realize that I'm no longer leaning into the sink—I'm leaning into her, with not so much as half an inch of space between us. My eyes dart across her face—she has freckles. I didn't remember that. Light brown freckles, dusted on her cheekbones. I'm close enough to smell her—her hair and her skin and her soap and her sunscreen. Those scents all mix together, turn as familiar as a long-ago memorized song that roars into your senses every time it comes on the radio, taking control of your heart and sending you back in time to the place you were when you first heard it. I smell her, and I'm back there—summer one all over again.

She turns to pull a pair of long silver scissors from the first aid kit. Lays them against my cheek near the gash. Flicks them open and closed. Pieces of dark beard fall across my forearm. "I've got to get this hair out of the way," she murmurs.

I don't say anything. Just close my eyes. Chelsea dabs and cleans. Dabs and cleans again. She's got a nice touch—gentle, without hesitation. The kind you immediately give in to. The kind of touch you trust without question.

A small wet brush tickles my jaw. "It's only liquid bandage," she says, as though to ward off any fear. "It'll keep it shut. I think all the blood's kind of deceiving—the cut's not really as deep as you'd think. There's one deeper pit where it looks like the hook initially hit, but then there's just a scratch. Head wounds bleed the most."

When she's finished, she turns me toward the mirror so I can see for myself. "I messed up your beard," she mutters as we both stare into our reflections.

Chelsea
STUMBLING BLOCK

Clint clears his throat as he backs away from the sink. "How'd your group do this morning?" he asks.

It takes me a few beats to get my head together. *He's talking about the tournament?*

"Well," I finally manage, "you do have Luke on the civilian team. I mean, now *there's* a fisherman. We have no shot, really. Never did. Even without the fishhook, I'm sure you would never feel the need to stick around for the official weigh-in."

"Luke's good, I'll give you that," Clint confesses. "In fact, I'm pretty sure his dad would tell you he played this tournament in his sleep."

"Literally!"

"Right. But my MD managed to catch a seventy-two-inch Northern Angler." He points to his cheek.

I chuckle quietly.

And stare at Clint.

Waiting for what's next.

"You're behind the postcards, I'm assuming," he finally says. "And all those supplies in the shop."

"You got Charlie to feed the hungry throngs the first day of cabin renovations. I wanted to return the favor. It wasn't all me, though. I had help."

264

"Yeah, so Kenzie warned me. How'd you get your hands on them?"

"The pictures? Rusty gave me a few of your old memory cards. Earl kept them."

"Well. Thanks," he whispers.

"How's your face?" I ask. "Couldn't have been too pleasant to have me mucking around in your gash."

"I'm glad you were there. In the lodge," he admits. He gets this funny look, like he instantly regrets saying it.

"Yeah. Me too. I hope—" I stop myself, shaking my head.

"Hope what?"

"I hope that you're glad I've been here for other reasons."

When he doesn't immediately answer, I say, "I saw you the other night, you know. At the waterfall."

And suddenly, the space between us shrinks.

I wrap my hand around his arm. And lean in with closed eyes, my head tilted back expectantly.

"What are you doing, Chelsea?"

I open my eyes. My face heats up. There I go again, jumping in when I shouldn't.

"What is this?" he asks, stepping backward. "Why are you here?"

"Because Greg—"

"I don't care what Greg did. Why did *you* come?"

"I love this place."

I can't read his face. I'm not sure if this declaration hurts him or makes him angry.

"You love—" He shakes his head, waves his hands. "What? Competition? Being able to show somebody you can do everything better than they can?"

That hurts. "Why would you say that?"

"Because it doesn't make sense. Look at what we're doing here—does it even feel like a real competition? Me helping you, you helping me? The dining room, the gift shop? What are the rules? Huh? I have no idea."

"But I wanted—" I blubber. "Being with you, I—"

"Time, Chelsea. It always comes back to that. It's been ticking down since the moment you got here. Maybe you don't have a boyfriend to go back home to this summer, but your life is still waiting on you. Same as the last summer you were here. I don't even know for sure when you're going to leave. How much more time we have. Till tomorrow? The day after that?"

"Clint," I plead, "you haven't let me—"

"What are we doing here? Huh? You and me."

"We're—"

"Falling into the same old pattern," he says. "I can feel it. This back and forth. This time around, though, the project that needs fixing isn't you, it's this place."

"Is that bad?" My heart feels like it's shredding.

"It's a rerun. And it'll have the same ending. Right?"

"Clint, we haven't had a chance to talk about it. The program that's waiting for me, it's—"

"Exactly. Here we go again. You have a master's to get to. What are you doing here, Chelse?"

"I don't like the way things ended."

"You want what? My forgiveness? Me to think you're fantastic so you can leave feeling good about yourself?"

"Clint—I—"

"There is absolutely no reason for any of this. None. It's all so temporary. This is ridiculous."

"Clint, you've got it all wrong."

"I do."

"Yes."

"Then promise me something."

I open my mouth. But nothing comes out.

"You can't. Promises take time."

I reach for him. But he slips away.

That night, I'm seated near the campfire, feeling like the real fire's somewhere inside me. A simmering anger is still glowing hot. Right now, I'm kind of mad at everyone—Greg for his stupid postcard and Rusty for enticing Chelsea to stay and Brandon for coming up here with her. And Chelsea, of course. I'm furious at Chelsea, popping up after all this time, dredging up stuff that probably would have been best left to settle down to the bottom of the lake, never to be seen again.

Mostly, I'm mad that she's still unable to give me anything. Not even a decent answer.

And I'm a little grumpy about the fact that I had to shave my beard. Not sure Chelsea had to cut so much of it off one side. Stupid thing had gotten to be a constant companion in a weird way.

Now that we've reached the end of the day—scores recorded, poles put away, the tournament set aside until sunrise—the teams have scattered. I'm here with Greg, Rusty, and most of her military team, cooking what we've caught on an open fire. Finishing off our plates with the baked beans and fried potatoes left by Chef Charlie.

We've got a few members of the civilian team, too, but most of them have opted for Charlie to whip their own catches into one of his gourmet specials up at the lodge, to be enjoyed in the comfort of the dining room.

Give me the lake and the moonlight any day.

But especially this day, when Chelsea's up at the lodge.

After polishing off the last smoke-seasoned bites, we swap stories. The kind only fishermen with a couple of beers in them can tell. Hemingway-inspired. *The one that got away* kind of tales (made up or not) about fishing trips to remote locations. Sometimes tropical. About a swordfish that broke a pole in half. About a two-day-long struggle with a white sturgeon that ended in tear-wracked disappointment.

Once the beer is traded, somewhere along the way, for Irish whiskey, our *one that got away* tales take a different turn. These are stories about long-legged catches. The kind with wavy hair and soft skin. These all have a decidedly sadder tone. Ending in *if only I'd* or *if I could see her again*. Even my regular, Dave, gets in on this one. Talks up a girl he knew in med school. He has to blow his nose on the tail of his T-shirt twice. One of the older guys, all gray haired and sunspotted, slides the cup of whiskey from Dave's hand before it drops to the dirt.

Greg eyes me through the whole scene. He's not much of a drinker. Not like Todd was. Tonight, he's drinking even less than usual. Holding a cup full of what has to be swamp-warm beer. Measuring my reaction.

I get it. I'm no dope. Greg's wordlessly warning me to listen to these guys. He's telling me not to blow it. Not to wind up, twenty years from now, being in the same boat: all grimy beard and bleary eyes, repeating a sad tale of regret to an equally bleary-eyed bunch of drunks. What Greg doesn't seem to realize is that some guys don't have *the one that got away* stories. They've got *wish I'd never seen her face* stories. Life would have been so much simpler that way.

Guests are beginning to trickle out of the lodge. Maybe, I think, some of them would like a moonlight tour. I, for one, would love to get back on the water, the only place where I can escape so many of my own thoughts. I head toward a launch, knowing without looking behind me that Greg's already coming along too.

<h1 style="text-align:center">Chelsea</h1>
FIGHT OR FLIGHT

I'm in the swing by the lake when Brandon decides to join me.

"Brought you two some dinner," he says, pointing to his tray of burgers and fries.

"Courtesy of Chef Charlie," I say.

"Thought you'd prefer it to the fish," Brandon says.

Blue's already licking his chops.

"Everybody's cleared out up there at the lodge?" I ask.

"Yeah—dinner's been done for a while."

"You should be playing. Maybe some of your new original stuff."

"Everybody was beat. Got day number two of the tournament starting before dawn. Hey. What happened to only playing songs people recognize? Huh? I figured you'd be at me to do a bunch of Top 40 stuff." He grimaces, shakes his head.

"Not when this place has been so good for your song-writing."

He grins as he throws a wad of fries into his mouth. After a giant swallow, he admits, "There are so many different sounds here. I mean, Missouri has its own kind of music, you know? The whistle of the cardinals. The screech of the crickets. Even our house in Fair Grove. There's a certain way the place creaks. How the porch stairs squeak. The high pitch of the wind wiggling its way through the windows. Here, though—when I walk, I hear more mourning doves than I did in Missouri. The sadness of the loons. The rushing water of that waterfall…This place has its own recognizable tone. A different melody and rhythm. I don't think I'd have ever written these songs back home."

"You definitely should be playing this stuff in the lodge. Or Pike's. Or both."

I stare at the person who has far outgrown his pesky-little-brother status, and suddenly have a lump that I need to swallow around. "Thanks," I say.

"For what?"

"Come on, Brand. This is way, way, way more than you ever had to do."

He shrugs. "I wanted to."

Blue whines. I offer him a burger patty, which he chomps in three swift bites.

"Can I ask what made you want to help out?" I ask.

"You act like you think maybe this is over. You want to go home."

I glance out at the water. "I'm not sure what that even means anymore," I confess. "Home."

"Are you looking for a way to get out of school?" Brandon asks. "Are you sick of it? I mean, not sick of it, but…you don't seem all that excited about two more years of helping Durst."

I take a deep breath, watching Blue gulp down burger number two. "You're right. I wasn't really excited about going back. But there was more to my wanting to help here. I felt like I had a chance to go toward something as much as I was trying to get away from something else. It's weird—I had these moments at MSU where I almost felt like a fraud, you know? Some big psych major telling people what they needed

272

to do to recover. What did I really know about any of it? What kind of expertise did I have? Here, though, I don't feel that way. I can't explain why. It's just—something was definitely missing. When I graduated, I mean. When I got here, I didn't feel that way anymore."

"Because of Clint?"

I tense up.

"Something happened between the two of you today," he guesses.

"He thinks I'm—I don't know. Here to mess with his head and then leave again. I think *he* wants me out of here. I've tried everything. The resort. The hockey kids. He starts to relax around me, and then out of nowhere, it seems like, he slams the door again. I wanted—"

"What? Another hot summer?"

I give him a look.

"I know what went on with you guys back then. You wanted what?"

"I wanted him to know it mattered. I mean *really* mattered. I felt that way when I saw Gabe at White Sugar. I mean, Mom's good and all, but you can get a wedding cake anywhere. I figured he came by in part because what we'd had was important. I still crossed his mind. Not like he wished we were still together. But it had meant something to him. And it felt so nice, to know that despite everything, I was still thought of in a kind way or a sweet way. I was thought of as somebody important. I wanted Clint to have that same feeling Gabe gave me."

"And?"

"And, okay, I wanted to feel like I did that summer. Like the world was on fire and everything was starting. It was so exciting—"

Blue whines again. I offer another hamburger. He

sniffs, but lays down instead. Two's enough.

"It's weird," Brandon says. "Last time around, it felt like the two of you kept pushing to be together, even though the rest of the world didn't really want you to be. This time around, it almost feels like the rest of the world keeps trying to shove you together, despite yourselves."

"It's this place," I say. "It's not a setting. Not a backdrop. It's alive. So calming. I felt it the first time we got here."

"It talks to you," Brandon agrees. "It's got a wisdom about it. But you do, too, Chelse. You can listen to yourself, you know. I don't care what Clint's been telling you. You shouldn't be afraid of your gut."

I sniff.

"Aw, don't get all squishy about it," Brandon moans.

"I'm not. I must be allergic."

"To dogs?"

"If I turn out to be allergic to dogs, I'm going to walk around with Kleenex jammed up my nostrils."

Brandon laughs in such a loud way that Blue turns to growl at him.

"You tell Mom and Dad you've adopted a dog?"

"Not yet. I—"

"Chelsea!" a voice cries out from somewhere behind my shoulder.

We both turn to find Ryan waving me over, wanting me to join him. He's surrounded by a few of the teenage boys from the tournament's father-son duos. "Lawn darts!" he shouts.

"Go on," Brandon says. "Catch you at the cabin later."

I nod. "I'll watch," I call out to the boys, carrying my burger and leading Blue toward their game.

They move the targets, trying outdo the kid who threw the last dart. To be more accurate, more graceful, more in control. Ryan plays while making sure I'm watching and giving him my *attaboy* nods of approval.

But that soon gives way to them getting crazily inventive: Instead of just throwing the darts, you first have to take three running steps. After that, you have to spin twice before throwing. Then it's a blindfolded round.

Night is creeping closer, like a cat. The game's showing no sign of slowing, so I head down to the nearby dock to light the smudge pots.

Blue trots along beside me.

And Luke follows along after Blue.

"Isn't it getting awfully late for you, buddy? Starting to get dark out here."

"Everybody always wants me to go to sleep," he groans. "I had twenty naps today."

"You did," I laugh.

"Yeah." He comes closer, points toward the pots that I light, one after another. "Those look like the things my dad was fishing with. Only bigger."

"Bobbers, you mean?"

"Yeah. Do those float in the water like bobbers?"

"Luke, these are on fire. The smoke is supposed to keep the bugs away. Don't get near them, okay?"

"Okay. But it would be neat if they did. If they floated on the water. While they were on fire. Do they do that?"

The sound of an engine puttering along draws my attention. It's one of the launches. I figure Clint's on it. Some sort of entertainment for the guests. A tour of the lake during sunset. Something nice and calm and restful before tomorrow's round two of the tournament.

What I wouldn't give to be on that boat.

"Chelsea?" Luke presses. "Do they float?"

"Don't think so. Come on, now—let's head back."

Luke sighs, his shoulders drooping. "It's boring over there. They won't let me take a turn."

"Yes, they will. I'll make them," I promise, whistling for Blue.

Luke sighs again, following reluctantly.

When we get close to the ongoing game, I start clapping my hands to snag the boys' attention. "Come on, guys," I announce. "Everybody gets a shot."

They all stop, scooting out of the way to give Luke his turn. He looks like somebody getting ready to make one of those million-dollar half-court shots, his face twisting into an expression of pure concentration and hope and effort. He launches the dart, but it flops to the ground maybe a foot from the toe of his sneaker. He sighs yet again—this time, the sigh is accompanied by a whimper that warns tears are soon to follow.

Ryan shoves the dart back into Luke's hand and scoops his brother into his arms. Luke lets out a surprised squeal as Ryan races across the course with him; when they get near the target, he shouts, "Throw it now!"

Luke drops the dart on the bullseye and squeals again. Suddenly, the rest of the guys are into it, too, passing a squealing, laughing Luke between them, then shouting to let Luke know when he can throw the dart to hit the target.

It reminds me of the way Dad used to put me on his shoulders so I could get the basketball through our driveway hoop.

The sounds of the resort dissolve as I drift further away, into old memories of playing the game. Of loving the game and the glory of winning. Of the way I'd always felt, on the court, that I'd be able to figure it out. If I lost a game, it hurt, but it also meant I was a step closer to understanding how to win against a similar opponent.

Right now, Clint's the one who acts like he's figured it all out. I'm the jerk who throws his life into chaos only to disappear again. Kind of like cicadas who show up to disturb everybody's sleep with their loud screeching every seventeen years.

The boys tire of Luke and return to their own game—pushing and tripping each other, grunting in disappointed failure or cheering with another hit of the bullseye. My eyes glaze as I remember, again, the freedom I knew when I was their age. Before any kind of disaster had ever struck.

A high-pitched scream finally yanks me out of my head.

I glance out at the lake. Could that have possibly come from one of the guests on Clint's launch? Did it sound more like a woman? Do we have any women in the tournament? I'm suddenly having a hard time remembering anything.

Another scream hits the air. But it doesn't in any way sound playful.

The scream has grabbed hold of the boys. They've stopped their game to glance out at the water.

"Can you tell what's—?" I start to ask them. My stomach flips as I glance about the grassy area. "Where's Blue?" I gasp. *Please don't let him be gone again.*

"Fire!" one of the boys yells. He points at the dock by cabin number four—which is engulfed, now, in flames.

"Oh, my God," I mutter, taking a few bewildered steps forward. The flames crawl, leaping, like they're challenging each other. Racing down the dock.

The scream erupts again—louder this time, more desperate. But it's not female. It sounds like a child.

"Where's your brother?" I ask, grabbing Ryan's arm.

Even in the twilight, I can tell Ryan's eyes are swelling in horror and the color is draining from his face. "I thought you were watching him."

No, I wasn't. I wasn't watching at all. And right now, all I feel is paralyzed. Afraid.

The flames are insidious, hungry. A furious red.

I start running, but I'm too slow—the dock is too far away. And besides, the screaming appears to be coming from the water, not the shore.

I lurch straight for one of Clint's motorboats. The engine starts easily. I turn on the headlights, illuminating the water in front of me. I have no idea what I'm doing, but there's no time to second-guess anything. I simply react.

Luke's still screaming. I know it's Luke. Who else? I can hear him over the engine—louder as I grow closer. I instantly start to mutter silent prayers: *Please let him be screaming in fear. Don't let him be hurt. Please just let him be terrified.*

I slow the engine as the boat light washes across two figures in the middle of the water. The water's fairly deep here—but not quite as deep as it would be a few yards farther out. Blue's here, doggy paddling frantically. Luke's using him as a raft, arms draped over his back to stay afloat. I turn off the engine and begin to call to Blue. Trying to make my voice sound soft and appealing, like nothing's wrong.

"Come here, buddy," I coo, trying to maintain a sense of calm. Trying to convince the poor dog—who's whimpering as terror engulfs him, too—that it's okay to come to me. My boat's safe. "Come here, guy. Good boy," I cheer, as he swims my way.

The growl of another engine seems to turn my way; another light washes across the water, smacking my eyes and blinding me for a moment.

A splash hits the air.

"Blue? Luke?" I shout.

"Got him," Clint calls.

When my eyes readjust, I make out his shock of black hair floating above the water. See his arms flying forward, windmilling as he swims toward Luke.

The launch keeps puttering along, inching slowly closer; Greg shouts something, but his words are garbled.

The orange glow of fire washes across Clint's face as he reaches for Luke, tugs him close, presses him against his chest. "Got him!" he shouts again, this time obviously for Greg.

Clint leaves Blue to doggy paddle for a moment as he swims toward my boat with one arm, still hugging Luke to his chest with the other.

I lean down over the side, grab hold of the back of Luke's soaked T-shirt. Clint pushes him up high enough that I can get my hands under his arms. I pull him into the boat; he's crying the whole time, and I'm trying to soothe him, assure him, "It's okay," even though I'm not entirely sure yet that it is.

"Just a second," I promise, because I have to leave him a moment to turn back toward the water. "It's okay," I say again, this time with more assurance as Clint grabs Blue by the collar and drags him closer.

Luke's crying grows increasingly louder as Clint and I repeat our rescue. Clint puts his hands under Blue's rump, supporting and pushing while I tug him over the side, into the boat.

I pant louder than Blue, letting the rush of having safely pulled both of them from the lake wash over me.

But I can't stop to rest. Not yet. Flames are gobbling the dock.

"I'm sorry," Luke whimpers as he holds tight to me. "I'm sorry, Chelsea. I knocked that bobber thing down. I wanted to see it float in the water. But it didn't fall in the lake. I didn't mean to make a fire. I was scared. I couldn't get out of the way. I had to jump in. Blue helped me."

"It's okay. You're safe now. That's all that matters," I say, still trying to offer him a slice of comfort.

"Chelsea, we've got to get moving. Take Luke back to shore," Clint shouts. "We've got more fire extinguishers in the main lodge. Meet me back at the dock."

But leaving him is the last thing I want to do. Because the fire is roaring and Clint's swimming closer to it.

Clint

Arms reach down from the launch to help pull me out of the water. Greg immediately steers us close to the burning dock while I wrench our extinguisher from the space near the steering wheel.

Without asking, one of the guests on board grabs hold of a bait bucket. Dips it into the water. Tosses it onto the fire. But the flames laugh at the feeble attempt.

Greg cuts the engine. Flashlights pop along the shore. Voices dance against the air. Shouting. "I've got the lodge extinguisher," Brandon calls. "And bait buckets—here, catch," Ryan calls out.

They're racing toward the dock, their feet sloshing along the edge of the lake.

The roar of Chelsea's motorboat grows louder as she returns. She's handed Luke and Blue off to one of the vets on the shore and has driven as close to the dock as she can; her boat putters to a stop, the headlight draping across the shallow portion of the lake.

She grabs the extinguisher from her own boat at the same time I finally pull the pin from mine. Simultaneously, we start to spray.

The flames flinch, recoil, like they're being hit with fists. Like they're taking blow after blow.

Other extinguishers kick in. Buckets are filled; water splashes against the dock. The flames sputter, even as shrieks and shouts continue to billow, grow louder, attack my ears.

But the shouts aren't exactly panic-stricken, not anymore. The crowd drawn by the flames begins to cheer, like fans at a game. We're all on the attack—even the humid lake air feels like a covering that's trying to starve the fire of oxygen. And still, we spray, we douse. As our water and foam knock down the orange fingers of fire, the screams of all the witnesses also begin to subside.

The fire dies.

Greg and I stand on the launch, wide-eyed, breathing heavily, coughing. Luke's still crying. But slowly, pleasant night sounds begin to filter back in. Crickets sing. Loons answer. Water sloshes gently against the shore, acting like a hand stroking a person's back in the most soothing way.

"Everybody okay?" I finally shout, the fear in my voice echoing across the resort. My clothes are plastered to my body. I'm soaked, covered in foam and ash and lake water.

"Chelsea?" Brandon's voice carries across the resort, darker and stiller now without the flames. "Where are you?"

"Over here," Chelsea calls. "How's Luke?" A splash hits the air as Chelsea climbs out of her boat. She's close enough to the shore to wade rather than swim. The sloshing sounds end, signaling that her feet have found the muddy bank.

I pick up a flashlight, flick it on and trail down the line of faces. I find Brandon patting Blue's head and trying to comfort him. What's happened has rattled the poor dog; he's panting worriedly and shaking. Even under the sketchy beam of my flashlight, that much is clear.

Luke, meanwhile, is now crying in his father's arms.

"I'm so sorry," he says as I wade toward them. "I should have been keeping a closer watch on Luke. I know he has a tendency to wander. He didn't want to be in bed while his brother was outside, and it was getting late enough that I was expecting him to collapse from sheer exhaustion at any moment." He shakes his head at himself, horrified.

"The important thing is if anyone's hurt. Luke's okay, isn't he?"

"Had a scare. No more," his dad says.

"Blue's okay, too, isn't he, Chelse?" Ryan asks.

Chelsea squats, letting Blue into her arms. "Yeah. Just wet. And shaken up. Like the rest of us."

"Are *you* okay?" I call out to her.

She turns to stare at me. She stares a long time. I'm not sure what to call what flows between us right then. Some kind of wireless connection. In the crisscrossing flashlight beams and boat lights, I like to think I can see her eyes darting back and forth, searching my face. The wheels of her mind are spinning. I'm sure of it.

"You need some help with any of this, coach?" Ryan asks.

"We can all stay to help clean up," Brandon offers.

"Not tonight," I say. "Greg and I'll pick up the buckets and the extinguishers. Make sure the boats are secure. We'll deal with the dock tomorrow, when it's light and we can get a decent look at the damage."

"No, Greg'll take care of the tournament tomorrow morning," Chelsea calls out. "No need to delay it. The dock's the only damaged area. You and I will work on it."

I want to say something to her. Something that matches the way I feel right then. All I can manage is, "Everyone, thanks, but you go on back to your cabins. Tomorrow will be here before we know it."

Chelsea
GOAL SETTING

It's time to set emotions aside, put the head down, get to work. I'm already in the zone before the sun rises—before round two of the fishing tournament even kicks into gear—tying my hair into a ponytail and tossing on the first pair of shorts I come to.

I take off toward the staff cabins, jumping up the front steps of the only one with the lights on. Start knocking insistently on the door.

Greg answers. Behind him, Clint's seated on the living room couch, a coffee cup in one hand and his head in the other.

I do an incredible imitation of Durst as I bark, "Morgan. You gonna sit and mope all day?"

He offers a crooked smile.

"What're you waiting for? Come on."

Flashlights dancing, we head to the scorched dock. Without full daylight, it's still not too easy to inspect the damage.

"Can't be too far gone," I say as Blue races between the two of us. "It was only on fire a few minutes."

I want him to see last night's fire the way I do. I replay it in my head like I once replayed the video of my last basketball game. Only this time, it's not a tragedy that fills my mind's eye; it's a near-miss. I can't quite get over it—with

284

Clint, we escaped what could have been a major catastrophe. We got through it.

We've done it before, sort of. The ATV accident of four years ago. It was terrifying then, but feels so small now.

I can't figure out how to say it—or if I should say it at all. Before I can make up my mind, an SUV rumbles down the main dirt path, followed by a delivery truck.

The SUV's door flops open. The light is getting hazy and soft, barely bright enough to see who emerges. "Hey, there," Kenzie calls, waving our way.

I race out to greet her. "What are you—"

"Word spreads fast around here—faster even than a fire. Luke's dad called the boys' mom to tell her what happened, and that was all it took. Suddenly, my phone was blowing up. That's why I called those guys." She gestures toward the truck, branded Rogers & Sons Hardware.

The driver side door opens and Mike emerges. "Hey, Chelse," he says. "Heard you guys had a rough night," he adds, rubbing Blue's head.

Clint hurries to help Mike unload nails and a nail gun. A table saw.

"Remember—these tools are rentals," Mike says. "Gotta get 'em back in decent shape."

I clear my throat. "The big— giant pipe thing—that's for—uh. That would be—?"

"To fix the pilings," Mike says. "From the sounds of it, that dock didn't burn all that long. I'm hoping all you need is some reinforcement. Kind of works like a sleeve around the pilings, see? Lot simpler than having to replace them."

I'm so grateful he's here. Blood rushes to my head. A minute ago, I was feeling a little sick, thinking maybe this repair job was going to be more like building a house than simply laying a few boards.

Mike laughs, obviously getting a kick out of the look of pure horror plastered on my face. "My brother's a contractor, remember? And lucky you, he's between jobs. He's on the way."

Together, the four of us finish unloading the supplies. Mike announces, "Gotta get back to the store. These tools are due back the minute you're done."

"What do we owe you?" Clint asks.

"More than you're obviously worth," Mike jokes.

"Ballpark."

"Nothin'. Seriously. I'm waiving tool rental fees and donating your supplies in exchange for advertising—er, on-line presence—uh—" He glances at Kenzie for help explaining exactly what it is he'll be getting.

Kenzie shrugs. But it's clearly her doing that we have everything we need. Even as we're spewing a bunch of thank-yous, she's already slipping back into her SUV. "I gotta get back, too," she calls.

Mike points to a white truck branded with an Old Pro Construction logo. Sean, his brother, has arrived.

There's no need for an introduction. Sean just starts pointing. Telling us to pull up scorched boards so we can get to work.

Once we've reinforced the pilings (correction: once Sean and his small crew reinforces the scorched pilings), it's all about measuring and cutting. One person holding the end of a board while the other feeds it through the table saw. Carrying the board to the end of the dock. Hammering it into place.

We find a working rhythm. As the noontime sun warms the lake, Sean slaps Clint on the shoulder and touches the edge of his ball cap in a kind of nod to me as he bids us both goodbye. We can take over; we've got this thing. Slowly, the sound of his truck fades into the distance. As does the sound of a launch puttering across the lake. And the voices of the guests fishing from it. Sounds like someone's snagged quite the catch.

It's only me and Clint—and the dock in front of cabin number four. The black, charred, and useless boards have all been stacked into mounds near the water's edge. We move in tandem as we continue to hammer back what was destroyed, our skin growing pink under the summer sun. Sweat turns our bodies as shiny as the surface of the lake as we pass containers of nails, connecting new planks; the air around us swells with the smell of sawdust and new, treated lumber. I keep pressing my palm flat on each new board we hammer into place, letting its warmth radiate into my skin. Glancing behind my shoulder, the boards we've already laid are starting to look like the lines in a notebook. Like paper waiting for some new sentences—waiting for a new story to be told.

But I don't want a new story, I think as I look at Clint. A new story requires a change of scenery and being surrounded by strangers' faces. No, I'd rather have a new chapter in a continuing tale.

CALM WATERS

"Hey, there," a voice calls, making us both jump. Chelsea and I stop hammering and glance up, finding Greg standing at the edge of the lake. "You two are making great progress."

"Thanks," I say, knocking once against the new, solid board beneath us.

"You two work well together," Greg adds. "Have been all summer."

I feel my back straighten and my chin lift as I take in the resort. The full picture, this time: The paint. The repairs. The paths. The beginnings of an herb garden by the lodge. My MD on his porch, feet propped on the railing as he turns the pages of a book. Rusty with a couple of vets zooming past on ATVs. Ryan and Luke giggling as they set paper boats out to sail on the lake. Brandon seated on a fallen log next to a bunch of the civilian team members, asking for random words and putting together a song off the top of his head. A round of laughter interrupts his attempt.

My eyes are still bouncing around the place as Greg steps away from the dock. He waves his arms, pointing in a *this way* motion, in the general direction of a hiking trail. A cluster of Rusty's vets follow.

Morning two of the fishing tournament is finished.

Catches weighed and a winner announced. A grocery van pulls to a stop in front of the main lodge—surely here to deliver ingredients that will allow Charlie to turn the tournament catches into lunchtime masterpieces.

The place is buzzing. For the first time all summer.

No. For the first time since Greg and Todd and I showed up, at Rusty's request.

"You know, we really have done a good job," I tell her. I lean on the *we've*. I hope she hears it.

"Yeah. Not just the dock, either."

I reach a hand out for her to shake.

Our palms touch; our fingers curl. Before she can pump my hand once in a formal coworker gesture, I loosen my grip, pull back. As our fingers slide against one another's, I tilt my wrist and slip my fingers between hers, curl them down around her knuckles. Her fingers bend with mine. We're holding hands.

Before I can get my thoughts to stop spinning, I draw her hand closer, kiss a knuckle.

A tear springs to her eye.

Our touch is unhurried. It's comfortable. Welcoming. We just keep holding on to each other. No flinching. No pulling away.

I smile, the warmth of her hand continuing to seep into mine, as we sit on the burned wreck we're rebuilding together.

The Next Day
Inside Kode
Baudette, Minnesota

Chelsea
Good Sportsmanship

"**N**o! No, no, no!" Makayla shouts, banging her fists on the table. Pounds it so fiercely, she actually shakes the webcam a bit.

My heart is still thundering away. Finally, I've said it out loud. Admitted to what I want, where I want to be. Durst and Makayla are the first two from back home that I've broken the news to. I'm hoping that the news breaking gets easier the more you do it.

Durst puts a hand over Makayla's fists, stops the thundering. "So who's getting you instead?" he asks. "You go to Minnesota to help a friend and wind up with a job offer?"

"I did," I say. "Rusty—the owner of the resort, and the

one I'll be working for—she asked me to stay on indefinitely. We had a long talk yesterday, and she agrees with me about this place. About what we could do here. This summer, we actually gave it something of a trial run."

"Some fishing resort?" Makayla asks. "How does that have anything to do with basketball?"

"Not just basketball. All sports. And more. This place—it's somewhere to get your head on straight. We can help anyone, any age. We had some luck with team building…" My voice trails.

"Chelse? You frozen?" Makayla asks.

"No—I—was thinking."

"About?" Makayla presses, impatient.

"How much there is left to learn. I mean, team building—we threw that phrase out a lot, didn't we, Durst?"

He shrugs, nods.

"You know, up here, my friend had a group of teenage hockey players—no matter what he tried, they weren't coming together as teams. We got them off the rink, and had the kids help with renovations at the fishing camp. They painted cabins. Worked on a few repairs. Even pulled weeds on the hiking trails."

"This is the resort you said your friend needed help with," he says.

"Yeah. And I know that it's not like every team could do the same. I mean—how much paint does a cabin need, right? But we could do so many things out here with them. Set them up at a campground and tell them they have to figure out how to start a fire. Make them cook their own dinner under the stars."

"What does that have to do with anything?" Makayla asks.

"I probably would have said the same thing, a few years

ago," I agree. "The teams who come will probably say that. But there's something about unplugging. Something about having to…look, it's not about the sport. It's not about learning the rules and figuring out how to squash the competition. It's not about being a star. It's about *playing* together. Learning to come together. Feeling like you're really in it together. Then you're—well. Then you're a real…team." My voice has gotten increasingly softer as I've spoken.

Because all I can think of is that dock. How we came together as a team of our own, me and Clint.

"Look, Keyes," Durst barks. I tense up. He's going to let me have it. I know he is. Leaving the program like this, last minute, it's…

"I'm going to tell you something." He points his finger into the computer's webcam. We're barely three minutes into this video chat, and I'm kind of regretting telling the two of them this way. I thought my face-to-face announcement would help soften the blow. All I'm doing is making the two of them angry.

In front of Kenzie, no less.

I squirm in the seat she's supplied me at the front of her office, where the lighting is best. Why'd she have to overhear what I was doing? Why'd I agree when she waved me inside her shop? Why didn't I tell her I'd do this on the sidewalk outside? Or in my car?

Blue raises his chin off his paws and whimpers.

"I will only sign off on this," Durst thunders, in a way that makes Kenzie's head turn my way, "if…" He sighs, lowers his hand. "If you'll be sure to give our teams a discount. And anyone else I send."

"Seriously?" Makayla asks.

"Sure. After all, I'm known as a broad-minded and understanding guy."

Makayla snorts a laugh.

Durst shushes her. "Got promise, Keyes. Team building. Getting heads back in working order. I like it."

I grin. "Thanks. I thinks so, too. And yes, you'll all get a big discount. Huge. Enormous."

"And we can still talk during the season," Makayla insists. "Anytime. No matter what."

"Absolutely," I tell her. After a pause, I add, "You can shoot me questions now that you're going to be filling my old position for Durst."

She frowns. "I'm not—he hasn't—"

"You will," I tell her and Durst both.

"Well, Keyes, what are you waiting for?" Durst growls. "Show me what you've got."

And the screen goes dead.

It's over. Hard to believe.

My phone starts ringing. When I answer, Mom instantly starts jabbering, "I had this feeling I needed to call. Motherly intuition."

"Yeah," I say, squirming as I watch Kenzie type away on her keyboard. Yet again, this is a conversation I would rather not have in front of an audience. "Look, about coming back. I think I'm—"

"You're going to stay. I was waiting for this call," Mom admits.

"I'm still not sure what Dad's going to think about it."

"I do."

"He's going to be upset."

"No, he won't. Chelse, he just didn't want you to lose who you are. Helping to get a business back off the ground—a business you'll be infusing with your love of sports—isn't losing anything."

"How'd you...Did Brandon talk to you?"

"He might've."

"You know about Blue, too, don't you?"

"Your dog? Yes. What'd Durst say?"

I laugh. "Of course you'd also know that I talked to him."

"Well?"

"He was basically his usual grumpy, yet supportive self. Makayla was there, too. And she was a little upset. But I told her—and Durst—they could call me anytime. I'd watch game vids, anything they'd like. And give any of the MSU teams a discount."

"You can bet they'll be there," Mom announces. I detect a real happiness in her voice.

"Well. Maybe. If this whole thing works."

"Oh, Chelse, the only reason you have a single doubt about it is that you're too close to it. Your dad and I both have enough distance to see clearly. Trust me. It's going to work out fine."

When we end the call, I raise my head to find Kenzie staring right at me. "*If* the whole thing works out?" she asks. "Isn't everybody on board?"

"Well. Rusty's agreed. And she's the owner, so that's what matters."

"But you haven't talked to Clint about it."

I shake my head.

"We need to fix that," Kenzie says. "I think I can help."

Clint
STILL FISHING

"**A**ll right," I say, my handclaps echoing through the ice rink, "that'll do it for today."

"Nun-uh," Luke says at my side, all singsong. He's giggling and he has an excited smile plastered to his face.

"Okay, you're right," I say. I pick him up—magnifying glass and all—and together, we leave the penalty box.

"Look, guys," I tell my players, "I want to thank you. I should have sooner."

"What for?" Ryan asks, tugging off his face mask and shaking his hair free.

"For all your help. At the resort. With the cabins. Getting the place back to where it once was."

"We didn't do much," Nick says.

"You did. You all did. You indulged kind of a crazy idea and you came together, and as a result, I'm really proud of how you conduct yourselves on the ice. Ryan, you were cool in the face of something frightening the other night, with the fire at the dock."

"Fire?" Travis echoes.

"I'll let him tell you the story. But for now, I just want to say how much I appreciate you all."

"What about me?" Luke asks.

"I'm especially glad to have you," I say. "My very own

assistant coach. And I'm glad your brother and the rest of these characters have agreed to keep coming to Lake of the Woods through the rest of the summer. Years ago, I had an idea for a boot camp, and it looks like I'm finally getting a chance to really do something with it."

"Is that all?" Ryan asks Luke.

"Nooooo," Luke says, dissolving into a new round of high-pitched little boy laughter.

"What—?" I start.

Luke points to a figure on the opposite end of the rink. A small, hazy figure growing increasingly sharper as it skates toward us.

It's Chelsea. She's wearing a knee-length skirt and a suit jacket—like something Kenzie would wear to Kode. In fact, I think I saw that exact jacket on Kenzie when I met her in her office. And her hair is piled into a bun on the top of her head.

She's not a natural skater. Not even close. But she doesn't fall once as she makes her way out to us.

"What're you—"

"I'm applying for a job," she says, handing me a sheet of paper.

"Your résumé?"

"Yes. I'm looking for part-time employment."

"What do you mean? Year round? Here?"

"Yes."

"Are you sure?"

"Yes."

"What about Missouri?"

"I'm pretty sure it's going to stay put."

My players snicker and smirk as only fifteen-year-old boys can.

"Aren't you going to ask me why I only want part-time

employment?"

My head is spinning. "I—okay."

"Because I am already employed full-time. At the Lake of the Woods Fishing Resort. Perhaps you've heard of it."

"I—you are? How?"

"The owner of the resort has hired me."

"Rusty?"

"Yes. I'll be working on upkeep and with her vets. But I'm hoping you have an open position, too. That you're looking for someone who can continue to work with athletes like your hockey players."

She leans forward. So close I can smell her hair. "Aren't you going to ask me about my five-year plan?"

"Should I?"

"Don't all interviewers ask about five-year plans? Isn't that a thing?"

I grin, deciding to play along. "Okay. Ms. Keyes, please tell me all about your five-year plan."

"I plan to continue to take classes here and there, work on my master's little by little here in Minnesota."

"What about Durst?"

"I've done what I can do for Mr. Durst, my former employer. I want to help build something, instead of doing little jobs for an athletic director.

"Staff would need to be added as Lake of the Woods becomes something brand-new. Something different than it's been before. Wheelers Point does family vacations. Your resort could become known as a center for healing. Water therapy. Team building. Help for former military members readjusting to civilian life. Did you know Charlie's actually a certified dietitian? Perhaps he could help with some herbal remedies or unlocking some connections between nutrition and overall well-being. We could even have yoga."

I grimace. "Yoga?"

"Yes. Yoga. It's all about healing."

"Healing," I repeat.

"You and I found plenty of that at Lake of the Woods, too, it seems," she says softly. She takes a deep breath and continues in her more professional tone, "Your sporting events could be part of that. Your fishing tournaments. I mean, nothing helps get a mind off its troubles like a nice competition, right? Or a few hours out on the serene lake? I would wager that's part of why your MD likes to come, yes?"

"I—yes, yes," I say, when Ryan nudges me with his stick.

We stare at each other for a moment.

"Therapy. Healing. Team building," she says. "They're all branches of the same river."

She eyes me like she's waiting for something.

"Is that it?" My pulse is thundering.

"That's never it," Chelsea says quietly. "I don't want to play against you. We could make a good team, you and me.

"Life isn't all about winning," she goes on. "I know that now. It's not all about coming out first. But if we can build a dock together, surely we could build this program. And if I'm there, taking up where Todd left off, I thought you'd have time to do Bemidji, too. We can get through the hard stuff together—and there will be some, surely. But we also have fun together. And I believe we have the same goals. Isn't that what everybody dreams of? Isn't that..." Her eyes search me for some sign. "Isn't that the real win?"

I hold her résumé close to my chest. "I'll—take it under consideration," is all I can manage. Chelsea's face falls. She turns and skates away.

The teams start shouting at me. But my brain is fuzzy, and it takes me a while to realize they're telling me, "Go!"

"Come on!" "What's wrong with you?"

I finally figure out how to make my feet work. I hand Luke over to his brother.

"Chelsea!"

She turns.

This is it. This is all I ever wanted her to do—to tell me that being with me is important. That it's what she wants. That *I'm* who she wants.

Who am I kidding? It's far more than I ever wanted. Or dared to dream about. One phone call—her to me—from her old dorm room over the past two years would have been all I wanted. But this? To admit she loves Earl's old place as much as I do? That she wants me *and* to be part of the same stretch of ground where my own life began? It feels like being chosen twice.

"I can't hire you part-time."

"Why?" she asks. "You need references, too?"

"Full-time," I tell her. "*I* want you full-time."

"You'll have to speak to Rust—" she starts.

Before she can get out so much as one more syllable, I grab her and kiss her.

To the team's uproarious applause.

After sunset, we take a drive together, back to the field where the two of us watched the firecrackers the night of my arrival. Clint parks, and under the moonlight, he reaches for me.

"You really are staying?" he keeps whispering, weaving his hands through my hair, his breathy words warm against my face.

"I'm not going anywhere," I keep whispering back.

He presses his mouth against mine—kissing me deeply and with more tenderness than he ever has.

He pulls back to chuckle, like he can't quite believe it. He places his hands on both sides of my face again, closes his eyes, and tilts forward so our foreheads touch. I grab both of his wrists, squeeze. Which makes him smile, let out another chuckle. When I pull my forehead away, a tear trails from the corner of his eye, runs down the side of his cheek.

"Are you okay?" I whisper.

"I'm perfect," he says, flicking the tear away and pulling me tight to kiss me again. His hands relax their grip as they trace my spine from my neck all the way down to my backside.

Clint digs his fingertips into my flesh again, then wraps his arms around me, squeezes. The pressure turns tight enough to constrict my lungs, but never gets uncomfortable. Our hip bones clash. Our legs tangle. I find the hem of his T-shirt, let my fingers slide along the skin right above his shorts.

He pulls away so suddenly, I stumble forward, throw my hand onto the dash to steady myself.

"Wait," I say as he jumps from the cab. "Where—?" I crack open the passenger door to follow him.

He hoists himself into the truck bed, saying, "The first thing you need to learn is that any respectable Minnesota girl keeps a quilt in her just-in-case stash."

"Minnesota girl?"

"That's what you are now. Isn't it?"

I smile. Yes. I'm a Minnesota girl. "Quilts for emergency picnics?"

"When we find you a truck of your own," he says, and the *we* part makes my stomach draw a loop-the-loop, "I'll insist on a few things. Tools to change a tire, tarps, a winter emergency kit, and a quilt." He's grinning as he tugs his own blanket free.

He snaps it open, spreading it across the grassy softness of the field.

We're suddenly two creatures who belong here—every bit as much as the birds roosting on the branches above. His hands are on my waist as we drop down to our knees together, moving in such a fluid motion that it seems as though the summer breeze has guided our bodies down to the earth.

He tugs my knotted shirttail free as I attack the buttons. Once the shirt falls from my shoulders, the sweet outdoor air glides like a warm exhale over my bare skin. The moonlight kisses my nipples before he does; his mouth is warmer than the day's lingering heat, and even after all these years, familiar. Clint's a place I've come back to that's all at once safe and comfortable and also full of the thrill of so many unknowns.

I touch him, running my fingers down his arms,

searching for a response—some way for him to tell me he feels the same way I do. I find it when he lets out a deep, throaty murmur at the moment our chests come together, two pieces whose edges curve and dip in sync.

His heartbeat bleeds through his chest into mine. He kisses my neck to the rhythm of my own pulse.

With our mouths together, he guides me from my knees to lie flat on my back. My shoulder blades find the blanket to be as soft and worn as a pair of favorite jeans. From this angle, the wildflowers circling the blanket tower over me. Some stalks are brown and dry—but instead of looking withered, they remind me of tree trunks. Sturdy. Solid. Not like fragile, fleeting blooms at all.

The smell of the soil explodes into my nose. The entire world is earthy and alive. Fertile. Full, always, of the next round of blooms ready to explode. And suddenly, we aren't so much moving together as growing together, twisting and weaving in new directions. We have shoots that climb moonbeams; we absorb the moisture from the humid air. This is not the love scene either one of us remembers. It's not the two of us racing after some kind of heat—lust, passion, whatever you want to call it. God, it was all so frantic back then. Because time was flying. And we were scrambling after it, the way we felt about each other. We knew, even when it was happening, that it was fleeting. Temporary. But this? It's a beginning. This doesn't feel like a crazy rush to grab onto something just for a little while before it's over. It feels like this thing between us has room. Like whatever we're feeling is alive and only starting to sprout.

He weaves his fingers in mine. I arch my back, dig my toes into a soft patch of soil beneath the hem of the blanket.

He clutches tighter to me; I press my face against his shoulder. A tear tingles against my eye. The way we touch isn't

a firecracker, popping with heat and disappearing.
The way we touch has roots.

CAUGHT

We lay right out in the open, twisted into each other. Until the night breeze brings its chill. We don't really want to, but we dress, fold the blanket. As Chelsea's placing the quilt back in the bed of the truck, though, she runs her hands down a waterproof drawstring bag.

"What's in here?" she asks.

"A tent," I say. "I've had it forever. Greg and Todd and I used to use it for out-of-town fishing…trips…" My words slow down as she smiles. It's one of those half-playful, half-devilish kind of grins.

There's no way we're leaving the field. Not now.

We pitch the tent and crawl inside. I drift toward sleep with her arms around me; I drink her in, all limp and sweet and smelling like sweat and exhaustion and love.

"So," she murmurs, "what do you think about that quote of yours?"

"What quote?"

"The one you recited to me. About love blooming once and being short-lived."

"That wasn't what it was about."

"I distinctly remember 'must be enjoyed a brief hour.'"

"You have that wrong," I say. "I never would have memorized that."

"You wouldn't."

"Nope. It's not true. It's a dumb quote."

She laughs, kissing me along the base of my throat.

"Hang on," I tell her, "this night deserves a toast."

I zip out of the tent long enough to grab my cooler. I hand her a bottle and raise my own. "To—"

"—tomorrow," she finishes.

We clink our bottles and drink.

She stares at me a minute before ducking out of the tent.

"Hey!" I shout. "Where're you—"

She returns rifling through her purse. "I've had this a long time," she admits, before pulling out my old Boy Scout compass. "Since your ATV wreck."

"Why'd you keep it?" I ask as she slides it into my hand.

"Earl saw me with it. Said if something rescued you once it could help rescue you a second time."

"Did you believe him?"

She runs a hand through her wavy blond hair. "I guess I thought maybe if I kept something of yours, it'd give us a reason to be in touch again. I took it and your postcard to college with me. Last time I picked it up, after graduation, there it was, pointing north."

"It always points north, Keyes."

When she gives me this look, I groan, "You're not going to say something corny about it pointing to me, are you?"

She shoves me, saying, "Shut-up! I'm allowed to be corny."

When my laughter dies down, she says, "I think about all the time that went by when I had that thing. All those days, months. So many years we missed out on—"

"Doing what?" I ask. "Going for coffee? Phone calls?"

"So many little things. Little moments. Learning everything about each other."

"My middle name's Nicholas," I say. "I listen to old Metallica songs when I jog. I've got an entire spiral notebook full of possible names for my beer, none of which are right. That the kind of thing you're talking about?"

"The way you say that makes it sound dumb."

"It's not dumb," I say. "It's incidental. Memorizing a bunch of stuff doesn't mean you really know someone. I mean really get them, know what makes them tick."

She nods, considering. "I bet I can come up with a name for this beer faster that you can."

"Another challenge? I'm game."

"You just wait, *Morgan*."

We stop, stare at each other.

"Can't be that easy, can it?" I ask.

"Why not? Why does it have to be complicated? *Morgan*," she says, looking into her bottle. "You could do a Morgan Stout, Morgan Pale Ale, Morgan—"

"Oh, man," I moan. "When am I going to have time for all this?"

"You already have access to a whole microbrewery. It's not like you're starting from scratch. Besides, you know your dad would be more than happy to sell it at the restaurant. And we need funding for all the stuff we're going to do with the teams who'll be flooding us with reservations."

"You act like we're going to be inundated. Like it's a foregone conclusion," I say.

"It is," she says simply. "Defeat is not an option."

I drape an arm over her shoulder. It's intended to be a hug, but it lasts so long, it begins to feel like we're holding each other, neither one of us willing to let go.

When I wake, it's to Chelsea whispering, "Hey, hey." She strokes my shoulder until I have no choice but to pop my eyes open.

Dawn has come and gone. Bright morning light streams through the open flap of the tent. She's leaning over me. Smiling.

I start to rise, finding my neck cramped up from the weird position I twisted myself into so I could fall asleep looking at her.

"You gotta see this," she murmurs.

I let out a single grunt against my sore, knotted shoulders before tugging on my shorts and following her outside.

"Look," she whispers. Not that she needs to. The entire field is in full bloom—lady slippers, flesh-colored and dewy, fill the entire landscape.

It's breathtaking. Even for a Minnesota boy who's seen more orchids than he can count.

I have so many things I want to tell her. That Earl drew Rusty a map out here, to this very place where the earth healed. That I don't feel the giant sinkhole between us anymore. That she knows this place as well as any of us—even Earl. That he would have loved her idea. More than that, he would have believed in it.

I settle on asking, "I ever tell you about the ancient orchid?"

"Ancient what?"

"Orchid. You know," I say, "every one of these slippers blooms once, only to wither. But one of them came back. Every single summer. Crazy flower must be a hundred years old now."

"Sounds like one of Earl's whoppers."

"Or a story that hasn't had enough time to come true yet."

She smiles at me, her hair billowing in the summer breeze as she stoops to touch the bloom of the closest lady slipper. The soft shade of pink on the petal is a perfect match for the blush on her cheeks.

Brandon doesn't fold his old concert T-shirts as much as wad them before tossing them into his last duffel bag. He glances up when he feels me lingering in the doorway.

"You know, there are plenty of weeks left of summer. I wouldn't even charge you to stay," I tease.

"Charge me! You owe me about a million dollars for my outstanding musical contribution. Not to mention working that fishing tournament. Man, the blistering sun. Mosquitoes buzzing. Extinguishing emergency fires. And don't even get me started on the cabins! The hammering. The painting. Lifting hundred-thousand-pound sofas…"

"Oh, boo-hoo. Poor you," I interrupt, which in sibling speak actually means, *You are absolutely right. I do owe you big time.*

"Besides," he adds, smashing the top of his duffel and zipping it shut, "I need to get back. Mom said they've got about six million cakes ordered for a family reunion. Every Highful for seventy-thousand miles. Oh. You probably still don't want to hear about the Highfuls."

With the mere mention of the name, I'm reliving it all over again, as I probably will for the rest of my life—the Highful twins' squabble. The spilled soda. My fall. My shattered hip.

Then again, without those Highfuls, we wouldn't have

had the same last family vacation. Maybe there wouldn't even have been one. Maybe I would have gone to a basketball camp. Maybe Brandon would have been busy forming a garage band with his high school buddies. Maybe life would have looked completely different.

Maybe I really don't hate the Highfuls at all.

"…and don't get me started on that Ross wedding cake," Brandon groans. "Mom says those two have changed their minds about it roughly twelve hundred times. They're driving her nuts." He cocks his head. "What a story I'll have to tell him when he asks where you are."

"You still can't believe I'm doing this. That I'm staying," I say.

"I knew when I saw you guys out on the dock. The one you also burned down."

"Hey, I was the rescuer. Not the burner. Need I remind you?"

Brandon's serious face begins to curl into a smile.

"Here it comes. I've been waiting for you to give me grief."

"No—I'm just. You know. Cheering for you. Gonna paint some giant '23's on poster board later today."

"Somebody else has my number now, you know."

"Nah, that number's always gonna be yours. Chelsea Keyes—Pride of Lake of the Woods. And you know, you really better be."

"I will," I promise.

"Oh, I'll know if you are. I'll be here. I gotta come back, since I never did make it to the record store."

"Record store?"

"Sure. It happens to be in town. Right down the street from a certain former resort worker turned professional web wizard."

"Brand, I told you, that's a flea market. And Kenzie said she has a boyfriend."

"Now, but later?" He holds his hands out.

"Pathetic," I scold him.

"Seriously, Chelse. I'll be thinking about you all the time. You'd better not be stingy on the texts."

I nod in appreciation, even though being serious feels suddenly awkward. "I have to admit," I say, "it felt really good to announce I was staying here. I even texted Nathan—my old psych study partner. Told him he'd have to find somebody else to cram with."

"Any new tidbits you want me to tell Mom? She's gonna grill me like crazy, you know."

"Just that I'm—well—"

"—happy as you ever were riding on the shoulders of your teammates after scoring the game-winning three-pointer," he finishes with a smirk.

I help him outside. He lovingly places his amps and duffels in the trunk while I buckle Francine into the back seat.

"What's hard to believe is that you're giving up the Camaro," he says.

"Oh, that chapter's over, too. Stick a 'For Sale' sign in the windshield when you get home. No way I could ever find a buyer for that thing up here."

"I'll send the money as soon as I sell it."

"I know you will. How do you think I'll look driving a truck?"

As he starts to frown, I say, "Give it a chance. It'll grow on you."

"I'm really glad, Chelse."

"About—?"

"This. All of it. I'm kind of jealous, actually."

"Really."

"Yeah. Really. I hope something like this happens to me. I hope I get to do something I love every bit as much as you love what you're doing. It fits you, you know?"

My eyes start to tingle and a lump swells under my vocal cords.

"I mean, but cooler. My gig will definitely be cooler."

"Brandon."

"Come on. This place is nice and all, but it's a fishing resort. I'm an up-tempo kind of guy. Hipper. Bopping along to my own syncopated rhythm, if you will."

"Brandon."

"I gotta find me a place where the Panama hats are everywhere, and the improv guitar is always playing."

"Actually, I'm pretty sure that was a fedora."

Which we both take as our cue to dissolve into our normal struggle to put each other in a headlock.

He squirms his way out. "Whatever. I gotta get on the road. It's a long drive."

I nod. "It is," I say, opening the driver side door.

Brandon climbs in, revs the engine.

I lean in through the window. "Call to let me know you get home okay."

"Sure thing, Ma," he jokes, and puts my old car in drive.

I see it all in a flash: the way Mom and Dad—and Brandon—had been standing on the walk outside our house in Fair Grove, waving me goodbye at the end of the summer four years ago. I was off on a new adventure. To college. On my own.

This time, starting off on a new adventure means I'm the one staying behind. I wave to Brandon, because I know he'll watch me in the rearview until he can't see me anymore.

"**S**ure am gonna miss you," Greg says.

"Yeah," I mutter, mostly because I'm only half-listening. I pace the porch, chewing on a thumbnail. Squint down the brown trail as Chelsea finishes waving to Brandon, Blue sitting patiently at her side.

I've been waiting for her to say goodbye to him. I didn't want to barge in on it.

Rusty leans against the porch railing of the cabin I've shared with Greg for the past year. Greg plops into a lawn chair and stretches his legs out. They share a look; Rusty wheezes a laugh.

"So glad this is a source of amusement," I grumble.

"What're you so nervous about?" Greg asks. "I'm the one whose life is about to change."

"What're you talking about?" I ask.

"Hel*lo*…I've had the pleasure—or is that pain?—of your company since we were kids. We've shared tents and basements and college apartments. We all lived together in this cabin. You and me and Todd. First, I lose Todd. And now, I'm going to be on my own."

"Rusty's only shouting distance away in her house," I remind him. "You'll be fine."

"How do you know? I spend hours at a time counting

moose, getting increasingly hungrier for human interaction. Maybe it'll be torture."

Greg glances at Rusty once more, and together, they wheeze out another laugh.

"You aren't going to convince that boy to change his mind," Rusty warns. "Trust me."

"Change his mind?" Greg says. "Who do you think got the girl back up here? I'm not trying to change his mind. But I do think the guy owes me. Like no man has ever owed a friend before. More than Chelsea owes Brandon. More than..."

I tune out. I don't care that I'm the brunt of their teasing. Not now, when the Camaro and Brandon are both disappearing down the main dirt path. I grab the last of my bags.

"This is not the teary-eyed Morgan who said goodbye to Todd," Greg says. "I'm a little offended."

"Oh, come on," I tell him. "I'm only moving fifty feet away. To cabin number four."

"Earl never did allow an employee to live in his guest cabins," Rusty reminds me. "Maybe I shouldn't allow this."

"Listen," I tell her, "Cabin number four is mine. It's always been mine."

"Ever since we were kids," Greg agrees.

I race down the front steps, toss the last bags into the back of the truck.

By the time I'm opening the driver side door, Rusty and Greg have turned their attention toward each other. Neighbors enjoying some evening conversation.

I jump in the truck, drive down to cabin number four. Catch myself thinking it's the shortest and longest drive I've ever taken.

As I kill the engine, I glance into the passenger seat. My skates are back. And so are the painted "C"s on each heel.

Chelsea opens the front door. Blue comes panting onto

the porch. And it hits me—I'm being greeted by my family.

I race up the steps. Chelsea wraps me into her arms. "Blue said he'd show you which room is ours."

"Oh, Blue said, huh?" I ask.

He trots inside the open door; it's officially just the two of us.

She reaches into my pocket and pulls out my old compass. Ever since she gave it to me, I've been back to carrying it around everywhere.

It points to her.

I grab her around the waist and pull her close—every bit as close as we were in the wildflower field. And she says the words that have been on my mind all day:

"Welcome home."

Epilogue

It's evening; the setting sun is casting its familiar orange watercolor wash across the entire resort. Night creatures are beginning to stir, creeping out of nests—the owls and the loons prepare to unleash their nighttime melodies.

Chelsea and Clint are singing a kind of night song of their own, sitting side-by-side in lawn chairs on the porch of their cabin, bare feet propped on the railing, dinner plates in their laps, their laughter spreading outward like the ever-expanding ripples made by a walleye jumping from the lake.

Nearby animals pause to cock their heads and listen. This laughter is a new sound, but doesn't create panic, not like the roar of cars that come and go, flying down the dirt road. Maybe because this is a sound with permanence. A sound that has moved in, that's now announcing it will be as hard to turn off as the constant pulsing beat of the waterfall.

Far more similarities than differences mark the two human voices; the pitch of their words may be octaves apart, but they speak in a nearly identical cadence, and they swoop in to finish the other's thoughts. The voices overlap, crisscrossing as they tease and play.

As the evening lingers, the night song also begins to include Blue's raspy breaths of deep, satisfied sleep.

A few animals tilt their heads at the clink of beer bottles and the clatter of forks as Chelsea and Clint devour the pasta they've made. It's a clumsy dinner, the kind made by people who are not used to cooking. But it's every bit as delicious as anything prepared by Chef Charlie.

When Chelsea's phone rings, she rushes to grab it up off the arm of her lawn chair. It's Brandon. It seems perfect that he would call now, in the middle of this new song. He needs to hear it, Chelsea thinks. The music of this night. She puts him on speaker; his voice trickles out, adding its own harmony.

Chelsea places her plate on the porch. She hasn't gotten around to dessert yet—one of the dark chocolate cupcakes that arrived earlier in the day from White Sugar sits between her fork and some unfinished vegetables. When she's through talking, she'll turn her full attention to the sweet, slowly peeling back the paper cup to take small bites. The sun will be completely set by the time she finishes.

"Next summer, we'll…" Chelsea starts, her alto notes creating a tune of pure happiness. She's already making plans—which cabin Brandon will stay in, whether her folks will come, the things they'll all do together.

Clint smiles; he loves being part of her plans. But daydreaming, planning—that's a form of escape, he thinks. And tonight, aren't they celebrating knowing that this is the opposite of escape? The resort is no longer Chelsea's part-time; it's home and work to both of them.

Yes, Chelsea has found her way back and she's here now in a way that belongs to both of them. This isn't the summer of four years ago; they aren't two kids who helped each other take flight, soaring off on their own separate journeys. Shouldn't they both be holding tight, right now, to knowing their names will be carved across the resort every bit as deeply as Earl's and Helen's? Shouldn't they be holding tight to this beautiful summer of lost and founds?

Like any good legend, their story already spans ages. Some chapters are years old, some only seconds. And maybe

Chelsea was right, maybe life isn't about wins and losses. But being here, right now, feels utterly triumphant.

Why dream up another scene that takes them away from all this?

"What do you think?" Chelsea asks him. "About next summer?"

But Clint shakes his head. Not now. Here, beneath the setting sun, the universal symbol of all things ending, they're finally at the true beginning of their story. There are acres upon acres inside both of them that neither has seen yet. Just as Clint spent years roaming the Lake of the Woods landscape, now, finally, they have a chance to explore each other—discover gorgeous, unexpected waterfalls of emotion, find cool welcoming shade, joy deeper than the lake they both love.

In the next few weeks and months, their feet will wear paths through their favorite sections of wildflower fields. In the next few years, they will wear similar paths in each other's hearts.

Together, they'll finally face their first rust-colored autumn, their first winter—a season whose icy beauty will surely equal the brilliance of the dew-kissed summer they're still sharing. Together, they'll watch the lady slippers sleep and wake again. But this small moment is itself as flawless as a daydream.

Why rush past this?

Chelsea sees all of that in his face, it seems. Her eyes grow hazy, and her words wind down. She agrees; there's no need, at this moment, to plan for anything. Not even for going back to Missouri to empty out a childhood bedroom, just as she'd emptied out her dormitory earlier that summer. One day, she and Clint will both be there, and she will show him the mementos in that room, the pieces she has preserved of the long, lovely life chapters that led her here. But she does not have to think about that now. She tells her brother good-night. She turns the phone off. And she reaches for Clint.

Their hands join; Clint tugs her closer, leans forward to meet her lips. Their kiss lingers. What lies before them is a sweet to be savored, nibbled at like Chelsea's cupcake, drawn out to make it last longer. Chelsea's lips tighten against Clint's as they stretch into a smile. Instead of pulling his mouth away, Clint leans still closer. He smiles back.

There's time.

It's hard to get back in the game—of life or love—when you're still playing hurt.

Once, she was a small-town celebrity. One of the most talented high school basketball players her hometown had ever seen. Bound for something far bigger beyond the city limits of Fair Grove, Missouri. But Chelsea's world changed when an accident on the court ended her days as an athlete. She struggles with the idea of no longer being a star—and has no real idea what life might hold for her next.

Once, he was a small-town celebrity. One of the most talented hockey players his hometown had ever seen. Bound for something far bigger beyond the city limits of Baudette, Minnesota. When an unexpected tragedy took his head out of the game, Clint was forced to hang up his skates. He swore he'd never put himself in a position to be hurt again, building walls around his heart.

When their paths cross one summer at a Minnesota lake resort, Chelsea and Clint are immediately drawn to one another. But wounds of the heart cut the deepest, and take the longest to heal. Will an unexpected romance end up causing Chelsea and Clint more pain—or finally heal their heartbreak?

Available Now
Visit HollySchindler.com for details

Holly Schindler is a multi-award-winning and critically acclaimed author of books for readers of all ages. She holds a master's degree in creative writing, has taught writing courses, mentored budding authors, and edited authors' work at all stages of professional development. A firm believer that reading is as creative an endeavor as writing, Schindler has also worked one-on-one with K-12 students, honing their literacy skills.

Schindler insists that nothing is quite as magical as a good story or an exciting "what-if." She is currently chasing down another "what-if" as she drafts her next book. She also loves hearing from readers.

If you'd like to get in touch, subscribe to newsletters, or view her full list of publications, please visit:

HollySchindler.com

www.ingramcontent.com/pod-product-compliance
Lightning Source LLC
Chambersburg PA
CBHW051218190726
48288CB00006B/2009